Greg,

Enjoy the new adventure!

My best,

Golden Torpedo

7/11/17

Other Emerson Moore Adventures by Bob Adamov

- *Rainbow's End* – released October 2002
- *Pierce the Veil* – released May 2004
- *When Rainbows Walk* – released June 2005
- *Promised Land* – released July 2006
- *The Other Side of Hell* – released June 2008
- *Tan Lines* – released June 2010
- *Sandustee* – released March 2013
- *Zenobia* – released May 2014
- *Missing* – released April 2015

Next Emerson Moore Adventure:

- *Chincoteague Calm*

Golden Torpedo

Bob Adamov

Packard Island Publishing
Wooster ❁ Ohio
2017
www.packard island publishing.com

www.Bob Adamov.com

This book is a work of fiction. Names, characters, places and incidents are either products of the author's imagination or are used fictitiously. Any resemblance to actual events, locales or persons, living or dead, is entirely coincidental.

First Edition • July 2017

ISBN: 978-0-9786184-6-9

(ISBN 10: 0-9786184-6-7)

Library of Congress number: 2017902636

Printed and bound in the United States of America.

Cover art by: Denis Lange
Lange Design
890 Williamsburg Court
Ashland, OH 44805
www.lange design.org

Printed by:
BookMasters, Inc.
PO Box 388
Ashland, Ohio 44805
www.Bookmasters.com

Layout design by: David Wiesenberg
The Wooster Book Company
205 West Liberty Street
Wooster, OH 44691
www.wooster book.com

Published by:
Packard Island Publishing
Wooster, Ohio
www.packard island publishing.com

Dedication

This book is dedicated to Wayne Valero, who passed away in early 2016 after incurring Creutzfeldt-Jakob disease. Wayne was President of the Clive Cussler Collectors' Society and had me speak at three of their annual conferences. Wayne became a friend and inspiration. His wit and friendship are dearly missed.

Creutzfeldt-Jakob disease (CJD) is a rare, degenerative, invariably fatal brain disorder. It affects about one person in every one million people per year worldwide; in the United States there are about 300 cases per year. CJD usually appears in later life and runs a rapid course.

The Creutzfeldt-Jakob Disease Foundation *(www.cjdfoundation.org)* will receive a portion of the proceeds from the sale of this book in memory of Wayne Valero. The address is The CJD Foundation, P.O. Box 5312, Akron, OH 44334, if you'd like to make a donation.

This book is also dedicated to Frances Wilbanks who passed away in October 2016. Frances was the wife of my good friend and fellow Clive Cussler Collectors' Society member, Ralph Wilbanks. I have fond memories of our times together at the conferences. Ralph discovered the Civil War submarine, *The Hunley*, and is the basis for the character Willie Wilbanks in this novel. And Ralph is a rascal like Willie.

They that wait upon the Lord shall renew their strength;
they shall mount up with wings as eagles;
they shall run, and not be weary;
and they shall walk, and not faint.

—Isaiah 40:31

Acknowledgements

For technical assistance, I'd like to express my appreciation to authors and shipwreck hunters Mike and Georgann Wachter of Erie Wrecks, maritime archeologist and U-boat hunter Joe Hoyt of the National Oceanic and Atmospheric Administration (NOAA), shipwreck hunter and underwater archeologist Ralph Wilbanks, Dr. Steven Meyer, Cpl. Shawn Bogart of the Collier County, Florida Sheriff's Office, Kim Fisher from Mel Fisher's Treasures in Key West, Avenger owner and pilot Charlie Cartledge, and Ed Seifert.

I'd like to thank my team of editors: Cathy Adamov, John Wisse, Peggy Parker, Julia Wiesenberg of The Wooster Book Company, Hank Inman of Goldfinch Communications, Andrea Goss Knaub, and the one and only Joe Weinstein.

The following publication provided reference material:
Great Lakes Folklore by Charles Cassady, Jr. copyright 2013 Schiffer Publishing. Ltd.

For more information, check these sites:

www.BobAdamov.com
www.cusslersociety.com
www.VisitPut-in-Bay.com

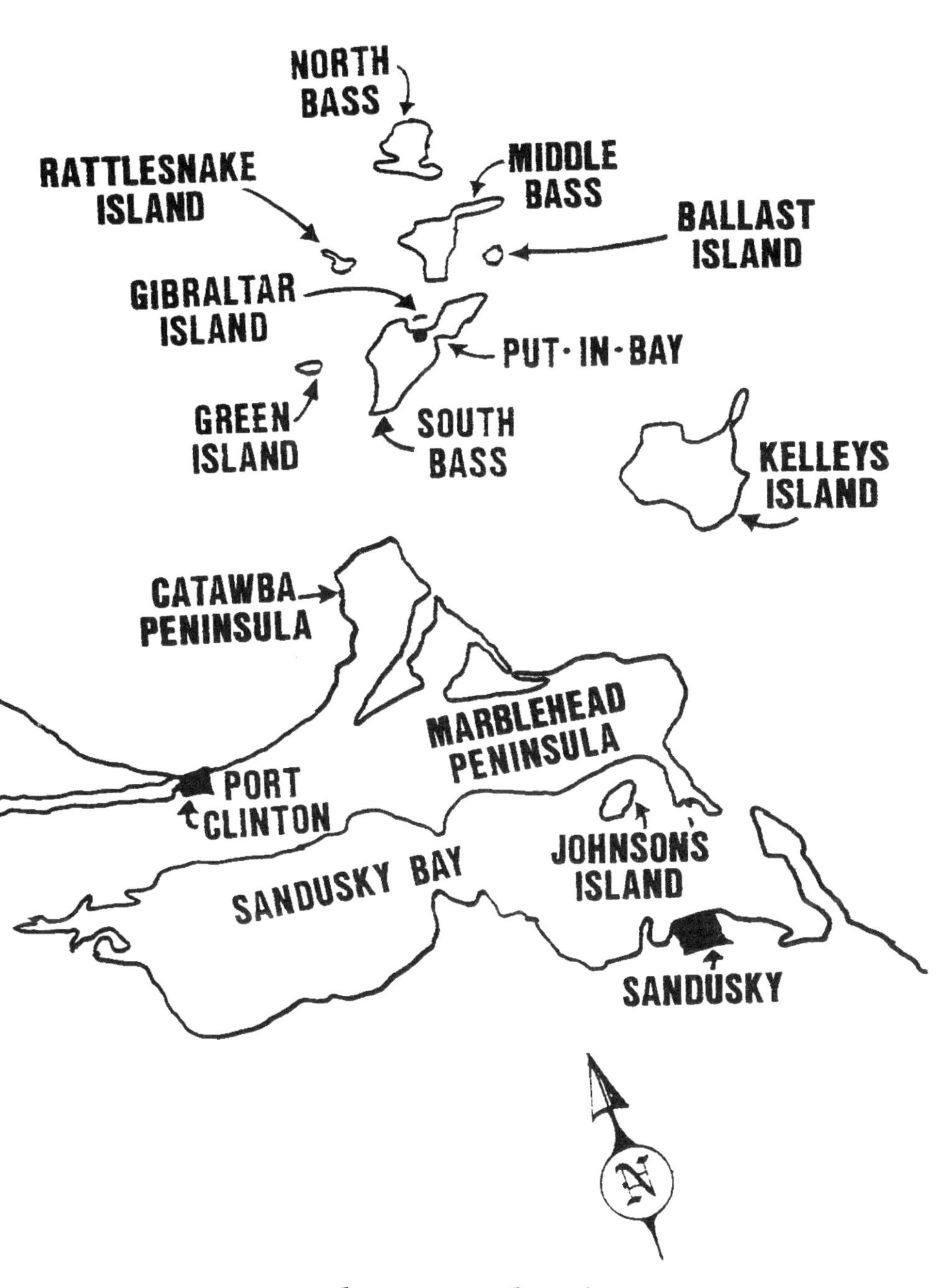

Lake Erie Islands

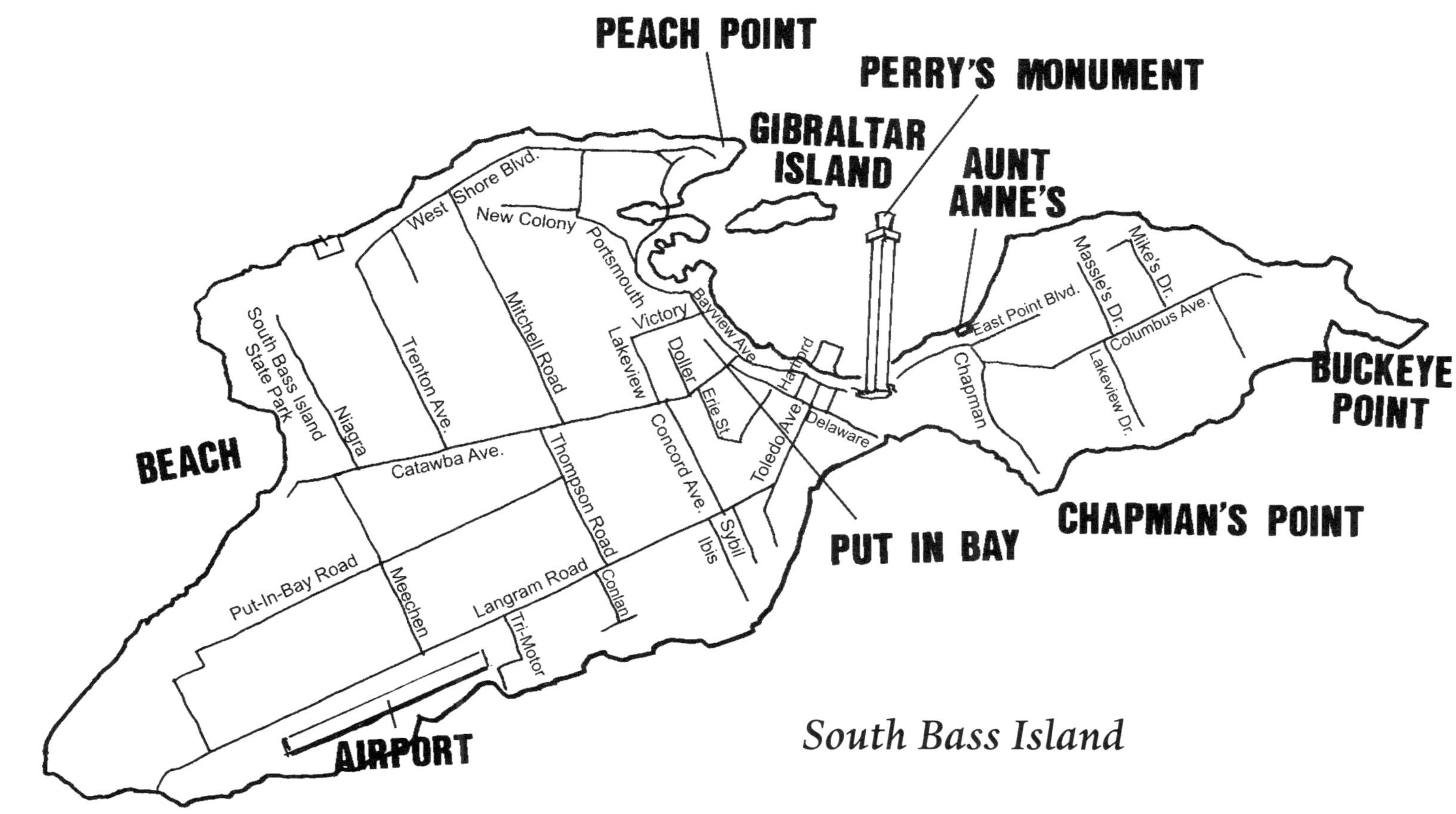

South Bass Island

PART ONE

CHAPTER 1

Early April, 1945
Key West, Florida

Charging her batteries as she waited motionless offshore for the two saboteurs to return, the German submarine *U-235* sat on the ocean surface as night turned into early dawn.

Three crewmen and the captain were stationed in the conning tower, scanning the shore for signs of the returning saboteurs. They were overdue.

Captain Zimmermann absentmindedly stroked his red beard as he peered into the emerging dawn. He was anxious. His gut churned as it had in the past when danger was near. It was like a sixth sense that warned him of impending trouble. That instinct would be right once again.

Fixing his gaze in the distance, he thought about having left Norway two weeks ago to begin this highly secretive and potentially deadly mission. It was German Chancellor Adolph Hitler's idea.

The leader of Nazi Germany had personally overseen the mission's planning. If it succeeded, Hitler was confident the mission's outcome would turn the tide of the war and Germany would emerge victorious.

Admiral Karl Doenitz, Germany's naval commander, had accompanied Zimmerman on the flight from Norway's Kristiansand Harbor to Tempelhof Airport in Berlin where they met Hitler at his headquarters. Doenitz introduced Zimmerman as one of the top five U-boat commanders in the fleet. As Hitler ranted about the importance of the mission, Zimmerman noticed a uniformed man sitting by himself. The man was staring intently at Zimmerman.

After the men endured Hitler's demagoguery for fifteen minutes, Hitler paused and beckoned to the seated man. "This is Dieter Gabor from the Abwher."

Zimmerman nodded his head in the direction of the sinister man from naval intelligence who had walked to the side of Hitler's desk.

"Herr Gabor will be carrying out the first part of your mission. It is critical that he succeed and you do everything possible to support him," Hitler instructed.

Zimmerman assessed Gabor. He was of medium build with jet-black hair and piercing dark eyes, almost the color of coal. He had an air of danger about him as he stood, dressed sharply in a crisp uniform.

The meeting lasted another fifteen minutes and ended with the three men being ushered out of Hitler's office to a waiting car that returned them to Tempelhof Airport for the return flight to Norway. Within five days, the U-boat was underway to start the secret mission.

The U-boat's two 9-cylinder, 4-stroke diesel engines gently powered her as she glided out of Kristiansand Harbor and ran continuously submerged for the next two weeks. After making safe passage through the English Channel into the Atlantic Ocean, Zimmerman felt sufficiently confident to surface each night to charge her batteries and run on the diesel engines. He maintained radio silence as was initially ordered by Admiral Doenitz.

Zimmerman's type XB submarine was the largest class of German U-boats with a length of almost three hundred feet, beam of thirty feet and height of thirty-four feet. Her speed ranged from seven knots submerged to seventeen knots on the surface and she carried a crew of five officers and forty-seven enlisted men.

After crossing the Atlantic, the U-boat surfaced one night off of the East Coast of the United States near the blacked out city of Savannah, Georgia. As two of the crew readied a raft, Zimmerman spoke quietly to Gabor, the special agent who would be rowing ashore to complete his dangerous mission.

"Dieter, I have something for you," Zimmerman said.

During the voyage and games of chess, he had enjoyed getting to know Gabor who single-handedly would wreak havoc on the U.S. government upon the successful completion of his mission.

"What is that?" Gabor asked as he gripped a suitcase in one hand. It was filled with civilian clothes and he was dressed as a civilian in a rumpled suit and cap.

"I noticed the knife you carry."

Gabor looked down at the Kreigsmarine dagger, which

hung from a scabbard on his belt and under his suit coat. The dagger had an eagle-shaped pommel with the eagle clutching a swastika surrounded by a wreath. The crossguard displayed the image of an anchor.

"Yes. What about it?" Gabor asked. His knife was always near.

"Here's another, my friend," Zimmerman said as he handed his Kreigsmarine dagger to Gabor.

"I don't need two," Gabor responded amid a sense of confusion.

"For good luck on your mission. Admiral Doenitz presented this to me personally and said it was a good luck piece. That's why none of my assignments resulted in the loss of a ship."

"I don't want your good luck piece," Gabor protested mildly.

"No. No. I insist. I want you to succeed on this special operation. You will forever change our chance for victory."

Taking the dagger, Gabor said, "Thank you. We certainly will meet after the war and I'll return it to you."

"I already look forward to seeing you again." Hearing a call from one of his crew, Zimmerman said, "Your raft is ready. You should go."

The two men confidently shook hands as Gabor thanked Zimmerman again before joining the two men holding the raft. He jumped aboard and the men pushed him away. He began paddling into the night and the crew dropped into the U-boat's open hatch before it submerged and continued the next part of its mission to Key West.

The warning shouts from one of the lookouts on the

conning tower allowed the remembrance to fade and brought Zimmerman back to present day reality, as he was still awaiting the return of the two saboteurs.

"Plane! Plane! Out of the east!" the lookout yelled.

Out of the rising sun, an American Avenger torpedo bomber suddenly dropped into view and began a run at the floating target. Methodically, the plane sent streams of .30 caliber rounds from its forward-mounted machine gun to the U-boat as its bomb bay door opened to deliver certain death to the German sailors.

"Dive! Dive!" Zimmerman commanded as his crew spotted the approaching enemy bomber and dodged the incoming .30 caliber rounds.

As the German sailors scrambled to slide down the ladder into the sub's relative safety, one crew member's chest erupted in blood as it was hit by several rounds. His body tumbled toward the conning tower deck.

With a quick look at his dead crew member, the captain took a final look at the approaching enemy plane.

Zimmerman's eyes widened as he saw a torpedo drop from the American plane. A shimmering glint of sunlight on the torpedo caught Zimmerman's attention. The instant reflection made it look like a golden torpedo. Ironic, Zimmerman thought to himself as he dropped through the open hatch and secured it behind him.

The warm waters of the Gulf of Mexico closed over the U-boat's bow as she sought the relative safety of the deep. It wouldn't make it though, as the Avenger's 2,000-pound Mark 13 torpedo struck near the stern, killing the men stationed there. Water began pouring in as a fire spread throughout the U-boat, filling it with acrid smoke.

Commanding his helmsman to take her to the ocean bottom, Zimmerman thought briefly about giving up his good luck knife earlier to Gabor. He quickly tossed aside his thoughts. Realizing there would be no tomorrow for his crew, he spoke solemnly on the intercom to his men. "We cannot let our cargo or any of us be captured. I'm sorry to say that we will sacrifice our lives to protect it. I salute you!"

Hearing the men's cheers echoing through the smoke-filled submarine, Zimmerman turned his attention to his charts. He needed to find the deepest area possible to hide his U-boat from the Americans while his crew raced to contain the fire.

Once they found themselves unable to make way, they would open the seacocks and flood the submarine, allowing her to sink to the bottom. The entire crew would drown, but Zimmerman was resigned to the cards fate had dealt them.

Zimmerman barked out a new heading which would take them southeast away from the Keys as the crew fought valiantly to contain the fire and seawater filling the U-boat.

The Avenger climbed as it successfully completed its bombing run and banked to circle its dying prey. But it soon lost the stricken U-boat as a tropical storm rapidly rolled in and the plane had to return to base.

After the storm passed, the plane and a destroyer returned to the area where the U-boat had been sighted. Although they searched the area, they didn't find it.

CHAPTER 2

A few days earlier

Savannah, Georgia, 1945

After burying his raft once he landed, Dieter Gabor walked with his small suitcase into Savannah as dawn was breaking and found the bus station. He checked the route schedules and went to a nearby restaurant where he ordered breakfast and killed time until the bus station's ticket window opened. When it was time, he walked back to the station and purchased a ticket for his next destination.

Learning that he would have to wait two days to catch the bus, he asked the ticket seller for directions to the nearest guest house. Pleased that a house was nearby, he walked the short distance and rented a room for two nights.

He used the alias of John Smith which was the name on his identification papers, on a letter from a supposed girlfriend postmarked in Buffalo, New York, and on a picture of the girlfriend that was inscribed to John Smith. Once in the room, Gabor set his suitcase on the small dresser, stripped off his clothes to his underwear and laid on the bed as he let out a long sigh and relaxed.

The stress of making the first leg of his journey was over. Gabor decided he would keep a low profile and stay in his room, venturing out only to dine by himself in the nearby cafe. He didn't want to raise any unnecessary attention towards himself.

As the thirty-eight-year-old relaxed, he thought about his past visits to the U.S. where he had attended college in Cincinnati, Ohio. He was then living with relatives and enjoying the large contingent of Germans there who had immigrated and settled on the banks of the Ohio River. After college, Gabor returned to Germany for additional studies in engineering and began working in aviation. He continued to take summer vacations in Ohio to visit relatives.

When war in Europe broke out, he had enlisted in naval intelligence, the Abwher. His work earned him a rapid rise within the organization and Gabor was pleased that his intellect and innovative approaches resulted in receiving additional training as a field operative. His successes attracted the eyes of his superiors.

Gabor's future would take an interesting twist in 1944 when the Abwher became a part of the Reich Main Security Office and under the control of Heinrich Himmler's Waffen-SS. Himmler had earlier worked with Hitler to develop a strategically important special mission and oversaw the selection of the one man to fulfill it. Gabor was a natural for the assignment and was quickly identified and selected. It was also a tremendous asset that he spoke fluent English without an accent and had previously lived in the U.S. for several years.

The two days in Savannah passed without incident and Gabor caught the bus to Warm Springs, which was located an hour southwest of Atlanta. The bus was nearly full with Savannah residents traveling to Warm Springs to escape the ravages of yellow fever that spring.

When Gabor arrived in Warm Springs late that afternoon, he checked into a small hotel on Broad Street, again using the John Smith alias. He walked upstairs to his room and dropped off his suitcase. Returning downstairs, he left the hotel and went for a walk. He wanted to see as much in person as he could since his only exposure to the area had been through studying maps.

He walked past the city hall and out of town. According to the map that he previously studied and now visualized in his mind, he knew it would be a short distance to the Little White House. He was anxious to scout the area before nightfall.

As Gabor walked, he thought about how much he enjoyed the expanse of hardwood forests that surrounded the village of Warm Springs. It reminded him of Germany's forests and the time he spent hiking there. As he neared the Little White House, he noticed the armed sentries who were on duty and patrolling the grounds.

Gabor decided not to risk being stopped and questioned. He instead turned and walked back to town, stopping to have dinner in one of the restaurants lining Broad Street.

When Gabor returned to his room, he opened his suitcase and pulled out the two Kreigsmarine daggers. He recognized his own because of his initials that were scratched into the blade below the hilt. He smiled as he developed an idea. He picked up Zimmerman's dagger and used it to scratch "DG235" on his blade in a subtle reference to himself and his U-boat captain and friend. Then Gabor used his own dagger to scratch his initials and 235 on it. He would use his own dagger for the mission, but keep Zimmerman's blade for good luck as he made his eventual escape.

Glancing at his watch, Gabor decided to catch a few hours of sleep before departing on his secret mission. He hoped for an overcast night to help mask his moves. He planned to carefully scout the grounds that evening and identify the sentry post as well as time the patrols.

After successfully completing the first part of his scouting mission without incident, he returned to his hotel. The next day he maintained a low profile and stayed in his room.

CHAPTER 3

The Little White House
Warm Springs, Georgia, 1945

The 90-degree waters of the springs edging the Pine Mountain hillside attracted visitors for years. They also attracted one U.S. president—Franklin D. Roosevelt.

For years Roosevelt had enjoyed the effect of the rejuvenating power the warm springs had on his polio-ravaged legs. He had a modest, six-room cottage built a quarter mile south of town so that he could spend as much time there as possible. Most of the rooms were paneled with Georgia pine. The cottage had a rustic air about it, but with a quiet touch of understated sophistication.

The one-story, wooden structure was built upon the side of a hill. It featured a combination living/dining room with flanking French doors that opened onto a sundeck where

Roosevelt would enjoy the view of a heavily wooded ravine.

There were two bathrooms and three bedrooms; one just for the president. Through a shared bathroom was Eleanor's bedroom. The bedroom for the president's personal secretary was on the other side of the house.

At 1:00 a.m. on April 12, Gabor secretively emerged from the woods near the cottage where he had been observing the rounds of the president's security detail. He had scouted the grounds the night before as he finalized his plans for assassinating Roosevelt.

Two guards were stationed at the front entrance to the cottage. He had noted that one guard would walk around the house every thirty minutes. He would have to time his attack carefully.

Gabor had almost missed the two dark green-painted sentry posts that were set in the edge of the pine woods to guard the rear of the cottage and the stairs to the sundeck and first floor. They weren't noted on the map of the property, which he had been given in Germany. It was only through the carelessness of one of the sentries lighting a cigarette that he noticed him. That and the sharp rebuttal called from the other sentry post.

When clouds overhead blocked the moonlight, he made his way quickly and carefully to the side of the cottage. As he moved, his eyes scoured the grounds for any movement.

When he neared the cottage, he made his way to Eleanor Roosevelt's open bedroom window. He looked inside and didn't see any movement, nor did he hear any sounds. He knew from what he had overheard at a Warm Springs restaurant that

Eleanor had not accompanied the president on his 41st trip to the cottage. It would be his last trip.

Gabor cautiously hoisted himself through the floor-to-ceiling window and into the room where he froze as he listened for any sounds which could signal a threat. Hearing none, he crept through the open door to the shared bathroom. Once on the other side, he slowly cracked open the door to the president's room and peered inside.

Next to the door, he saw a small lamp on the pine nightstand. Its soft light illuminated the president's features. The president's eyeglasses and cigarette holder were also on the nightstand.

Gabor carefully inched the door open and entered the room. Standing next to the sleeping leader, he could hear the president's laborious breathing. Hearing nothing to create concern, he moved toward the bed and looked down at the ashen gray face of the sleeping man. The war had taken its toll on his health. It was difficult to hide.

The agent allowed a smile to cross his face as he reached for his Kreigsmarine dagger, which hung from a scabbard on his belt.

He grasped the white celluloid handle with gold wire wrapping and plunged the dagger into Roosevelt's chest.

In response to the dagger piercing his heart, Roosevelt's body suddenly jerked. His eyes starkly opened with momentary shock, then glazed over as he died. FDR, America's wartime president, was dead.

As Roosevelt's body relaxed, Gabor released his hand from the dagger and checked the president's pulse to confirm he was dead. Gabor stepped back and looked at the message the Third Reich had delivered to the U.S. News of the assassination would set back the Allied advance into Germany. Hitler would be pleased with the blow that had been struck against the leader of the American people, showcasing the power and lethal reach of the Third Reich.

Satisfied with his accomplishment, Gabor's focus next turned to escaping successfully. He carefully exited the room the way he had entered by returning to Eleanor's bedroom. He looked at his watch and saw that only ten minutes had passed. A quick kill and run, he smiled to himself as he peered out the window. Seeing nothing of concern, he dropped to the ground and crossed the yard into the nearby woods. He quickly made his way back to town and checked out of his room that morning.

During breakfast, he watched a number of military vehicles race through town and head toward the Little White House. Although there was a lot of activity, word of Roosevelt's assassination had not made its way to town. Gabor was glad as it made his escape easier. He was able to catch an eight o'clock bus to Atlanta. From there he travelled north to Cincinnati where he planned to have his relatives hide him until the end of the war.

As Gabor travelled, he bought newspapers and looked for headlines announcing the assassination of Roosevelt. Instead, he found newspaper headlines announcing that the president died in the late afternoon of April 12th of a cerebral hemorrhage while sitting for a personal portrait. There was no mention of an assassination. Gabor guessed what had happened, and he was right. The assassination was covered up by the U.S. government so as not to cause fear in the U.S. or among the Allies. Gabor's successful mission would forever be lost to history.

PART TWO

CHAPTER 4

Present-day
Eastern Lake Erie

Twenty miles north of Erie, Pennsylvania, and four miles west of Long Point, Ontario, a team of divers had been working for several days in Canadian waters. They were on board a 40-foot workboat, the *Eerie Dearie*, which was anchored next to the sunken sidewheel passenger steamer, the *Atlantic*.

The 267-foot *Atlantic* was steaming from Buffalo to Detroit on August 20, 1852, at 2:00 A.M. when disaster struck during a heavy fog off of treacherous Long Point. The propeller freighter *Ogdensburg*'s bow struck the port side of the *Atlantic* as the *Atlantic* veered across its path. The collision caused the *Atlantic* to sink in 150 feet of water.

The ship carried 600 passengers, far in excess of her capacity. Most of them were Norwegian and German immigrants. It was estimated that 250 passengers lost their lives when the ship sank.

The ship's safe contained $1 million in today's dollars of American Express gold. It was no surprise that the safe and its contents quickly became the target of a number of salvage operations over the following six years. In 1856, the gold was recovered by a group of successful treasure hunters.

The *Eerie Dearie*'s divers weren't focused on the *Atlantic*. They had found another nearby treasure to target instead: the first submarine in Lake Erie. They were in the initial stages of recovering that vessel, which was developed by Lodner Phillips in Michigan City, Indiana.

Phillips had a reputation for building submarines. In 1845, he launched his first submarine on Lake Michigan. It was constructed of wood with copper sheeting and had a hand-operated pressure cylinder, which controlled buoyancy. It was forty-feet-long and four feet in diameter. Over the years, Phillips experimented with a number of designs. In 1851, he designed a self-driven craft that was sixty feet in length with a seven-foot beam and a top speed of four-and-a-half-knots. It had an onboard air supply and could stay submerged for four hours with twenty to thirty people on board. Two glass observation domes admitted light and it also had artificial cabin light for deep descents as well as for casting illumination outside of the hull.

In 1853, Phillips was asked to bring one of his submarines to Lake Erie to aid in the search for the gold on board the *Atlantic*. When he submerged the twenty-foot-long vessel to 100 feet, it developed severe leaks and he was forced to surface and evacuate. Phillips repaired the submarine and tested it for leaks. During a test, one of its lines broke and it sunk near the *Atlantic*. Over the years, lake silt covered the sub and created a sunken treasure of its own.

Shipwreck hunters from Lake Erie Wreck Divers (LEWD) had worked with a Canadian team from Niagara Divers to secure the necessary licenses and permits from Canadian authorities to search for and dive upon Lodner's submarine once they had found it. Using side-scan sonar and sophisticated 3D imaging collected over two summers, they had found the mother lode three weeks earlier.

Teams of divers, using large tanks of trimix, had worked in shifts in the 150-foot-deep Lake Erie water to clear the silt away from the submarine. A combination of strong currents, cold water and physical exertion impacted a diver's trimix usage and amount of time they could work. Their bottom time was restricted to approximately twenty-five minutes in waters where the visibility varied from five to twenty feet.

Trimix is a special type of underwater breathing gas whereby a portion of helium is added to the conventional mix of oxygen and nitrogen, thus enabling divers to extend their time under water and at depths beyond those recommended for recreational sport diving. Only properly trained and skilled divers typically use underwater breathing gases other than normal air, which consists of approximately 21 percent oxygen and 78 percent nitrogen.

The *Eerie Dearie* would stay on station for five days at a time when the weather permitted. She made weekly trips to Erie to replenish her fuel, food and any necessary gear and to rotate in new dive teams. At times, dive teams from Canada rotated in to help with the silt removal.

Things went south on their fourth day out in mid-June. The morning dawned with calm seas and no hint of any problems. The captain and deckhand were working with the divers to ready their gear for the day's work assignments.

"Like glass," a six-foot-two, tanned, dark-haired man said as he gazed at the lake waters. He spoke softly, but in a confident tone. He was in his early forties and lived with his wonderfully aged Aunt Anne in the popular island resort village of Put-in-Bay, Ohio. It was located in Lake Erie's western basin on South Bass Island about halfway between Cleveland and Toledo. The man's name was Emerson Moore, an award-winning investigative reporter with *The Washington Post.*

"Love diving during days like this," his friend Mike Althaus commented. Althaus owned New Wave Dive Shop in Port Clinton.

"Yeah, and you owe us big time for being invited to dive," Rod Wachter, the head of LEWD, teased Moore. The graying Wachter could have passed as Moore's brother. "I really wanted to invite Scuba Kat to dive with us. She's much better to look at than you, Emerson!"

"Hear! Hear!" Althaus smiled at Wachter's comment about Althaus' nice-looking wife, although Wachter's wife was also easy on the eyes. On top of that, she was in the Women Divers Hall of Fame. She had been scheduled to rotate in on this tour, but had to cancel due to a family emergency. Her place was filled by a last-minute substitution, who wasn't as experienced as the rest of the team.

The substitute's name was Itsy Icarian. He was the kind of guy who couldn't catch a break. Bad luck seemed to follow him wherever he went. His combination of bad luck and clumsiness was a sure recipe for disaster—but he was an available diver when they needed one the most.

"So you got me, you lucky guys!" Icarian chimed in right before he tripped over some gear and went sprawling on the deck.

"You really should wear your glasses, Itsy," Moore said as he watched the thin-as-a-beanpole Icarian slowly get to his feet.

"I can see well without them," Icarian proclaimed as he rubbed his bruised knee.

"Okay, Double I," Moore joked using the initials from Icarian's first and last names.

"Let me think about the last few days," Wachter said. "You dropped a box of food in the water when you tripped on the dock in Erie. You then knocked a plate of chow off the table at dinner the other night. And then you ..."

Moore interrupted. "And don't forget that unexpected wave yesterday that sent you plopping in my lap!"

"Lap dance time," Althaus shouted with glee.

Moore grimaced at the thought. "Not from Itsy!"

"Okay, guys. So I'm a little clumsy. But I can dive!" Icarian said boldly.

Almost in unison, the other three divers looked at each other with raised eyebrows. They also had big grins on their faces.

Icarian had been a hanger-on at Althaus' New Wave Scuba Center. When he overheard the phone conversation between Wachter and Althaus, he begged to replace Wachter's absent wife on the dive. Althaus was hesitant. So was Wachter. They told him to stand by while they tried to find an alternate. They couldn't and so they reluctantly allowed Icarian to join them.

The nervous and high-strung Icarian was kept on a short leash during the trip, especially after he put potato chips in the other three men's drysuit booties. He thought it was funny, but the men didn't appreciate the delay caused by the need to clean their booties.

The first dive team for the day was Althaus and Icarian. They geared up and Moore geared up as the safety diver, who was on standby near the dive site as an emergency first responder for the team. While the two men went over the side, Moore took a seat in the Zodiac. Wachter had already settled aboard the craft and was leaning against the outboard. In case of an emergency, Wachter would navigate the Zodiac to a position on the water for Moore to drop overboard.

"Welcome aboard my yacht, the *SS Wachter*," Wachter kidded as he breathed in the fresh lake air and watched the surface for an emergency float.

Sitting with his mask dangling from his neck as he also scanned the lake surface for an emergency signal, Moore commented, "I like these inflatables. I've got one at the bay, but I'd like to get a bigger one. I told Jerry Matsos over at Island Marine Sales that I'd buy a Briggs from him one day."

"Don't wait too long. You've got to enjoy the small things in life, Emerson," Wachter solemnly advised.

Down below, Althaus was in the lead and carried the business end of an air gun, which he would point at the silt to wash it away from the sub. As he descended along the ascent line, he was followed by the air hose that was connected to a generator on deck. Icarian followed Althaus.

When they reached twenty feet below the water surface, Althaus stopped to secure a bailout bottle of pure oxygen to the line. He saw Icarian slowing his descent and preparing to affix his bailout bottle. Althaus continued dropping to the bottom, reveling in the unequalled calmness of being submerged. He loved being lost in the depths of any body of water. He dropped through two thermoclines and shuddered as he realized that the water temperature was much colder than the previous day.

When he reached the bottom, he was disappointed by how murky the water was, severely restricting visibility, which was better the previous day. With no time to waste, he aimed the pressure gun and began washing away more of the silt.

Above Althaus, a nervous Icarian renewed his descent after he clumsily allowed his bailout bottle to slip from his grasp and drop into the murky lake bed below. Knowing that he would need the bottle for his safe ascent back to the surface, Icarian chased after the disappearing bottle.

When he reached the bottom, he anxiously searched for his dropped bottle. As a result, his breathing became more rapid and his heart rate increased. Panicking because he couldn't find his bottle in the murky water, he quickly became disoriented. He didn't know which way to turn to reach Althaus and the sub.

Icarian glanced at his dive watch and air pressure gauge. He was surprised at how much time he had spent in the water and the amount of trimix he had expended. He wasn't thinking clearly and wasn't sure what to do with his ascent and the required safety stops since he didn't have his 50/50 bottle. He decided that he better shoot up a bag.

Reaching for the orange safety bag on his belt, he filled it with air from his regulator. He released it, allowing it to shoot to the surface with a line that had one end secured to his belt. The bag broke through the surface about fifty feet from where the divers had descended.

Above, Wachter and Moore were watching the lake surface as they discussed the progress they were making on recovering the sub. The team was on track for next week's arrival of the work ship that would assist in raising the sub from the lake bottom.

"Trouble!" Wachter said in a serious tone when he spotted the bobbing deco bag. He started the Zodiac's engine and immediately piloted the craft to the bag.

"Oh, boy!" Moore said as he pulled up his mask and inserted the regulator in his mouth. As soon as the Zodiac reached the bag, Moore rolled off the craft with double tanks of trimix and two 50/50 bottles. He didn't know what to expect as he began following the line down.

Moore's heart was beating strong and fast as the spike in his adrenaline created an artificial high. He quickly followed the line downward, scanning the water in all directions for signs of trouble. He was on high alert and ready to swiftly react.

As he neared the lake bottom, he spotted Icarian and swam over to him. As Moore approached, he glanced at Icarian's eyes and saw they were filled with panic.

Fear had paralyzed Icarian until he saw the 50/50 bottle that Moore had brought. Icarian wildly reached out to grab the bottle and soar to the stop point. He had no willpower and wanted to swim upward as fast as possible. It was an action that could end Icarian's life and endanger Moore's as well. Moore held up his hand for Icarian to calm down, but Icarian ignored him and grabbed one of the bottles. Before Icarian could start a panicked ascent, Moore grabbed hold of him and shook him violently. Moore's head shook from side to side as he sought to calm the overwrought diver. At the same time, Moore placed his hands firmly on Icarian's shoulders to comfort and calm him.

Finally, Moore saw the wild-eyed look in Icarian's face disappear and his lost senses gradually return. His breathing normalized. Moore gave Icarian a thumbs-up to signal the start of a slow, controlled ascent to the first safety stop point.

Icarian nodded and also gave Moore a thumbs-up as Moore grasped Icarian's wrist to lead him up the ascent line to the first safety stop point for a timed decompression. When they reached the stop, Moore motioned for Icarian to place the mouthpiece for the 50/50 air mix in his mouth as Moore repeated the action. They waited for ten minutes before rising to the next stop point, where they floated for another ten minutes before starting their final ascent to the surface.

When their heads emerged from the water and next to the Zodiac, they saw that Althaus was on board the work boat. He had exited the lake about five minutes earlier and shed his gear. He was peering anxiously at the two divers in the water.

"You okay?" Althaus called.

"We're fine!" Moore yelled. "Now," he added.

Turning from helping Icarian climb in the Zodiac, Wachter shouted to Althaus in a teasing manner, "It was hero time for Emerson!"

"What a surprise! And no women around to swoon at your heroics!" Althaus kidded.

Moore threw a good-natured punching motion out toward Althaus. "Just as long as I make your wife swoon!"

"Hey! Private property! Besides she swoons whenever I enter a room," Althaus joked.

"Yeah. Yeah. Scuba Kat only has eyes for me," Moore countered.

Interrupting their fun-filled exchange, Wachter turned his attention to Icarian. Wachter's tone was pointedly somber. "What happened, Itsy?"

Icarian explained what had happened earlier with dropping the bailout bottle at the safety stop shortly after beginning the dive. Moore, who had climbed aboard the Zodiac, soon described the eventual rescue.

Wachter listened intently before he spoke.

"Panic below is one of the worst things a diver can do," Wachter lectured. He was upset with himself in allowing Icarian to dive with them and had decided that he wouldn't be making any more dives with the team.

"I know. I couldn't help myself," Icarian said nervously.

"You won't be doing any more dives for us, Itsy," Wachter said firmly.

"But, I ..."

Wachter's stern look stopped Icarian's pleading.

"Nice job, Emerson," Wachter commented as he looked over at Moore, who was stowing his gear.

Moore shrugged off the compliment and looked at Icarian. "Just a bit of itsy bitsy trouble, right Itsy?" Moore tried to cheer up the crestfallen diver as Wachter started the Zodiac's motor and headed it to the dive boat.

CHAPTER 5

Heineman's Winery
Put-in-Bay, Ohio

A week passed since the diving incident and Moore had returned to his aunt's house on East Point on South Bass Island. He had been puttering around the garage and decided to get a glass of wine and some cheese at Heineman's Winery.

He walked into the house to let Aunt Anne know that he'd be gone for a while. He found his spry aunt seated on the front porch overlooking the bay.

"Beautiful day," Moore said as he looked at the various boats entering and departing Put-in-Bay's harbor.

"I never tire of this view," she responded with a big smile. "Ever!"

Moore was glad that he had moved in with his aunt a few years earlier. She had lost her husband and Moore had lost his son and wife. Together, aunt and nephew would often privately commiserate about their losses. Besides, he enjoyed using her island home as his idyllic base of operations. Being an investigative reporter, it didn't matter the location of his domicile. Additionally, he still had the houseboat on the Potomac River in Alexandria, Virginia, to use whenever his editor wanted him back in nearby Washington, D.C. for meetings.

"I'm going to head over to Heineman's Winery. Would you like to come with me?"

"No. I'm just going to relax here Emerson. Maybe you'll meet a nice girl while you're out and I wouldn't want to be in the way," she said as she thought about a couple of the pernicious women with whom he once had been involved.

Moore rushed over to his aunt and bent down to give her a big hug. "Why do I need anyone else when I've got the prettiest girl on the island right here," he teased as he planted a soft kiss on her cheek.

Pushing him away, she spoke with mock anger. "Go on. You get on your way. You're nothing more than a spouting wordsmith! Go use your sweet talk on some nice, young thing. Not me. I'm over the hill."

"You're always the apple of my eye," Moore teased back.

"Out! Out with you," she urged. "And please bring me a bottle of their Pink Catawba!" she shouted as he walked back through the house.

When he reached the garage, he climbed into his late uncle's 1929 Ford Model A truck. The classic cream vehicle had a tan top and green fenders. His uncle had replaced its original 40-horsepower, 4-cylinder engine with a 289-cubic-inch V8 engine. He had also replaced the standard three-speed transmission with an automatic and a floor shifter. The truck was tricked out with lots of chrome and a spotless rich brown leather bench seat.

Moore started the little truck and backed out of the garage. In a minute, he was driving along Bay View and past Perry's Monument on his left and the harbor on his right. Driving past DeRivera Park, he turned left onto Catawba Avenue and followed it out to the winery.

Heineman's Winery dated back to 1888 when an immigrant and entrepreneur from Baden, Germany, named Gustav Heineman, arrived on South Bass Island. Knowing about the island's rich, fertile soil and cool, temperate climate—ideal for growing flavorful grapes—he started the winery.

After parking the Ford to the side of the building, Moore walked into the winery, greeting the third, fourth and fifth generations of the Heinemans—Louie, Ed and Dustin—as he entered. Moore was envious of the Heineman family. He had always wanted to be in an environment where he could work with family members.

Stopping at the wine bar, he ordered a glass of Pink Catawba wine and a cheese plate and bought a bottle of wine for his aunt. He then walked over to a nearby table, took a seat and began to enjoy his tasty treat.

He overheard a couple seated behind him discussing the recent death of a family member and a knife from World War II, which had belonged to their grandfather. Moore was intrigued about the knife and thought he recognized the woman's voice. When he swiveled around in his chair, he recognized the woman. It was Connie Mueller, an attractive islander in her late twenties with large, chocolate brown eyes.

"Connie! I didn't see you when I walked in," Moore exclaimed.

Mueller leaned toward Moore and gave him a quick peck on the cheek. "I didn't see you either; otherwise I would have given you a kiss sooner, Emerson. I don't think I ever did repay you for rescuing me from that group of guys at the Beer Barrel that night!" she smiled appreciatively.

Moore remembered it and the run-in with her biker boyfriend later that same night. "No problem." Seeing that she was seated with another woman, Moore asked, "Where's Boozer?"

"Home. You couldn't pay him to come to a winery. If the place doesn't serve beer, he won't come," she said with exasperation. "When I left, he was sitting on the porch with his third beer and throwing rocks at a beehive. I told him that he better quit, but he doesn't like listening to people."

"You might be nursing him when you get back to your place."

"He's a big boy. He can take care of himself, although sometimes I think that boy has no sense—throwing stones at a beehive! Sounds like a recipe for disaster to me!"

"I'll say," Moore agreed, as he imagined the burly biker casting his stones.

"Emerson, this is my cousin, Chris Casenheiser. She's up visiting since my father passed away."

"Hello, Chris," Moore said to the good-looking blonde who smiled at him.

"Hello, Emerson," Casenheiser said.

Turning to Mueller, Moore spoke softly and said, "I'm real sorry about your father's death."

"Thank you, Emerson."

"His name was Herman Gabor, right?"

"That's it."

"I knew who he was, but never had a chance to get to know him better," Moore explained. "He lived out on Peach Point, right?"

"Right."

Finishing his glass of Pink Catawba wine, Moore commented, "I couldn't help overhearing your discussion about your grandfather's knife."

"Yeah, it's really cool," Connie responded. "Some sort of World War II knife."

"That sounds interesting," Moore said.

"It's at my dad's house. We found it while we were cleaning it out," she explained. "If you like World War II memorabilia, you should come over. We found the knife and a couple of other things in a small locked chest. When we were growing up, Dad wouldn't let us see what was in the chest. But with Dad passing away, I found the key on his key chain and opened it."

"I'd be interested in seeing the knife."

"Do you have time to come over to the house now?" Mueller asked as she and Casenheiser stood.

"Sure," Moore replied as he rose from his chair and followed them out the door.

"Follow us," she said as the two jumped into a parked golf cart.

"Give me a second. I'm over there." Moore pointed to his truck. Moore hopped into the truck, started it and followed the golf cart to the house on Peach Point near the Ohio State University facilities. The house was on the west shore of the island and had a beautiful view of evening sunsets on Lake Erie.

Parking the golf cart in front of the garage, the two ladies hopped out and opened the overhead garage door as Moore parked and joined them.

"I've been moving some of the stuff out of the house. Getting ready for a garage sale," she explained.

"That's always tough to do, going through a parent's belongings and having to dispose of things," Moore offered as he followed them into the garage and to a chest, which sat on the workbench.

"It is," she agreed. "This is the chest I told you about. It belonged to my grandfather, Dieter Gabor." She produced a key and unlocked the medium-sized, metal chest. She opened the top to reveal a Kreigsmarine dagger with a white celluloid handle and a gold wire wrapping. The dagger had an eagle-shaped pommel with the eagle clutching a swastika surrounded by a wreath. The crossguard displayed the image of an anchor.

Mueller reached inside the box and reverently withdrew the dagger before handing it to Moore.

Moore turned the dagger over as he admired its fine workmanship and intricate detail. "This is a keeper, Connie," he murmured. When he saw DG235 scratched into the blade, he asked, "Any idea what this is about?"

"Let me see." Mueller peered at the blade in Moore's hand. "I'd guess the DG stands for my grandfather's initials. I don't know what the 235 means."

Moore felt his natural curiosity pulling him in. "I'd like to check this out."

"You want it? It's for sale," she said. "I'll throw in the trunk and its contents, too. One less item for me to sell at the garage sale."

Moore turned his attention from the exquisite dagger to the trunk. "What else do you have in there?"

She withdrew a small package of envelopes that were held together by string. "These letters from my grandfather to a man here on the island when he was trying to find a job here. He moved here from Cincinnati and lived the rest of his life here after the war."

Mueller smiled with a conspiratorial look. "I read them when I opened the trunk. After all of those years of not being able to see the contents, I had to read them Emerson."

Moore grinned. "I understand. Anything more in there?"

"A few maps of South Carolina and Georgia. They're in German." She handed a map to Moore.

Looking at the map in his hand, Moore commented, "Looks like they indeed could be World War II vintage. Was your grandfather in the service?" While he waited for a response, he saw that there was a penciled path from Savannah to Warm Springs, Georgia, on one of the maps.

"Don't know," she mused. "He died before I was born and

Dad didn't want to talk about my grandfather's past." She pulled out a folded knit cap and handed it to Moore. "Does this help, Emerson?"

Moore examined the aged cap and found the Kreigsmarine insignia on the cap. "Well, he was either in the service or came across this somehow."

"There's a scarf in here and a couple of worn shirts. Nothing more. What will you give me for the whole batch of stuff, including the chest?"

The two negotiated briefly and reached an agreeable price. Moore paid Mueller and left with his newfound treasures. His mind was beginning to wander with ideas about the knife—interesting, contrived and highly speculative ideas that were so typical of an ace investigative reporter like Emerson Moore. He drove into the village and over to the Chamber of Commerce office where he parked. He first stopped to buy some pastries for his aunt from the Village Bakery.

"Hi Pauline. Hi Beth," Moore called out as he entered through the front screen door. Pauline Garstock was the highly energized owner of the bakery and a constant source of encouragement to Moore whenever he needed it. Her daughter, Beth, worked for her mother in the bakery during the summer months and then returned to her home in Costa Rica for the rest of the year.

"It's about time you came in here, Mister," Pauline teased when she saw Moore.

"Hi Emerson," Beth called from the back where she was busy finishing an order.

Moore waved. "Pauline, it's only been a week," Moore started.

"How am I ever going to get you to put some weight on?" she joked.

Ever since his conditioning and training in Cedar Key, Moore had lost weight and become more muscular. He had continued many of the exercises he had learned and was frequently running to maintain his physique. "I need to keep it off, but that doesn't prevent me from buying a few pastries for my aunt and me."

"I know. Sometimes I see you running down the street," Pauline commented. "When are you going to join Beth and me for some yoga? You should try it. I do it every day. Keeps me limber."

"Maybe one of these days. I have a workout routine I follow."

Moore smiled to himself. Pauline was an amazing woman whose vim and vigor was not defined by her advancing age, but instead was driven by a deeply rich spirit within her that defied the exuberance of many women half her age and younger.

"You let us know and we'll get you limbered up, too. Now, what can I get you?"

Moore carefully selected his delectable pastries and paid for them. As he was leaving and walking through the covered porch between the bakery and chamber, he heard a familiar voice call.

"Just like I expected. You walk by here with your uptown, brownstone Washington D.C., East Coast, hoo-hah, 'who-dey?' nose up in the air Mr. Pulitzer Prize Winner and don't say hello to people who simply care about you, a lot!"

Moore stopped in his tracks smartly, and turned toward

the open door to the chamber. He could see a sixtyish-looking blonde standing in the doorway. She had a large smile on her face.

"Linda!" Moore exclaimed as he walked over to her and gave her a big hug. "I didn't know you were on the island."

"Excuses, excuses," a voice called from behind Linda. "If he knew you were visiting on the island, he would have made a point to stay away," the woman's sister shouted jokingly.

Jumping right in, Linda said as Moore released her from his hug, "Now just you remember which of us sisters is the nicest," she smirked.

"Are you kidding me? That boy can't remember a thing. He has a hard enough time trying to tie his shoelaces in the morning. And it's really hard because he's usually wearing loafers," the sister called.

"Hello, Maggie," Moore said as he started to hold out his arms to hug his good island friend Maggie Beckford.

"Don't kiss up to me, buddy. You've done your damage."

Moore persisted and advanced reservedly towards her.

Pushing his outstretched arms aside, Maggie teased, "Huh-uh. Don't touch me. You've got cooties!"

"I thought cousin Jimmy gave you the cooties," Moore teased back as he referred to her alter ego.

"Watch yourself, buster!" Maggie threatened.

"Bringing us goodies?" Linda asked.

"They're for my aunt, but go ahead and take one," Moore said as he started to open the pastry box.

"You're too easy. That's why we enjoy picking on you, Emerson. We don't need any of your cookies," Linda said.

"Yeah. And it would be just like you to try to make my sugar level skyrocket," Maggie teased. "You know I'm diabetic, you clown!"

"Why do I continually put myself through this with you two?" Moore asked to no one in particular.

"Because you have to walk by here on the way to the bakery, dumb ass," Maggie said with a warm smile.

"Besides, you like us, deep down in that cold heart of yours," Linda added.

"Only you two!" Moore said. Changing the center of their conversation, Moore asked Linda, "How long are you here visiting?"

"A couple of weeks."

"She'd stay longer, but then she'd have to pay me rent," Maggie quipped.

"What have you been up to?" Linda asked as she ignored her sister.

"Not too much. I've been taking it easy."

"Heard that you recently lost your memory," Linda mentioned.

"And finally your virginity!" Maggie cracked even though she knew that Moore had been married in the past.

"I don't know. I can't remember. What was your name again?" Moore retorted to Maggie before looking at Linda. "Yeah. Tough time. Still have nightmares. It's hard to really know what was a dream and what was real."

Suddenly Emerson had a thought. "Linda, you live in Georgia, don't you?"

"Yeah. Why?"

"Where in Georgia?"

"Southwest side of Atlanta."

"Ever get to Warm Springs?"

"I do. That's where President Franklin D. Roosevelt went to relax." Before Moore could ask another question, Linda continued. "They've turned his place into a museum. I'm on the museum's advisory board and volunteer there."

"You do?"

"That's what she said, Mister. You losing your hearing, too?" Maggie chimed in.

Ignoring Maggie's comment, Moore looked directly at Linda. "Could you come out to my truck? I'd like to show you something," he said with a renewed sense of anticipation.

"That's a line if I've ever heard one," Maggie said with a sly grin. "Linda, you be careful with pretty boy, especially if he wants you to go for a ride," she good-naturedly warned her sister.

Linda smiled as she stood to follow the handsome Moore. "Only in my dreams," she said wistfully as Moore walked through the door. She followed close on his heels.

When she arrived at the truck, Moore had the chest open. He rummaged through the clothes and extracted the map. Opening it, he displayed it to Linda, "Does this mean anything to you?"

Linda studied the map for twenty seconds. "A map with a line drawn between Savannah and Warm Springs? No. Not really. Should it?"

Moore looked at Linda's eyes and saw that they were focused on the open trunk. The Kreigsmarine dagger was partially uncovered. Her eyes progressively widened in astonishment. "Where did you get that dagger, Emerson?"

"I bought it from a friend. Estate sale," he explained without going into detail.

"There's a knife like that in the Little White House's office safe. I saw it once when our museum's director had the safe door open," she responded.

"Really?" Moore asked as he withdrew the dagger from the chest and handed it to Linda.

Linda chuckled as she examined the dagger. "Yeah. I got in trouble that day. I reached in the safe and picked up the knife and looked at it. When the director turned around, he got angry fast. Told me to put it back and not say anything about seeing it."

Moore's interest was significantly piqued. "Are you sure the daggers are identical?"

"They are. I won't ever forget what the one in the safe looked like. Not something I'd expect to find at the President's residence." She looked at the initials and numbers scratched into the dagger's blade. "The one in the safe had something scratched on it too, but I don't remember what it was. I only saw it briefly."

"You going to be lollygagging all day or ride back to the house with me?" Maggie called from the open window of her van which she driven up to Moore's vehicle.

"The mean sister calls me. I better get back in there," Linda said as she handed the dagger to Moore and started walking toward her sister's van. "It was great seeing you, Emerson."

"I hope to see you before you leave the island," Moore called after her as she waved. His mind was reeling as he thought about possible connections. As he climbed into the truck, he decided that he needed to spend some time on the Internet and search the possibilities. He was jacked up and getting high on life—an investigative reporter's life.

CHAPTER 6

That evening
Istanbul, Turkey

A figure walked on a quiet nighttime street after dinner at a nearby restaurant. Imad Uzun was returning to his apartment to finish packing for his flight the next day. He also needed to go over the plans that his terrorist cell had prepared. He would be responsible for carrying out the attack.

Not far away, two CIA spotters tracked his movements. As Uzun approached a parked SUV, a bomb planted in a spare tire on the back of the vehicle exploded, sending a burst of shrapnel across a tight radius and into Uzun's body. He was killed instantly.

The spotters slipped away quietly into the night and headed for Uzun's apartment. They were anxious to get their hands on the documents before anyone else had a chance.

They parked across from the front of the building and watched the street for any unusual activity. Seeing none after allowing twenty minutes to expire, they exited the vehicle and walked across the street to the apartment building.

One of the spotters extracted a set of tools and expertly picked the lock on the front door of the building. Cautiously, they opened the door and walked up the two flights of stairs to Uzun's apartment. When they arrived at the door to the apartment, the first spotter picked the lock while the second acted as a lookout.

Hearing the latch unlock, the spotter slowly opened the door as he flashed a light into the room. Seeing nothing out of the ordinary, he whispered to his companion to join him as he walked into the room. He continued to flash his light around to be sure that no danger was lurking.

When his companion entered the room, he closed and locked the door behind him. He flicked on the light switch, unknowingly completing the circuit. A huge explosion instantly filled the four-room apartment, killing the two men.

Multiple fires rapidly spread throughout the apartment building and were followed by shrill cries for help. Confused and scared tenants rushed into the halls and stairways as they sought escape from the blazing inferno, which threatened the entire building.

Across the street in a five-story apartment building, a watcher stepped away from the window. From his perch in a fifth-floor apartment, he had watched the two men leave their car and break into Uzun's building. He had a smile on his face, knowing that the beneficiaries of his tip weren't alive to make any connection to him. He had already been in the apartment and stolen Uzun's documents. He had also wired the explosives, which the spotters had ignited.

Smiling, the double-crosser turned away from the burning hell across the street. He picked up the briefcase filled with Uzun's plans and left the rented apartment. Within minutes, he hailed a taxi and disappeared into the midst of Istanbul.

CHAPTER 7

Liberty Aviation Museum
Port Clinton, Ohio

"Good burger," Moore said as he finished the last bite. After completing his daily workout, Moore had caught the early Miller Ferry to Catawba so that he could meet with Dick Rathmell at the Tin Goose Diner, a throwback to the family diners of old. The diner was connected to the Liberty Aviation Museum, located next to the Erie-Ottawa Regional Airport.

The museum had two hangars, a workshop and a WWII-themed three-story control tower. Each of the hangars were filled with military and classic vehicles and memorabilia, including uniforms as well as a flyable Ford trimotor transport plane, a trimotor under restoration, a B-25 Mitchell bomber named "Georgie Gal," a bright yellow AT-6 Texan trainer and a Stearman Model 75 biplane. Also displayed was a local favorite—a PT boat named *Thomcat* after local Port Clinton resident Lenny Thom, who in WWII served as John F. Kennedy's executive officer on PT109 when it was damaged and sunk in the Solomon Islands during 1943.

A friend of Moore's had shared that Rathmell was restoring a Grumman TBF Avenger torpedo bomber. Moore was beyond intrigued and genuinely imaginative in his inner speculation about all he had encountered thus far in his pursuit of a potential story. He had set up lunch with Rathmell, who soon after was giving Moore a tour of the blue Avenger.

"Yep. They've got good food here. You should try the milkshakes," Rathmell suggested.

"Milkshakes are a weakness of mine. Especially the old-fashioned thick ones, but I better not. They have a way of sticking to my ribs," Moore laughed.

"Ready to check out the restoration?" Rathmell asked.

"Sounds good to me," Moore said as he pulled cash from his pocket and paid the bill. He followed Rathmell out to the hangar to see the Avenger.

"Where did you find this beauty?" Moore asked.

"Naples, Florida. It was too good of a deal. I couldn't pass it up."

"Do you know where she saw service?" Moore asked as his eyes roved over her aged surface.

"Yep. She did anti-submarine patrols off of Florida, mostly around Key West. She then saw duty as a trainer before she was sold off," Rathmell answered. "She's got folding wings so she wouldn't take up unnecessary space on an aircraft carrier. See how her wings are mid-way up the fuselage?"

"Yes."

"That way the Grumman designers were able to give her a large bay. You could fit her with a 2,000-pound torpedo or four 500-pound bombs or an extra fuel tank."

"Is that a machine gun in the back?" Moore asked as he looked at a turret mounted behind the cockpit.

"Yep. That's a powered turret for the rear gunner. Had a .50 caliber machine gun. She had three of them. There was one in the nose for the pilot and one tucked into her belly for the bombardier/belly gunner to use."

"So, she had a crew of three?"

"Yep. That was standard then."

"You mentioned that the Avengers did anti-submarine patrols?"

"I did. They were perfect for long endurance and provided a stable weapons capacity. A lot of them were used in hunter-killer groups in the Atlantic." Rathmell sipped his coffee, and then asked, "Did you know they hunted Japanese subs in the Atlantic, too?"

"No. I had no idea. I didn't realize that the Japanese submarines were active in the Atlantic during WWII. Really? They were?"

"In the mid-1940s, the Japanese used specialized 350-foot long cargo submarines to transport rubber, quinine, tungsten and molybdenum. The Japs traded them for German radar, bombsights, vacuum tubes, optical glass and ball bearings. One Japanese sub, the *I-52*, was monitored by U.S. intelligence when it departed Singapore in March, 1944, to rendezvous with the German sub *U-530* in June in the mid-Atlantic."

"Did they exchange the cargo at sea?" Moore asked.

"No, the Japanese crew picked up a German sailor to guide her to port at Lorient on the French seacoast. That's where she'd be unloaded. But she never made it."

"An Avenger got her?"

A smile crossed Rathmell's face. "Yep. She was on a nearby carrier, the *USS Bogue*. The intercepts had pinpointed her location and the plane flew over her, dropping flares to light her up that night. They caught her on the surface. They ended up getting her with a Mark 24 'Fido' acoustic torpedo. This was payback for the Great American Turkey Shoot."

"What?"

"Yep. That's what they called it."

Moore smiled as he listened to the veteran. He was amazed by the wealth of knowledge the man had.

"During the early years of the war, German U-boats were sinking ships off the entire east coast of the United States. They were an unstoppable juggernaut until 1942 when torpedo planes like the Avenger began hunting them down." Rathmell patted the fuselage with pride.

"One area where U-boats concentrated their attacks was around Cape Hatteras and the Outer Banks off the North Carolina coast. It became known as Torpedo Junction. The Germans called it The Great American Turkey Shoot. It was an area where ships gathered to form into convoys before heading across the Atlantic. Wolfpacks of U-boats waited like hungry wolves, licking their chops to attack the ships.

"Prior to the middle of 1942, there were no blackouts in the area. Lights from towns and passing cars on coastal roads helped silhouette the waiting ships and assisted the U-boats in torpedoing them. The U-boats seemed invincible. It was a disaster until the Avengers showed up and turned the tide."

"I had no idea," Moore commented in awe.

"As U-boat sinkings increased, a number of U-boats moved to attack ships in the Gulf of Mexico. They focused on attacking tankers from Texas to Louisiana. One tanker, the *Virginia*, was sunk at the mouth of the Mississippi River."

"I've never been aware of this."

"Bet they didn't teach you about that in school. Not much was said about U-boat attacks off the U.S.; the government worked hard to squash newspaper stories so as not to panic the public. The government covered up a lot during the war, or so I've been told."

"Imagine that. Government cover-ups!" Moore said sarcastically. "How do you know so much?" Moore asked.

"I was in the Air Force and love anything to do with planes, especially Avengers. My grandfather worked in intelligence during the war and he told me quite a few stories. That's why I don't believe everything that I read in the media. Too many cover-ups going on to mold public opinion."

Moore reacted quickly. "Not in anything I write or the writers I know," he countered. "And with the Internet, I believe there are more avenues to get the truth out."

"Well then, you must be the exception. It happened a lot during the war based on what I heard from my grandfather." Rathmell moved closer to the plane. "Climb up if you want, Emerson."

Moore climbed onto the wing and thoughtfully peered into the cockpit.

"I'm still restoring it. It's not finished, as you can tell," Rathmell called up to Moore.

"Looks good to me," Moore responded as he studied the controls and wires that were dangling in the plane. "What are these numbers scratched on the side?"

"They would be the latitude and longitude of the last sub they sunk, in descending order. This one sunk a sub off of Key West in April 1945, so I've been told. Some planes have a number of those scratched in by the bombardier. He'd scratch one on the side as the war was nearing the end. If they sunk another sub, he'd scratch a line through it and scratch in the newest sinking location."

"Sort of like a memorial," Moore mused out loud.

"You could call it that if you wanted."

Moore climbed down from the plane and gazed at the work being done on the Ford trimotor restoration.

"Come along and I'll show you what we're doing back here and then take you up front to see the rest of our museum."

"Thanks," Moore said as he followed his tour guide. "I appreciate the tour and the history lesson."

CHAPTER 8

One week later
Warm Springs, Georgia

After a morning jog through Warm Springs and taking in the surrounding forests, Moore showered and grabbed breakfast at a small diner a couple of doors away from his hotel. He drove thirteen hours the previous day from the shores of Lake Erie so that he could meet with the Little White House curator. Without saying anything about the dagger, he was able to set the meeting on the basis of background research for an upcoming *Post* story.

Leaving the diner, he drove his Ford Mustang convertible with the top down the short distance from his Warm Springs hotel to Roosevelt's Little White House nestled on 1,700 acres in the pine woods of Harris County's Big Pine Mountain. Finding a parking spot, Moore parked his car and cast a quick look at the wispy morning sky to check for any signs of rain.

Seeing none, he opted to leave the top down.

Moore walked past the combination garage/servant's quarters and the guest house to the one-story, white cottage set on the edge of the hill. It was built of Georgia pine and constructed in the Colonial Revival style. He saw a bespectacled man with a slight build standing like a posted sentry near the front entrance. He guessed it was the museum curator, Peter Nehrebecky.

"Mr. Nehrebecky?"

"Yes," the man responded as he extended his hand. "You must be Emerson Moore."

Returning the handshake, Moore said, "Yes. I appreciate you taking time from your busy morning to meet with me, Mr. Nehrebecky."

"No problem. No problem at all. And call me Pete." Nehrebecky led Moore inside the pillared entranceway into the house. "I understand you'd like a tour of the house so you can write a story for your newspaper?"

"Right. I'm doing initial research for a possible story in *The Washington Post*."

"Okay, then. Let's get started," Nehrebecky said as he walked through the doorway and into the kitchen as Moore followed. "I usually have tour guides conduct the tours, but I decided I'd conduct yours."

"Thank you. I appreciate it."

"As you likely know, we are in President Roosevelt's Little White House, his personal presidential retreat which saw its construction completed in 1932 when he served as Governor of New York. Following his 1933 inauguration as our nation's

32nd president, FDR maintained this special residence. He so enjoyed his personal retreat for many reasons and made a total of sixteen visits while serving as president. It was rarely visited by the First Lady, his wife Eleanor, though she did have her own personal bedroom that you are about to see. Following FDR's death, this house and most of his personal property were willed to the Georgia Warm Springs Foundation. The Little White House was first opened to the public as a museum in 1948. Today, it is known as Roosevelt's Little White House State Historic Site and operated by the State of Georgia.

"So let's begin. This is the kitchen area where Daisy Bonner prepared Mr. Roosevelt's meals, his first through last." Nehrebecky pointed out items of interest in the kitchen, including Roosevelt's favorite device—the ice cream freezer.

Next, they walked through FDR's personal secretary's bedroom and onto the sundeck that overlooked a ravine filled with pines. Moore noted the two wooden guard shacks set along the edge of the woods.

"What a beautiful view," Moore said with admiration.

"It's relaxing. It has a calming effect."

"They had security this close to the house?" Moore asked as he pointed to the guard shacks.

"Right," Nehrebecky responded. "And in front, as well as walking patrols on the grounds. There was also a checkpoint at the front gate when you drove onto the property. Couldn't be too careful when we were at war."

Moore nodded his head with understandable agreement.

Walking through two open French doors, they entered the rustic living/dining room with its stone fireplace and naval paintings on the wall. Moore was struck by how spartan the room was. He assumed it was in stark contrast to the rich furnishings one would expect to see in Roosevelt's home at Hyde Park, New York.

Moore noticed that bookshelves lined the wall of both sides of the fireplace and a wooden ship was displayed on the mantel. "I like that ship model."

"The president and one of his Secret Service agents built that ship out of scrap lumber left over from the construction of the cottage," Nehrebecky commented in response.

"Nice work. When again was the house built?"

"1932 and all of the wood for the house came from this very property. He bought the site in 1927. He liked this parcel specifically because the mineral springs here seemed to rejuvenate his polio-ravaged legs. There's a pool on the grounds that I can show you, too," Nehrebecky offered.

"I'd like to see it."

"This is the room where Roosevelt was sitting on the afternoon of April 12, 1945. He was posing for a portrait painting when he suffered a massive stroke and died."

Nehrebecky was reverently silent for a couple of minutes as Moore walked around the room, trying to imagine the scene on the day the president died. The only discernible noise to be heard outside was a distant lawn mower being used to manicure the grounds.

"His bedroom is right through here," Nehrebecky said softly as he went through the open doorway into the adjoining bedroom.

Moore followed Nehrebecky through an open doorway

into a room with a double bed.

"This is the president's bedroom and through this shared bathroom, we enter into Eleanor's bedroom," he said as he walked through the rooms and out through the entrance hall and onto the covered portico. "Any questions so far?"

"Just one," Moore offered. He opened up the photo gallery on his cell phone and displayed the picture of the Kreigsmarine dagger from Connie Mueller's grandfather, Dieter Gabor.

"Does this look familiar to you?" He watched Nehrebecky's face closely for any reaction and was glad that he did as a shocked look crossed Nehrebecky's face.

"Where did you get that picture?"

"I took it."

The shocked look was replaced by a puzzled look. "I thought you said this was your first visit here."

"It is."

"Then where did you get this?"

"It's a picture of a friend's dagger. Look familiar?"

"No," Nehrebecky said quickly as he sought to compose himself.

"That's strange. I heard that there's an exact duplicate of this locked in your safe here."

"You heard wrong, Mr. Moore. You're mistaken," Nehrebecky spoke rapidly.

"But, I …"

Nehrebecky cut him off. "I told you there's nothing like this here. Let's continue our tour, Mr. Moore."

Moore noticed the abrupt change in Nehrebecky's

demeanor. It was like someone turned off the faucet of friendliness that had gushed out only a few minutes earlier. Moore indeed was very suspicious.

The balance of the tour was uneventful and Moore found himself returning to his car by midafternoon. Before he started his car, he pulled out his iPad and researched Daisy Bonner's name. He found her obituary and a list of her family members. He then searched several names and found that a granddaughter still lived in Warm Springs. He located her address and then set his GPS for her home. He had a hunch and wanted to immediately follow up on it.

Ten minutes later, Moore parked his convertible in the driveway of a modest two-story frame home with a large porch on a lot with several pine trees. As he walked up the front steps, he heard a dog start barking. The little dog was on the other side of the screen door and jumping up to see the approaching stranger.

"Settle down, Sheba," a voice called from the back of the house.

"Hello, anyone home?" Moore asked as he knocked on the door, which started the dog barking again.

"Be right there," the woman shouted over the barking dog. Within fifteen seconds, she was approaching the door. "Settle down I told you, Sheba," she said. "Can I help you?" she asked with a southern accent.

"Yes, please. I'm looking for Donna Vaughn."

"That would be me," the redhead responded as she looked at Moore with her sparkling blue eyes.

Pretty lady, Moore thought to himself. He guessed that she

was in her early fifties. "Donna, I know it's rude of me to drop in without calling, but I wanted to see if I could get your help. I'm Emerson Moore and I'm an investigative reporter with *The Washington Post*." He handed her a business card.

"What can I do for you, Mr. Moore?" she asked as she ran her hands quickly through her short hair.

"I'm working on a story about President Roosevelt's death and wondered if I could ask you a few questions about your grandmother, Daisy Bonner."

Vaughn's demeanor changed as her outgoing, vivacious personality shifted and she became very serious. Her smile disappeared and her pursed lips tightened.

"You sit down on one of those chairs," she said. "I'm going to get us a pitcher of lemonade and be right back." She didn't wait for a response from Moore as she turned and disappeared toward the rear of the house.

Moore settled into one of the wicker chairs and waited. He thought he heard Donna and a man talking through the open window behind him. Within minutes, Vaughn returned. A man followed her.

"Here's a glass for you," she said as she handed a green glass filled with lemonade and several ice cubes to Moore before dropping into one of the chairs. "This is my husband, Russ."

Moore started to stand, but Russ waved him back. "Don't need to be formal around here, Mr. Moore."

"Then you need to call me Emerson," Moore replied to the tall man who resembled Clark Gable in appearance and voice.

"I can do that."

"Good."

"What can we help you with?" Donna asked.

"As I mentioned, I'm writing a story on the Little White House and FDR's death. I've just taken a tour there and gathered research material on the Roosevelts' time there. I understand that your grandmother, Daisy Bonner, was the cook there."

"The one and only. She served Mr. Roosevelt his first meal and all the way through to his last meal," Donna answered. "This was Mawmaw's house. I inherited it when she passed. I'd come over here and she'd tell me all kinds of stories about what went on in that Little White House and some of the famous people she got to serve meals to."

Over the next thirty minutes, Donna told Moore the stories she had heard from her grandmother. Moore took copious notes.

As Donna sat back, Moore said, "This has been very helpful and I appreciate everything that you told me. Did your Mawmaw say anything about the day that President Roosevelt died?"

Donna's demeanor again changed to a not-so-lighthearted tone. She seemed to recoil in her chair and became observably withdrawn. She hesitated. "What do you want to know?" she inquired.

"It was a cerebral hemorrhage in the afternoon, right?"

She stared at Moore and nervously wrestled with her emergent response. Then, she softly spoke, "That's what they say."

Moore drilled in. "I'd like to know what your Mawmaw

thought."

Watching the woman closely, Moore innately sensed that she was reluctant to respond. He thought there was more here than what she wanted to share.

"You sure you're not with any government agency?" she asked, suspicious. A fearful look crossed her face.

"Not me," Moore responded. "Let me show you, if I please may." Moore Googled his name on his iPad and showed her. "You can see I'm an investigative reporter, with *The Washington Post*, that is.

The couple looked at the iPad screen and Russ pointed to one line on the display. "You won a Pulitzer Prize?"

"Yes. Years ago," Moore proudly, but modestly, answered.

Russ turned to his wife. "I think this is the one."

Moore reacted with a deeply perplexed look on his face.

"I think you're right," Donna agreed. She looked at Moore's glass. "Let me get you some more lemonade, Emerson." She didn't wait for a response as she stood abruptly and walked into the house.

While she was gone, Moore and Russ chatted about life in Warm Springs.

Donna returned within five minutes with a pitcher and a sealed envelope. She refreshed Moore's glass and set the pitcher on a wicker end table before plopping back into her chair. She turned and purposefully looked at Moore while holding the envelope in her hand.

"Mawmaw gave this envelope to my mother and my mother gave it to me. Mawmaw's instructions were that one day a man would show up to ask questions about the president's death and we'd be able to tell if he was the right man. We also had to be certain that he wouldn't have anything to do with the government. Well Emerson, Russ and I believe you're that man. So, we are supposed to give this envelope to that man. It's sealed and none of us know what Mawmaw wrote before her passing."

"Thank you, Donna and Russ. I'm honored that you've decided to give this to me," Moore said as she handed the yellowed envelope to him. "I'll open it up and tell you what it says."

"No, don't do that," Donna implored. "Mawmaw didn't want us to know what it said. My mother also honored that request for years after receiving it from Mawmaw, who said it would be dangerous for any of us to know. Please honor our trust in you, Emerson and don't tell us."

Russ had a smile on his face. "You have no idea how hard it is for Donna not to know what's in there. It's going to distress her for some time."

"You hush, Russ. My mind is made up. I'll let this go now that we have Emerson here."

Looking at the sealed, aged envelope in his hand, Moore simply uttered, "Thank you both; I will honor your trust in me."

Seeing that look of relief upon the couple's faces, Moore continued, "I should probably hit the road. I've taken up enough of your time today."

They exchanged farewells and Moore anxiously returned to his car. After pulling out of their driveway, he drove a short distance and pulled to the side of the road. He was anxious to read the contents of the letter. The pending euphoria was overwhelming. Retrieving a small pocketknife from his console, he carefully slit open the envelope, extracted the letter and unfolded it. He settled back to read it, noting it had been written only two years after Roosevelt's death.

Dear Whoever You Are,

I told my daughter that you'd show up one day and I want to set the record straight. I been hearing all the rumors about Mr. Roosevelt's death and read some of the stories in the newspapers. They are not true.

I was the only cook Mr. Roosevelt had since he built his house here. There was no way anyone could have messed with my cooking to put cyanide in his food. I know that he didn't drink anything with cyanide in it either. That's not what kilt him.

Before he went to bed on April 11th, Mr. Roosevelt asked me to serve him his oatmeal in his room for breakfast. When I knocked on his bedroom door the next morning, he didn't answer. I thought he was in the bathroom, so I opened the door and walked in with his breakfast tray.

I saw him in bed and I screamed when I saw the knife sticking out of his chest. I screamed and dropped the tray. Then, I ran over to him. That's when Mr. Hassett came in and walked me out. I was crying and he yelled at the Secret Service men to come in. Dr. Bruenn came in, too. They told me to go home and not to speak to anyone about what I saw. I did as told and I cried the whole way.

The knife in Mr. Roosevelt's chest had a German swastika on its handle. It was the Germans who kilt him.

Later that day, Mr. Hassett and some government goons came to my house and threatened me. They said if ever I breathed word about what I saw that day, they'd make me and my family disappear. I've kept my mouth shut.

Now you do what you have to do with what I just told you in this letter.

The letter was signed by Daisy Bonner and dated April 12, 1947.

Moore was in a state of perpetual disbelief. In his trembling hand, he held a document that he believed proved that FDR had been assassinated and the story about him dying from a massive cerebral hemorrhage was in fact false. He might have the basis for a story about a government cover-up.

After delicately returning the document to its envelope, Moore decided he needed expert advice. He picked up his cell phone and called his old friend Steve Nicholas in Washington D.C., who agreed to see him the next afternoon.

Moore returned to his hotel and checked out. Then he began the eleven-hour drive to his houseboat docked at the Washington Sailing Marina on the Potomac River in Alexandria, Virginia. The threat of danger was so thick within the folds of the secret letter that he wondered the entire drive if someone was watching him.

CHAPTER 9

Washington Sailing Marina
Alexandria, Virginia

After spending the night in Henderson, North Carolina, Moore finished his drive to Alexandria the next morning. He turned left off of George Washington Parkway and drove down the peninsula's tree-lined Marina Drive, which ended at one of Moore's favorite restaurants, Indigo Landing. As his car followed the lane on Daingerfield Island, Moore gazed at the rows of docked boats as they gently rocked in the light breeze. The marina held a number of sailboats, powerboats and houseboats.

Moore found a parking spot near "A" dock and pulled in. Grabbing his suitcase, he headed for "A" dock as he took in deep breaths of the fresh morning air.

As he walked, he glanced at the Potomac and smiled as he saw a number of sailboats taking advantage of a friendly wind. He headed down to the *Serenity* and stepped aboard the 1987 Adam cruising houseboat with twin 170-horsepower Detroit diesels. She was 60-feet long with a breadth of 20 feet. Her flying bridge was huge and, according to the previous owner, could hold up to 50 people for a party.

The accommodations included the stateroom with a queen-sized bed, a crew's quarters with two side-by-side single beds and a sofa bed in the lounge. The boat also had a head with full bathroom facilities. The modern galley was located aft of the living room. The interior was trimmed in a highly glossed teak wood and contained hunter green carpet.

After stowing his gear and going over the houseboat to check it, Moore walked the short distance to Indigo Landing. The low green structure on the banks of the Potomac provided an island-like atmosphere with its overhead paddle fans and teak wood decor. From its large windows, Moore could view the Washington Monument and the Capitol. He also could view the party deck where a local singer was providing island music to the crowd of young Washingtonian office and government workers.

Moore was seated on the first tier and ordered an ice water with a splash of cranberry juice. When the waitress returned with his drink, Moore ordered the day boat scallops with goat cheese polenta and an herb emulsion. He quickly devoured his lunch and returned to the houseboat so he could do additional research on conspiracy theories about Roosevelt's death and plan for his meeting with Nicholas later that afternoon.

CHAPTER 10

Nicholas' Office
Washington, D.C.

Behind the Supreme Court building was a residential area consisting of a collection of homes of varying styles. One townhouse in particular, situated on East Capitol Street NE and within a block of the Supreme Court, did its best to blend in with the others. The owner didn't want to attract any undue attention from the outside.

From the inside, though, it was unique amongst the other homes in the area. It had an underground tunnel that connected to the Supreme Court building. It also connected to a separate tunnel linking the Supreme Court building to the Capitol. The tunnels were there so that the home's occupant could easily make his way unnoticed from his residence to testify or consult at closed-door Congressional intelligence committee hearings. At times, the intelligence community members would make their way through the tunnels to the owner's home for consultations. The tunnels also provided him access to the service garages beneath the Supreme Court building and the Senate where waiting government vehicles could whisk him away to meetings at the White House.

Steve Nicholas owned this unusual home. He had taken early retirement as assistant director of the top secret National Intelligence Agency. Nicholas' career had skyrocketed as he moved from intelligence agency to intelligence agency within the U.S. government to strengthen their covert activities. His expertise, at which he was unusually adept, was code breaking and cyber warfare, but he also had covert field experience early in his career.

In the cluttered home office, the late afternoon sunlight was trying to penetrate the partially closed wooden shutters. The office was filled with fine leather chairs, a large mahogany desk and several bookcases. Its walls were filled with pictures of Nicholas with presidents and senior members of Congress.

Moore found a parking spot nearby and exited his car. He walked up to the townhouse and pressed the doorbell as he looked up into the lens of a camera and smiled. When the door buzzed and unlocked, Moore entered and closed the door behind him. He walked down the hallway to Nicholas' office. There he found the balding 68-year-old sitting behind his large desk. He was wearing a gray sweater monogrammed with the name Georgetown University and a plaid shirt. He looked more like someone's favorite grandfather than a human depository for highly sensitive intelligence data.

"Thanks for making time for me, Steve," Moore started as he dropped into one of the chairs in front of the desk.

"Always a pleasure to help you Emerson," Nicholas smiled.

"As long as you don't use me," Moore responded in a serious tone. Moore was still smarting for playing the role of a patsy for Nicholas during a previous search for the Nazarene's Code.

"Aren't you ever going to forgive me?"

"You burned me once, my friend. I'll trust that you won't again," Moore said, slightly irritated. He wanted Nicholas to be wary of using him again.

"Believe me. I won't." Changing the topic, Nicholas said, "Thanks for giving me a heads-up yesterday. I did have a chance to research Roosevelt's death." Nicholas split his attention between Moore and the two 22-inch monitors in front of him while his fingers flew across the keyboard.

"This could be a huge cover-up by the government," Moore said as he watched.

"Could be," Nicholas agreed. "You said you had a photo of the dagger?"

"Yes. Right here," Moore said as he located the photo in the picture gallery on his smartphone and showed it to Nicholas.

"And your friend saw it at the cottage?"

"Yes."

"And then you have this letter from his cook, Daisy?" Nicholas asked.

"Right." Moore withdrew the letter from the yellowed envelope and handed it to Nicholas.

After he read it, Nicholas handed the aged letter back to Moore. "FDR's death has always been a mystery heightened by clouds of secrecy. There were several reasons that key government officials or other countries then wanted him killed. He opposed using the atomic bomb on Japan, which offended the generals. He wanted to give Palestine to the Arabs and opposed the creation of Israel. He wanted to dismantle the British colonies and help them become self-governing."

Nicholas continued. "At the Yalta conference, Roosevelt caved in to Stalin's demands for ceding the biggest part of China and Hitler's booty in Europe. He also agreed to a hands-off policy with the Communist party in the U.S. None of our statesmen were thrilled with FDR's concessions. Neither were our generals or admirals."

"And it would be a huge victory and morale booster for the Germans, too, if they could assassinate him," Moore added.

"It would also irreparably demoralize the American public."

"And the world. What a coup for the Third Reich to be able to announce that they had assassinated America's President Franklin D. Roosevelt!"

"I did check some records that I have access to and read that Hitler's propaganda chief, Joseph Goebbels, rushed into Hitler's office to share the great news of Roosevelt's death."

"I bet he wasn't pleased that the cause of death was reported as a cerebral hemorrhage," Moore suggested.

"The reports show that Hitler went into a fit of rage. So, I believe that gives your theory more credence." Nicholas added, "You may not have known that Hitler was growing a beard and was going to shave off his mustache so he'd be disguised."

"What for? I thought he and Eva Braun committed suicide inside the bunker and their bodies burned."

Nicholas smiled like a Cheshire cat. "Are you sure? Or did he escape to Argentina? There were all kinds of rumors." When Nicholas saw Moore's brow furrow, Nicholas said, "But we digress. Let's focus on Roosevelt."

Refocusing, Moore said, "You almost lost me."

"I know. Let me tell you a bit about Roosevelt's medical condition. His cardiologist, Dr. Howard G. Bruenn, certified that he died of a cerebral hemorrhage. The president's blood pressure was dangerously high. There are reports showing it 230/126 in 1944. On the day he died, the reading was 300/190, or so they say."

"That's sky high!" Moore commented.

"Right, and the doctors didn't have strong diuretics, beta blockers and ACE inhibitors to reduce it back in 1945. There were also rumors going around that his death was caused by a mole suspected of being a deadly melanoma. He had one above his eye, which disappeared in pictures a couple of months before his death. If they didn't get the mole in time, the melanoma could have caused his death."

"I also read about rumors that he committed suicide by putting a small silver pistol to his head and pulling the trigger. That would explain the closed-casket," Moore added.

"Yes, I read that, too. Or did Eleanor murder him? He had both of his mistresses at the cottage when he died. Lucy Mercer and Margaret Suckley were there at the Little White House retreat. Eleanor may have become jealous. There also was the woman who was painting his portrait, Elizabeth Shumantoff."

"The Russian?" Moore asked, as he recalled reading about her, too.

"Yes. Elizabeth Shumantoff was Russian, but I don't think the Russians were behind this. There were rumors that Shumantoff, Mercer and Suckley worked for the British Secret Service. Interesting that they each immediately disappeared from the scene and were never questioned about his death."

"Intriguing," Moore commented. "I was surprised by how fast Roosevelt's body was whisked away from Warm Springs. They had a special train ready for his corpse on April 13th to transport his body to D.C."

Nicholas nodded his head. "The Secret Service violated Georgia law which required an autopsy. Looks like they did everything they could to avoid a medical examination by state officials."

Nicholas continued. "It would be interesting if FDR's body could be exhumed now in the present day and a full forensic examination conducted. It would most likely reveal the true cause of his death and potentially support your theory."

"I don't think that's going to happen," Moore deadpanned.

"I agree. If it were cyanide poisoning, the body would have turned black within hours, although people with circulatory problems sometimes turn dark very quickly. I find it curious that his body wasn't embalmed. It was as if they didn't want anyone seeing the body. Even his family was not permitted to view the body."

"I missed reading that in my research," noted Moore.

"Timing of the entire burial process is fascinating. From the time of his death to his burial, it was only seventy hours. Less than three days."

"Sounds suspicious," Moore suggested.

"Don't you find that amazing? He dies on April 12th and is buried on April 15th in his estate in Hyde Park after lying in state in D.C."

"Yes. Amazingly quick, for a U.S. president," Moore suggested.

"There's more to this," Nicholas shared. "His medical records originally were locked in a safe at Bethesda Naval Hospital. They disappeared within 48 hours of his death."

"It's like a shroud of secrecy descended on this entire incident. Sounds like a huge cover-up by the government," Moore suggested.

"I'll dig around with some of my contacts and see what I can uncover," Nicholas said. "Some folks may want the lid kept on this, you know," he said with a tone of caution.

"That's what makes revealing this stuff so enjoyable," Moore grinned.

"And dangerous, too," Nicholas added.

"I'll be careful," Moore assured. "I'll leave you to your research," he said as he stood.

"Do you want this letter back?"

"No. You keep it for now," Moore replied. "I have a picture of it on my cell phone. Let me know if you find anything." Moore headed down the hallway to leave. Within minutes, he was in his car and headed back to the newspaper office for the balance of the afternoon.

CHAPTER 11

The Washington Post
Washington, D.C.

After parking his car, Moore walked up 15th Street. He neared the tan brick building that held the offices of *The Washington Post*. He was carrying a cup of coffee, which he had purchased from Starbucks, located half a block away at the intersection with K Street.

He walked up the four steps and turned left into the lobby.

"And look who just walked in. We need to get you one of those 'Hello, My Name Is …' stickers to wear Emerson. You haven't been around for awhile!" exclaimed the slightly overweight, black female security guard seated in the security booth that guarded the entrance to the elevators.

"Hi Emily," Moore cheerfully greeted her. "I've been busy."

"Yeah, that's what I heard. You went missing on us not long

ago. How's that memory of yours doing? Is it okay now?"

"Good," he smiled. "I still have some nightmares and wake up in a sweat at night."

"Oh come on now. I wake up some nights in a sweat. And honey, it's not from any dream," she teased with a wink.

"TMI!" Moore teased back as he swiped his employee badge and walked through the security scanner. "I bet you have some interesting stories to share."

"And not one of them would make it to print. Have a drink with me one night and I'll tell you a couple," she said seductively.

"If I was only in town more often, Emily," Moore sighed.

"Sure. Sure. I bet you say that to all the women!" she said as she thought what a fine-looking man Moore was.

Moore blew her a kiss as the elevator doors closed in front of him.

When the elevator reached his floor, Moore walked briskly to the entrance of John Sedler's office. Moore's hard-nosed, but soft-hearted editor had his back to the entranceway as he reviewed a story on his monitor.

"John?"

"What is it now, Emerson?" Sedler grumbled as he recognized Moore's voice. Sedler whirled around in his chair.

"You getting grayer?" Moore asked as he noticed the advanced graying of Sedler's hair although it contrasted nicely with his ebony-colored skin.

"Thanks to guys like you, I am. You worry me to death at times," he replied. "You do need to be in here more often," Sedler said in a firm tone. "You can help mentor some of these younger kids who are here. And they can teach you more about the social media stuff."

"I keep on top of it. But I'll try to do better at being around more. You know I'm off investigating," Moore explained.

Sedler nodded. "Sure you are. Like sailing the inviting blue waters of Lake Erie." Sedler didn't allow Moore to make a retort as he continued. "And what are you working on now?"

Moore quickly brought him up to speed on how he stumbled across the Kreigsmarine dagger, his visit to Warm Springs and his subsequent meeting with Nicholas.

Leaning back in his chair, Sedler said, "That does sound enthralling. I've heard a lot of the rumors, but this is the first time that anyone has brought up a dagger and has a letter from FDR's cook."

"Two daggers. And they both exist."

"Go ahead and run with it, Emerson. See what you can come up with and keep me apprised. Could be a compelling story about another government cover-up and you know how much we enjoy breaking stories on them."

"Thanks, John. I'll let you know." Moore stood and left the office confident that his boss was pleased. He headed to his drab little office cubicle amidst the welcoming jeers from some of his co-workers. He responded to their good-natured kidding and questions about his memory loss and adventure with Jimmy Diamonds.

After he went through some of the paperwork on his desk, he spent the rest of the day and early evening with some of the younger staff members as Sedler had suggested. Afterwards, he returned to the houseboat where he spent the next day working.

CHAPTER 12

Three days later
Put-in-Bay, Ohio

The late morning sun cast a shimmer upon the water as Moore sat on the dock in front of his aunt's house on East Point. He had finished his morning jog and workout, and then showered before coming out on the dock. As far as Moore was concerned, nothing was more relaxing than enjoying the view of the harbor from his waterfront perch. He loved watching the boat traffic in and out of the harbor and seeing the crowded marinas and the sailboats bobbing at their mooring buoys.

After he wrapped up his chores on his houseboat three days ago, Moore had driven back to his island home on South Bass Island.

Moore glanced at his watch and saw that he needed to leave for his lunch meeting at Mr. Ed's with his good friend and legendary island entertainer Mike "Mad Dog" Adams. He walked to the garage and started the Model A Ford truck.

He drove past Perry's Monument and around DeRivera Park where he found a vacant parking spot on Delaware Avenue across from the entrance to Mr. Ed's. When Moore entered, he didn't see Adams on the outdoor patio or inside. He saw that the rooftop patio wasn't open.

Just then, Ed Fitzgerald, the affable owner of the bar and restaurant, walked by.

"Looking for Mad Dog?" Fitzgerald asked.

"Yes."

"He's out back at Mist," Fitzgerald answered.

"Of course he would be." Moore grinned. "Thanks, Ed."

"You know Mike wouldn't be too far from the pretty sights here!" Fitzgerald grinned as he referred to his sprawling outdoor pool area with a swim-up bar and a tiki bar.

"I should have known better." Moore chuckled as he headed alongside the building to the pool complex. As he walked next to the bamboo fence surrounding the pool area, Moore could hear loud music booming along with the sounds of people partying and jumping into the pool.

He walked through the entrance and looked at the sheer abundance of thong-laced, firm and deeply tanned bodies in and around the pool as they gyrated to the deejay's music. There were pine trees and twelve-foot-high rock walls at both ends of the pool. Water cascaded from waterfalls into the pool, which made it all quite the popular island pleasure palace.

The pool was ringed with reclining lounge chairs and dotted with a number of umbrella-shaded tables. There were four VIP cabanas, three VIP lounge chairs and a number of VIP tables complete with bottle service. It was again party time on the island, an almost daily affair during Lake Erie summers.

"Emerson!" a voice shouted from the U-shaped tiki bar to the right of the entrance. Moore turned and saw the ponytailed entertainer sitting on one of the bar stools as three fans spun overhead. The burly Mike "Mad Dog" Adams had been an island fixture for over 35 years as he entertained tourists with his singing prowess and sharp humor from the stage at the island's Round House Bar.

"Good to see you, Emerson," Adams said as he looked up from his menu and stared over Moore's shoulder at two attractive blondes at a nearby table. "I think I should get one of them on stage with me." He slyly winked at the women who giggled at his attention.

Looking over at the table and back to Adams, Moore asked, "Fans?"

"They're beautiful, aren't they?" Adams replied.

"You saying that all beautiful women are your fans?" Moore asked.

Adams chuckled in response. "What are you going to have, Emerson?" he asked as he picked up his menu.

"I'm going for the Big Chubby burger. You?"

"The Hangover burger."

"Rough night?" Moore asked.

"No, Emerson. I just love these Hangover burgers. They've got American cheese, bacon and a fried egg with Ed's signature Bloody Mary sauce on the side. What's not to love?"

"I'm not a fan of any concoction with Bloody Mary

involved," Moore said as he wrinkled his nose.

"You wimp, Emerson. Come on. Live dangerously!" Adams teased.

"Like I don't?" Moore quipped, thinking back to some of the earlier misadventures in which he was involved.

"I guess you do have a point there. I've lost track how many times Sam Duncan and I had to rescue your ass," Adams said good-naturedly.

After Adams and Moore placed their food and drink orders with a server, Adams swung around in his chair and faced Moore. "How's the memory doing, Emerson? You still having flashbacks and nightmares?"

"I am," Moore said, nodding. "Sometimes I can't go back to sleep and I end up walking out to the dock to sit and stare, rather blankly and a bit forlornly, too. When I get tired enough, I head back into the house."

"You were lucky you weren't killed. Remember I told you that Jimmy Diamonds wasn't somebody to fool around with. But, my friend, you didn't listen to the wise and sage Mad Dog, now did ya?"

"Yeah, you were right," Moore agreed as the two touched on a recent reporting adventure where Moore had been seriously wounded and suffered temporary memory loss that resulted in him believing he was a hit man for the mob.

"You're looking good. You still working out?"

"Yes. That training the guy in Cedar Key, Florida, gave me really toughened me up. I don't want to lose everything that he taught me or put the few extra pounds back on. I try to work out every day, but not the regime he put me through."

"You have anything new that you're working on now?"

Moore related the story about the German dagger, his trip to Warm Springs and visit with Steve Nicholas in D.C.

"Sure sounds like a cover-up to me. That Nicholas guy that you mentioned. Isn't that the guy I had come on stage to blow my conch during one of the shows?"

"Yep. I owed him and I enjoyed seeing him getting embarrassed."

"Glad I could help you out especially after you told me what he did to you, the little creep!"

Moore felt two arms go around his waist and a woman lean tight against him with her breasts pushing firmly into his middle back. Her lips moved next to Moore's right ear. "Hello, Emerson. Guess who?"

"I'm not sure," Moore answered before turning to Adams. "This happens to me all of the time," Moore quipped as the woman tightened her grasp around his waist.

"Oh sure it does, Emerson," Adams said as he eyed the dark-haired woman with wide brown eyes. "Honey, when you're done with him, you can come over here and do the same to me," Adams teased. "Or even more!"

"Oh, I'm not sure I can let go of these abs of steel. You've got a regular six-pack going there," she said as she ran her fingers from Moore's waist up to his chest.

"Okay, Connie. I know it's you," Moore said as he turned around and she gave him a quick peck on the cheek with wetted lips.

Adams interrupted the two. "So, tell me Connie. How much did he pay you to come up and do that in front of me?"

"He doesn't have to pay me anything. I'd do this for free," she said while stroking the side of Moore's face.

Moore grinned as he enjoyed the touch of her fingers. "Is Boozer here?" Moore asked as he recalled how jealous her biker boyfriend could be.

"No. He ran off with some redhead," she joked.

"Got to watch those redheads, Emerson," Adams said with a sharp twinkle in his eyes.

"Any time I can," Moore retorted.

Mueller playfully struck Moore's arm. "And what about us brunettes? What's wrong with us?"

Being very comfortable with Mueller, Moore looked her up and down. "Not one thing. Not one thing," he repeated admirably.

"You better say something nice like that after I tracked you down. I stopped over at your house and your aunt said I could find you here," Mueller said.

"What's up?"

"I found something else that you might be interested in."

"What's that?" Moore urged.

"I didn't realize that my grandfather had a small safety deposit box at one of the Port Clinton banks. When I went to the mainland to check it out, I found a couple of rings and an old watch. I also found this paid receipt from a hotel in Warm Springs, Georgia. I remembered you seemed real interested in the maps that had Warm Springs on them," she said as she handed the receipt to Moore.

He found it difficult to contain himself as he opened the receipt. It was for two nights stay on April 10th and 11th in

1945. The receipt was made out to John Smith.

"Did your grandfather go by any other name?" Moore asked.

"I thought you'd ask that question." She handed Moore an old black and white photo. "I found this photo in the safety deposit box, too. It was with a letter mailed from Germany after the war ended from Ernst Knorr to my grandfather's address here. That's him in the photo."

Moore looked at the photo showing Dieter Gabor and another bearded man posed next to the conning tower of a U-boat. Moore peered at the U-boat number, but it only showed *U-23*. The rest of the number, if there was more, had been cut out of the picture by the margin.

Moore turned the photo over and read the date on the back. It was dated March, 1945. Moore turned and surprised Mueller with a tight hug.

"This could tie your grandfather, if he was John Smith, to Warm Springs when Roosevelt died," he said, elated, as he squeezed her tight.

"Maybe you two should get a room," Adams teased as he raised his right eyebrow.

Realizing what he was doing, Moore released Mueller.

"Now, look what you went and did Mad Dog!" Mueller kidded. "I was just beginning to enjoy myself."

"Honey, I bet you enjoy yourself all of the time!" Adams said with a cheesy grin.

Mueller responded with a chuckle. "I better be off. Great day to cruise around the island." Before she started to walk away, she handed Moore an envelope. "The letter and photo were in here. I can't tell you what the letter says since it's written in German."

Taking the envelope, Moore cracked a broad smile, "Thank you, Connie. This could be very helpful. I'll get it translated and let you know."

"No problem. You should join me for a cruise some time, Emerson."

"That would be fun," Moore responded as he pictured himself on the back of her Kawasaki Drifter 800 motorcycle with fat fenders, chrome wheels and his arms firmly around her narrow waist.

The two men admirably watched as she walked away, and then they turned their attention to their food that was growing cold.

"She's real easy on the eyes, Emerson," Adams said taking a bite from his Hangover burger.

"That she is," Moore agreed as he bit into his Chubby burger.

The two bantered between bites as they finished their meals. Adams then headed over to the Round House Bar for his afternoon show and Moore returned to his aunt's house on East Point.

When he returned, Moore scanned in the letter, envelope and photo, then emailed it to Steve Nicholas, asking him to translate the letter since he was fluent in German. While waiting for a reply, he did an Internet search for *U-23* to see what he could find.

He found *U-23*, a U-boat that sunk seven vessels and one warship during the war. It was scuttled in September 1944 off the coast of Turkey to prevent capture by the Russians. Based on his review of the U-boat's records, there was no way to tie that U-boat to service near the U.S. He also checked the other U-boats in the "20" series, but didn't find anything of interest.

Moore was frustrated. His head was pounding from a migraine headache and he wasn't thinking clearly. He pushed his chair back from his desk and stared out the window at the bay simply in an attempt to clear his mind of all its clutter.

Suddenly, Moore's cell phone rang. It was Nicholas calling.

"Emerson, how is your day going?"

"Frustrating. Did you get my email?"

"I did and I translated it. That's why I'm calling. I think Gabor and John Smith are the same person."

"Why?"

"Let me read the letter to you. It's basically a note.

Dear Dieter,

Thank you for writing to me. I have many nice memories of our time serving the Fatherland together. I've enclosed the photo I took of you before you went to sea. Thought you would like it.

—Ernst Knorr

"Doesn't really link Gabor to Smith," Moore said with a note of dejection.

"No, but it does show that Gabor was in the military and aboard a German U-boat for some reason in March, 1945. I also checked out Knorr. He was in the German Abwher as was Gabor, which explains their service together. Knorr was stationed in Norway at a naval base in 1945 while Gabor was in Berlin."

"That's interesting."

"It gets even more interesting. Gabor seems to have dropped out of sight in March, 1945. There are no further references to him in Germany."

"So it sounds like we have the same guy and he surfaces in the U.S. and ends up as Dieter Gabor in Put-in-Bay," Moore surmised.

"And was he John Smith during the balance of the war and while he waited for the war to end?"

"And why would a U-boat bring him to the U.S.?"

"Looks like the *U-23* brought him," Nicholas proposed.

"And, I don't think it was the *U-23*," Moore countered. "She was sunk in 1944 and the photo was dated March, 1945."

"I'd suggest checking all U-boats sunk off the Unites States coast after March, 1945, but we don't know if the U-boat he might have been on would have escaped unscathed," Nicholas said.

"True."

"I'm missing something. I know that I'm not putting two and two together. I'm just not thinking clearly this afternoon," Moore said as he rubbed his brow, trying to ease the pain of the migraine.

"I checked on Knorr and he died in 1953 from cancer. My guess is that trail is cold."

"I really need something that concretely ties Gabor and Smith together as the same person," Moore lamented.

"You keep looking and I will do the same as time permits," Nicholas said before ending the call.

CHAPTER 13

The next morning
Put-in-Bay, Ohio

After his morning workout, Moore walked out to the edge of his aunt's dock and jumped into the water to cool down. The late morning sun was gradually warming up the day. He emerged from the water and was toweling off when his cell phone rang.

Moore picked up the cell phone and saw the caller ID reveal that his ex-Navy SEAL buddy, Sam Duncan, was calling him. "Hi, Sam," Moore spoke into the phone.

"Hey E. How are things going?"

"Another day in paradise, my friend. Nice and peaceful," Moore replied with a sense that Duncan would be disrupting his peaceful paradise.

"Good. Good. How'd you like a little adventure, E?"

Moore smiled at Duncan's leading question. He was right. The Master of Disaster again was going to get him up to his ears in some troublesome quest. "I'm listening," Moore responded quietly.

"Great. I've been invited to go on a hunt for a sunken German U-boat here in Key West. Something's come up on my end and I can't go. I thought you might like to sub for me. Excuse the play on words." Duncan chuckled.

"Going on one of your clandestine CIA assignments?" Moore probed.

"Now you know I can't answer questions like that E," Duncan countered.

"I know, but I have to ask. Are you in Key West now?"

"Yes, but I'm leaving in the morning. I can leave a key and you can use my place until you and the team depart. You'd be involved in diving on this one."

"Have you been talking to Nicholas?" Moore asked, suspicious that the two had talked.

"Yes. He called me and updated me on your interest in U-boats and FDR's death. When I had to bow out this morning, you were the first person to come to mind for replacing me. Interested?"

It wouldn't hurt to listen to Duncan's story, Moore thought. "Tell me about it."

"During World War II, Key West had submarine pens positioned inside of the outer mole at Truman Annex with up to 35 diesel subs using it as a base. There was a mooring field southwest of Key West Harbor for surface vessels. Our Navy had laid 3,500 mines in a zigzag pattern in the channel to make navigation difficult. One U-boat found out the hard way. She sunk northwest of Key West after striking one of those mines. Probably trying to get in close to sink one of our surface vessels."

"Is that the one you were going to dive on?" Moore asked.

"No, hold on a second. Let me continue, E. Ships from the Gulf of Mexico would enter the Atlantic close to here. So, this area was a great place for U-boats to lurk. There was an incident in April, 1945, when three saboteurs were landed by a German U-boat on Tank Island."

"Never heard of it," Moore commented.

"It's now called Sunset Key. It's the island you see from Mallory Square."

"Okay. I remember."

"The Navy had the tank farm on the island to separate it from the submarine pens in case there was an attack from the air," Duncan explained. "The three saboteurs were captured and the sub that landed them is the object of the search. It was sunk by an Avenger as it tried to escape, or so they think, based on the oil and flotsam that was found."

"An Avenger?" Moore perked up as he thought about Rathmell and the Avenger he was restoring.

"Yes. There were a number of them based here."

"And who wants to find it and why?"

"Some guy named Eli Karam," Duncan disclosed. "Let me tell you what I see in an email I have about him. He obtained funding for the mission and will be the lead researcher. Karam received a master's degree in Aegean and underwater archaeology from Oxford University and then followed this with a Ph.D. in anthropology and archaeology from Brown University. He became Director of the Archaeological Diving Unit in Greece where he assessed historic wrecks for the Greek government. He is said to be fascinated by ship technology of all periods and has investigated wrecks ranging from Bronze Age cargo carriers to a 20th century Russian nuclear submarine."

"He found a Russian nuclear sub?"

"Yes, and with Russian assistance. He's an expert in modern sonar technology for the study of wrecks and high-resolution multi-beam sonar."

"And what is so important about the U-boat that he wants to find?"

"Karam apparently has done a thorough research job on this. He learned that the captured saboteurs said that the U-boat was a type XB, the largest U-boat built. It doesn't say here, but I wonder if it was transporting gold, diamonds and art treasures stolen by the Nazis to South America."

"Think Karam would be after the gold and diamonds? I'd guess the artwork would be ruined," Moore surmised.

"Could be. I understand the guy is tight-lipped, but he has the funds and is moving forward quickly."

"Why the urgency?"

"I don't have a clue."

"Why did he invite you?" Moore queried.

"He didn't. A friend of mine got me invited. Do you know Willie Wilbanks?"

"Never met him, but I've read about him. He's a shipwreck hunter, isn't he?"

"One of the best. Willie is a maritime archaeologist. He has an M.A. in maritime history and underwater archaeology from East Carolina University's Maritime Studies Program. He specializes in maritime history of the Great Lakes, the Keys and World War II."

"Sounds like you have a dossier on everyone," Moore observed.

Laughing softly, Duncan said, "E, you should see the one I have on you!"

"Pretty bland, I'd venture."

"Not really." Duncan continued with his discussion about Wilbanks. "Willie's the principal investigator on this search. You'll like him. He's just full of Southern charm and a quick wit. He's right up there with our buddy Mad Dog."

"Another rascal!" Moore guessed.

"Aw, come on now. You love surrounding yourself with rascals. We make life interesting for you."

"And dangerous!"

"I convinced Willie to get Karam to add you to the team. Their research ship is in Key West now. Are you game, my friend?"

Moore thought a moment about how much he'd enjoy diving off of Key West, despite his busy schedule. "Sure. Why not? I'll let Sedler know. There might be a story here." Moore thought he better clear this high adventure with Sedler, who was his immediate boss.

"What's the name of the research ship?" Moore asked.

"You'll love this," Duncan chuckled quietly. "It's named *Dark Side*."

For some reason, Moore instantly felt a chill run up his back. "Sounds ominous to me," he commented.

"Nothing to it. I work on the dark side all the time," Duncan teased. "Now you can too."

"That just makes my day." Moore had a bad feeling in his gut with a sure sense of growing and tantalizing trepidation. He indeed was a man who leads a life of danger and one who was beginning to again believe that the odds were against him seeing too many more tomorrows.

"Still going to go?"

"Sure. Just another challenge."

"I'll reload your cat lives for you and make sure you're back up to nine," Duncan added.

"Thanks. I've got a feeling I'll need them." Moore said as they ended the call. He paused for a brief moment of reflection, and then called Sedler at *The Post* to secure his approval for the dive trip.

CHAPTER 14

The Schooner Wharf Bar
Key West, Florida

The prior forty-eight hours had been busy for Moore as he wound up his projects at the house on South Bass Island and prepared for his flight to Key West. After his plane landed, he caught a cab to Duncan's mobile home on United Street where he found the hidden key that Duncan had left for him.

Throwing his gear into the mobile home, he returned to the waiting cab for the ride to the Schooner Wharf Bar at the foot of Williams Street. Duncan had arranged for Emerson to meet with Karam and the ship's captain late that afternoon at the popular bar overlooking the historic seaport.

Glancing at his watch, Moore noted he was fifteen minutes early, so he took a seat at the bar.

"What'll it be?" the middle-aged bartender asked.

"Rum and Coke. No wait, let's go off script here and I'll instead try the añejo margarita, please."

The bartender quickly prepared the drink and set it on the bar. It was a house special and consisted of Patron Añejo tequila and Grand Marnier. It was a moment to just be somehow different and not typical Emerson. Moore watched as the bartender prepared another drink, mixing an ounce of Galliano and amaretto with two ounces of half and half. Next, he shook the mixture in a cocktail shaker with ice and strained the contents into a chilled martini glass. As the bartender started to walk away, Moore asked him, "What do you call that drink? I haven't seen that mix before."

"It's a golden torpedo," the bartender said as he walked three steps and served it to a tall blonde.

"Never heard of it," Moore murmured aloud to himself.

"Emerson Moore?" a deep voice asked from behind Moore.

"Yes," Moore responded as he slowly spun around in his seat to identify the source of the voice. Standing in front of him was a dark-skinned man with a hawkish nose. Two dark brown, sunken eyes, like of a human skull, stared back piercingly at Moore from a face with high cheekbones, bushy eyebrows and a graying beard. He had a medium build and average height with oversized hands. His age was approximately early fifties.

"I'm Dr. Eli Karam," he said with a touch of entitled arrogance. "You are the replacement diver on our team?" he asked.

"That would be me, yes," Moore said as he continued to size up Karam. This is a guy who would be challenged in social settings, Moore thought.

"Tell me about your diving experience."

Nonplussed by his attitude, Moore explained his diving background, including the dives on the sunken destroyer in the Cayman Islands and the pre-Civil War submarine in Lake Erie.

"You sound more like a recreational diver to me," Karam said with a disdainful look.

"If you mean that I don't have the pedigree that you have, you're right. But I'm qualified to assist you on this dive. Otherwise, why would I have been contacted?"

Before Karam could respond, a shouting match at one end of the bar disrupted them. They turned and saw a white-haired man with a white beard swing at the bartender, who easily ducked the roundhouse blow. The white-haired man swore, slurring his words and fell to the ground.

"We better help him," Karam said with a disparaging tone. "That's our boat captain."

Moore frowned. He didn't like the way this was starting out. He followed Karam over to the captain and helped stand the captain back on his feet.

"No more drinking, Hoppy," Karam said as he looked at Moore. "Help me take him to the ship."

The two men half-carried the captain out of the bar and down the dock to an 85-foot vessel. The name on the side of the bow read *Dark Side*. It appeared to be distressed. It needed paint and the equipment looked rusty and worn.

They were greeted by two deckhands to whom Karam barked orders. "Take him below and get him some coffee. We leave in the morning and I want him sober."

Karam turned to Moore. "If you have anything you need to get done today, go and do it. I want you here promptly at six in the morning to depart."

"I'll be here bright and early," Moore said as he turned and walked away. He headed down Williams Street and turned right on Caroline, enjoying the architecture of the houses as he walked. When he reached Duval Street, he turned left and continued the few blocks to one of his favorite Key West watering holes, Jack Flats. It was located near the intersection of Fleming and Duval and across the street from busy Margaritaville. The popular sports bar has big screen TVs over the bar and pool tables in the back.

There were two reasons that Moore headed to the famous island restaurant. He was going to enjoy one of their fresh grouper sandwiches and he had a meeting there with Willie Wilbanks.

As he entered the restaurant, he called Wilbanks on his cell phone.

"If that's you standing in the doorway, bud, turn to your right," the voice answered.

Moore turned and saw a fiftyish man with a gray mustache and thinning hair seated at a table next to the open floor-to-ceiling window, which overlooked Duval Street. "Hi Willie," Moore called out as he walked to the table, shook hands and took a seat opposite Wilbanks, who was starting his third rum and Coke.

"Glad we hooked up," Wilbanks said as he raised his drink to his lips.

"Me, too. And thanks for working to get me aboard as a

replacement for Sam."

"Be careful in what you wish for," Wilbanks said. "Me thinks this is but the calm before the storm." His mischievous eyes twinkled as he spoke. "You been out to the *Dark Side*?" he asked.

"Yeah. Just came from there. Met the captain and Karam."

"They're an odd twosome. Hoppy Hopkins used to be one of the best boat captains around here until he took up drinking. That guy had a nose for shipwrecks."

"What made him start drinking? Divorce?" Moore guessed.

"No. Worse. He had a ship go down. All hands were lost except Hoppy. The worst part of it was that his two sons were on the crew. His wife had passed years before. The two boys were the only family he had. He never was the same after he was rescued. He's just waiting for death. Ready to cast his last anchor."

"Will he be able to stay sober for the voyage?" Moore asked.

"He better. From what I heard, Karam said no liquor on board. So, I'm enjoying my last drinks today. I'd suggest you do likewise."

A server in a low-cut top appeared at their table and Wilbanks lost all comprehension of what they were talking about as he engaged the attractive, busty server.

"Lawdy, look at what we have here!" Wilbanks said as he spoke to the waitress. "Honey, you just made my pulse go into overdrive! You made me lose my breath and my mouth go dry!"

The server smiled. She knew his type and didn't let it bother her. "I can get you another server if that would help."

"Oh honey, just tap your heels together three times like Dorothy and take me to Kansas with you!"

"You have to excuse my friend," Moore stated.

"No problem," she grinned. "What can I get you?"

"I'm not a woman, but if I was, I'd be having hot flashes whenever I'm around you," Wilbanks murmured.

"I can't get you any of those, but the grouper is good today," she offered, ignoring Wilbanks' comments.

Wilbanks reigned himself in so she could take their food orders and Moore's order for a rum and Coke. After she left, Wilbanks watched her walk away.

"You know, Emerson, I make bad decisions when I drink." Wilbanks said before downing a big gulp of his drink.

"I can tell. Are you that way with all women?" Moore asked as he imagined Wilbanks, Duncan and Mad Dog hanging out together. What a hoot that would be, Moore thought.

"She not only brightened my day, she set me up for tomorrow and the next four days!"

"Easy boy," Moore teased as he tried to return to their conversation about their mission. "That Karam is a strange duck. Very aloof and condescending."

"Yeah, he's weird all right. I don't like him. He's like a hemorrhoid."

"A hemorrhoid! How's that?"

"He's a pain in the butt when he's around and a relief when he goes away."

Chuckling at Wilbanks' humor, Moore asked, "Then why did you join up to work with him?"

"Plain and simple. It's the money. It's really good! Karam sure is in some damn hurry to find this U-boat."

"Why?"

"It has something to do with that old rumor about Hitler escaping to Argentina."

"Oh?"

"Hitler was last seen on April 20, 1945. It's long been rumored that Hitler escaped through an underground tunnel which led to a subway station that took him and a number of high-ranking Nazis by plane from Tempelhof Airport in Berlin to Spain where they boarded a U-boat for Argentina to plan development of the Fourth Reich."

"So, Karam thinks Hitler's body might be on board?" Moore asked.

"No. The one Karam is looking for was sunk earlier in April, '45. But it could have some of Hitler's personal items, artwork and gold or silver."

"Still doesn't explain why he's in such a hurry."

"No, it doesn't. And this rush has caused him to throw together a weird crew. Have you met any of the others?"

"Not yet. I saw a couple on board when we dragged Hoppy over to it."

"I'd call it the ship of misfits and that includes you and me for taking part in this." Wilbanks paused as the server set the grouper sandwich in front of Moore and blackened mahi-mahi sliders in front of Wilbanks.

"Looks delicious," Wilbanks teased provocatively.

"Customers have been enjoying them all day," the server responded.

"I wasn't talking about the food. I meant you," Wilbanks kidded.

The server turned to Moore. "Is your friend like this all of the time?"

"We just met, but I do think he has an ornery streak running through him," Moore quipped as she turned and scurried away.

Taking a bite as he watched her walk, Wilbanks continued. "When she bent over, I could see clear to the promised land." Then he added, "These are good. You should try one."

"Nope. Love their grouper sandwiches. I'm addicted to them. I try to stop here for my first meal every time I'm in Key West."

"Getting back to the crew. Bingo Knowles is from the Bahamas. He's a deckhand and our cook. I've run into him before on crews. Funny guy and great cook. Not sure he's got a lot of sense. Sometimes, I think he couldn't find his way to the head even if he had a GPS."

"How is it that he's such a great cook, then?" Moore asked.

"I don't have the slightest idea. Maybe it's that left brain, right brain stuff."

Moore grinned and nodded as he listened.

"Devlin Sloan is a deckhand. Irish guy. He does all of the mechanical work. I've crewed with him before. Pretty good at mechanics, but he's got a few loose screws, too. When he's not thinking, I don't think he could find his ass if he had both hands in his back pocket."

Moore laughed. "I'm just the right amount of crazy to fit in with this crew." He knew he was going to enjoy Wilbanks' wit.

"Let me take you from crazy to dangerous."

"How's that?" Moore asked.

"Karam brought one of his assistants from Greece. Guy's name is John Carpos. He'll be involved with analyzing images and diving. Have you met him yet?"

"Not yet."

"That boy's got a burr in his saddle. Kind of edgy. Wears his black hair slicked back with a ton of lard. You better keep an eye out for him. He gives me the heebie-jeebies!"

"Thanks for the warning," Moore said. "I'll be wary around him."

"I'll be running the side-scan sonar and handle some of the technical duties. Everybody on board can dive. And you said that you saw the ship?"

"Yes, Karam took me out to it," Moore answered.

"What did you think?"

"It should be salvaged."

"My exact thoughts. It's a mess. When you try to do something like this at the last minute, you can't always get the best equipment. The ship is a disaster. The only thing she has going for it is that Sloan is a master mechanic. That man can get anything humming."

"That's reassuring," Moore commented.

"As long as she stays afloat," Wilbanks added. "The only good thing about this last minute stuff is that it benefits us."

"What do you mean?"

"They have to throw together a team at the last minute. Finding good people like you and me is critical to their success. That's why we'll get paid so well for this expedition."

"Sam didn't tell me about getting paid," Moore said. "Believe it or not, my motivation to be here isn't money. I just like the adventure and history."

Wilbanks went over the generous pay plan. "Well, you're sure to get adventure with this bunch. As for me, now you know why I'm a part of this."

"I do," Moore responded as he thought about how he could use the extra funds to buy a couple of things for his aunt.

Wilbanks drained his glass of rum in a few gulps and set its empty remains firmly on the table. "I am sufficiently fortified. Duty calls, forthwith." Wilbanks looked at the bill and threw some cash on the table. "This one is on me."

"Thanks," Moore said as the men stood and shook hands.

"I'll be seeing you in the morning." Wilbanks walked away.

"Bright and early," Moore responded.

"Welcome to the Mad Hatter's tea party," Wilbanks yelled over his shoulder as he headed down Duval Street to the ship.

Moore grinned. He liked Wilbanks and would enjoy working with him. He walked to the curb and caught a pedicab back to Sam's mobile home on United Street. He wanted to go through his gear and get a good night's sleep.

CHAPTER 15

The next morning
Key West Historic Seaport

After fixing himself a quick breakfast, Moore caught a cab over to the seaport. He walked down the dock, carrying his duffel bag and scuba gear.

As he approached the *Dark Side*, he saw Karam and Wilbanks standing together as they observed the crew preparing for departure.

"Well butter my butt and call me a biscuit! Look who's up early," Wilbanks called when he spotted Moore.

"Nice welcome," Moore responded to the mischievous Wilbanks. "Morning Eli," Moore said to Karam, who seemed to have a permanent scowl etched into his face.

Without reciprocating the greeting, Karam turned and yelled as Moore started to board. "Sloan, show him where to stow his gear."

The wiry, red-haired Irishman grabbed Moore's duffel bag and pointed to the gear rack. "Stow your gear there and follow me," he said with an Irish brogue.

Moore followed his directions and stowed his scuba gear. He then turned and followed Sloan, who was disappearing below deck. When he caught up to him, Sloan was throwing Moore's duffel bag on a berth.

"Got berthing space for twelve here," Sloan explained as Moore looked at the bunk beds, stacked three high. He had dry-cracked lips and half-rotten teeth. "My first name is Devlin."

"Emerson Moore," the reporter replied, introducing himself as he looked around the filthy cabin. Gum wrappers, used plastic cups, pennies, matchbooks and empty potato chip bags littered the floor like flotsam. Above the entryway, two bumper stickers curled in the heat. They read "Loon A Sea" and "Get Naked."

Sloan noticed the concerned look on Moore's face. "Feels like home doesn't it?"

"Maybe yours, but not mine," Moore sternly replied. He was used to a more professional setup for a crew.

"Good news. I just repaired the head. Used some duct tape. Should work fine now," Sloan added.

"Wonderful," Moore replied as his concern grew.

Pointing to his left, Sloan said, "Shower is over there. It works just fine although it's a bit of a tight squeeze."

"And what do you do?" a man asked with an air of distrust as he entered the berthing area while Sloan scampered topside.

Moore turned and saw a rough-looking thirty-five-year-old with a scar across his cheek. He had a dark complexion and dark beard and hair. He had dry-lidded eyes that reminded Moore of a lizard when he closed them.

"Diver."

The man peppered Moore with questions, "What about your equipment skills? What's your area of expertise? You experienced with side-scan sonar?"

The guy definitely had an attitude, Moore thought as he sized him up. It also seemed like he had a hair trigger and would be quick to anger. Probably very capable in a fight, Moore thought.

"Not really."

"Then what are you here for? This is no trip for amateurs," the man continued.

"I'm here to help, especially with the diving," Moore explained. He sensed that this guy was relationally challenged.

Without introducing himself, the man turned and walked into the forward compartment, which had 200 square feet of dry lab space and scientific equipment.

Moore shrugged his shoulders and returned topside where he bumped into Sloan. "Who's Mr. Happy down below?"

"Real jerk, isn't he? 'Tis John Carpos. Karam brought him. No one likes the guy. He's not a full shilling, mind ya!"

Moore furrowed his brow to show a basic lack of understanding. In response, Sloan made a circular motion with his forefinger by his ear to indicate the guy was crazy.

"Is he always like that?"

"Fer the three days that he's been here, he has."

Their conversation was interrupted by a disturbance on

the dock where Karam and Wilbanks were confronting a Bahamian.

"This should be good," Sloan chuckled as the two watched the exchange. "That's Bingo Knowles—our cook."

"You're not bringing that on board," Karam was challenging Knowles, who was preparing to lift a crate off a cart and carry it aboard. The crate was a foot high and two feet wide with a length of four feet. It was made of pine and birch and had a small lid on top. Inside the crate were eight cackling chickens.

"I always take chickens to sea wit me. We get fresh eggs for a few days, then we have fresh meat. You'll see. You'll get tired of eating fish every day," the Bahamian said.

"Chicken of the sea," Sloan said quietly to Moore, who grinned as they continued watching.

Hopkins spoke up. "Won't hurt anything, Eli," he said to Karam.

Karam looked at Knowles, who was still holding the crate. "Go ahead," he said, "You can keep them. Just don't let them get loose."

"Everyting be cool, mon," Knowles grinned as he boarded the ship.

Hopkins pointed to the stern. "Bingo, stow them there for now."

Knowles carried the crate to the stern and set it down. He then bounced back to the dock and grabbed the handles of the pushcart when he stopped dead in his tracks.

Walking toward them and pulling a large duffel bag on wheels was a tough-looking, hard-bodied woman in her mid-thirties. She had skin the color of honey and hair as dark as the dead of night. She walked with an air of confidence and independence.

"Looky here," Knowles said as he watched her approach. His face was filled with a lecherous smile as he gazed at the woman in short shorts and a blue denim work shirt with the shirttails tied at her slim waist. Her taut stomach showed.

"Good morning, sunshine. Bingo is my name," Knowles said in a sing-song manner.

The woman stared dagger-like right through Knowles as she closed the distance between the two of them.

"Sweetie, you're my morning pick-me-up." Knowles wouldn't quit.

"I'm nobody's pick-up," she responded coldly.

Ignoring her comment, Knowles continued, "Did someone mess with the thermostat here? I'm just heating up!"

The woman ignored him as she walked by.

"Keep walking, tramp, I've got all kinds of girlfriends," Knowles said, angered at her lack of responsiveness.

Upon hearing the comment, Sloan commented to Moore, "He's got all kinds of girlfriends all right. They're all plastic, blow-up gals."

Moore chuckled and drew a widening grin.

Sloan decided to jump in on the harassment of the well-built female as she neared the boat. "I need to wipe the drool from my chin, baby!"

"Knock it off," Karam yelled angrily. "This is Asha. She's my daughter!"

Sloan apologized quickly as a panicked and wide-eyed Knowles, pushing the handcart, disappeared down the dock. Knowles, who believed he was having an out-of-body experience of oddly directed focus and uneasy jitters, was beginning to feel the overshadowing presence of doom. He was getting spooked before the ship ever departed.

Karam continued. "Asha will act as our research assistant."

Hopkins leaned in to Karam and spoke in a hushed tone. "We don't have any separate berths for women."

"That's no problem. She can take care of herself," Karam assured.

"And make no mistake about it. I can take care of myself," Asha said coolly as she hoisted her duffel bag on board.

"Willie," Karam called.

"Yes?"

"Show Asha to our berths so she can stow her bag."

"Thanks, father," Asha said as she started to follow Wilbanks.

Karam smiled at his daughter and then spoke to Wilbanks again. "Then show her our equipment so she knows what she has to work with."

"I'd like to show her my equipment," Sloan said quietly as she walked by to join Wilbanks.

Ignoring Sloan, Asha quickly took in Moore and gave him a brief smile before going below deck.

Her smile to Moore was not lost on Sloan. "So, what makes you so special, dude?"

"Nothing. Nothing at all," Moore responded as he thought how attractive Asha was.

"She smells beautiful," Sloan said as he sniffed the air.

"Sloan!" yelled Karam.

"Yes?"

"Go help Willie and her stow her gear," Karam ordered Sloan who disappeared below deck.

Catching up to her, Sloan showed Asha the three-tiered bunk beds. "What do you prefer—on top, on the bottom or maybe in the middle?" he asked lecherously.

Ignoring his sophomoric innuendo, she tossed her gear on the lower bunk, and then shrieked loudly, "This is a pigpen. I want this mess cleaned up."

Hearing her comment topside, Karam yelled below deck to Sloan, "Clean it up, Devlin."

"I didn't make the mess," Sloan countered.

"You do as I say," Karam said sternly. "I'll send Bingo down when he returns."

"And get me an extra blanket in case I want to hang it from the middle bunk for privacy," Asha said stonily.

"I'll find one for you," he said as she went topside to rejoin her father.

When Knowles returned, Karam sent him to help Sloan. Wilbanks, who had been uncommonly quiet, returned topside and stood next to Moore.

"I guess I'm a bit shocked," Moore said.

"Shocked that we have a beautiful woman on board?" Wilbanks asked.

"No, shocked at how quiet you are. In the less than 24 hours I've known you, this is the longest period of time that I haven't heard you make a wisecrack—especially an inappropriate one at the appearance of a beautiful woman."

"I may appear to be a rogue sometimes, but I'm not stupid. There's a time to crack jokes and a time to be quiet. I had an inkling that now it would be wise not to make any cracks around her. You saw how much trouble Knowles and Sloan got in?"

"Yes."

"Not a good thing. You probably didn't notice that Carpos was glaring at everyone?"

"No, I didn't yet."

"Just be careful and watch yourself, Emerson."

Around ten o'clock, Hopkins started the boat's engines. Contrary to the ship's appearance, the diesel engines reliably caught and hummed thanks to the work of Sloan. Knowles and Sloan released the lines and Hopkins slowly guided the craft out of the bight and around Key West.

Moore was standing midship as they passed Fort Zachary Taylor on their port side and overtook an old freighter on the starboard side. The freighter's name caught Moore's eye. It was named *Mongo*. Several of its crew lined the side and waved at Carpos, who was standing in the bow. Moore tried to identify the country under whose flag she sailed. He had no idea.

"Carpos and Moore. Come below deck," Karam called out before he returned to the large salon area in the bow.

The two men did as they were told and rushed below deck where Karam had called a meeting with Wilbanks, Moore, Asha and Carpos. Asha spread out a chart of the area they intended to search.

"From what we learned in the archives, we firmly believe that the U-boat sunk in April was the *U-235*."

When he heard the number of the U-boat, Moore's eyes widened. He wondered if his search for *U-23* should have been for *U-235*. He then remembered the scratched number on the dagger as 235. He was kicking himself for not making the connection sooner and wondered if there was a link to Dieter Gabor. He leaned in to listen closely.

"The historical reports show that an Avenger torpedoed a U-boat off of Tank Island in this area." She pointed to a spot west of Tank Island. "The pilot reported that he hit the U-boat, but couldn't stay in the area to confirm where she sunk."

"Why?" Moore asked.

With a look of disappointment on her face from the interruption, she looked up at Moore and answered, "An approaching tropical storm chased it back to base and his plane was out of fuel."

"I see."

"Do your homework," Carpos snapped as he glared at Moore.

Moore ignored him as Asha resumed her analysis. "It would be logical that the U-boat would run to deeper water which takes us then in this direction." She pointed to an area south of Key West where the chart showed water depth levels of 77 feet to 492 feet before increasing to a depth of 902 feet. "We're not sure how far into the Straits of Florida the U-boat would have gone as it was sinking."

"That's right," Karam said as he stepped closer to the table and pointed to the chart. "We're going to target the area between the Naval Operational Training Area and the Explosives Dumping Area." Karam sensed that Wilbanks wanted to speak. "Willie?"

"I'll be analyzing the side-scan sonar's imagery." Wilbanks was referring to the towfish, which resembled a torpedo, packed with technology rather than explosives. As it was towed behind the ship, it transmitted signals to the ocean floor that were bounced back and created an image of what it found. "We'll be using a side-scan sonar and a magnetometer as we crisscross various grids during our search."

"Nothing new here," Carpos said in a condescending tone as he looked at Wilbanks. "Want to dumb it down so that Moore can understand that it's like a lawnmower making passes across the yard to cut grass?"

Wilbanks didn't comment. His only response was an icy stare.

Moore was going to react, but decided to let it go. This Carpos was a real piece of work, Moore thought.

Karam intervened. "Well said, John," he said in defense of his assistant.

For a fleeting moment, Moore wondered if he could swim to shore and leave this cuckoo's nest.

"Once we are able to see detailed images showing that we've located the U-boat, we will dive on her," Karam said. "Questions?"

No one spoke.

"Okay, let's get busy," Karam ordered.

"Come on, Emerson. You can help me with the side-scan sonar," Wilbanks said as he turned to leave the ship's cabin. Moore followed him to the stern where Wilbanks began to swear.

"Those guys are a trip," Moore offered.

"Ya think so?" Wilbanks asked sarcastically. He was still seething from the demeaning treatment he had received. "Those boys need to be schooled by a Southern gentleman like me."

"Then we'd be in real trouble," Moore said in a joking manner as he tried to relieve the edginess in Wilbanks' voice.

"Oh, crap!" Wilbanks exclaimed when they reached the stern and he saw the sonar towfish.

The portable chicken coop was stored next to the towfish and it looked like one chicken had been able to escape from the coop. It had defecated on the towfish.

"Bingo!" Wilbanks yelled as Moore grinned. "Get your butt up here!"

Within seconds, Knowles appeared on deck. "Yeah, boss?"

"Get that chicken away from my towfish!" Wilbanks stormed.

"She got away when I fed them," Knowles explained. "I couldn't catch her."

"You better catch her now or I'm going to wring someone's neck—and it doesn't matter whether it's the chicken's or yours!" Wilbanks fumed.

Moore joined the frustrated Knowles in trying to corner the errant fowl and between the two of them, they were able to catch her and return her to the crate.

"And clean up this chicken poop from my towfish," Wilbanks directed Knowles, who quickly bent to the task in order to ease Wilbanks' rage.

Turning to Moore as Knowles worked, Wilbanks added,

"I'm a bit protective of my equipment."

"I'll say," Moore smiled.

Suddenly a ruckus broke out in the pilothouse. The three men turned to look and saw Karam shouting at Hopkins as he threw several bottles of liquor overboard. "I told you that there would be no drinking on this expedition. None!"

Hopkins' eyes narrowed as he looked at Karam and Carpos. It looked like Carpos was about to pounce on Hopkins.

"Do you have any other bottles hidden on board?" Karam asked.

"No," Hopkins lied.

Karam and Carpos stormed out of the pilothouse and returned below deck.

"I can see we're off to a good start," Asha said as she walked toward the three men in the stern.

"I just hope this isn't a sign of what this trip is going to be like," Moore said as he looked at the beautiful woman.

Knowles, who had finished cleaning the towfish, walked by on his way below. "Baby, too bad you're not a fireman," he said with a lustful look in his eyes. "I got a fire that you could put out."

Without hesitating, Asha stuck out her foot, sending Knowles flying face-first to the deck. "Don't talk to me that way, ever," she cautioned him in a tone that meant business.

Knowles picked himself up and scurried below.

"I think he's harmless," Moore said.

"Maybe, but with some guys you've got to set very clear boundaries up front. And he's one of them," she said while lowering her Thom Browne silver-mirrored aviator sunglasses over her eyes.

"Some guys have no respect for women," Wilbanks said with a twinkle in his eyes.

"Look who's talking!" Moore countered, knowing what a flirt Wilbanks could be, based on what he had observed the previous evening at dinner.

Asha didn't comment as she turned to look out on the horizon.

"I think you've irritated her," Moore said, observing how Asha's body had stiffened.

"Asha, I meant no offense," Wilbanks proffered.

"None taken," she replied.

"Your body language says otherwise," Moore observed.

"Perceptive, aren't you, Emerson?" Asha asked as she raised her sunglasses to the top of her head and looked at him.

"Try to be," he grinned.

"I am, too," Wilbanks said, not wanting to be left out of the interaction.

Asha looked at Wilbanks and back to Moore without commenting.

"This is going to be quite an adventure," Moore said as he changed the topic.

"It is. My father has worked hard to pull this all together," Asha shared.

"It's got to be very special for him to be so close to finding this U-boat," Moore said.

"It is. He's found U-boats in the past. But this one has been a long-time dream of his."

"I'm going to head back below," Wilbanks said, satisfied that his towfish was secure and realizing that he was an intruder on their conversation.

"See you later," Moore said.

"Bye," Asha added.

After Wilbanks left, Moore asked, "I wondered if I could ask you a question."

"Sure. Fire away."

"I was wondering about your father. Is he always so arrogant?"

Asha chuckled. "Don't mistake arrogance for intelligence. He is a very smart man and doesn't suffer fools easily."

"I wouldn't call any of us fools," Moore responded.

"How about our friend Bingo?"

It was Moore's turn to chuckle. "I guess I was thinking more about Willie and me."

"You're taking it too personal, Emerson. So is your friend. Just let it go and focus on finding the U-boat."

"And that Carpos gives me the creeps. What's with that guy?"

"Now that one is a bit rough around the edge. But not to worry. He's solid. He's worked with my father for a long time. He's his right hand assistant. Gets things done and is very protective of my father and what he wants to accomplish."

"And how about you?" Moore asked.

"What about me?"

"Have you always worked for your father?"

"Why?"

"I was just curious."

"No. I'm more of a free spirit. We moved a lot. While my father was working on his Ph.D. at Brown University, I got my bachelor's degree in underwater archaeology. When father took an underwater archaeology job in Greece, I decided to kick around in the U.S. for a while."

"You are strong-spirited," Moore said in recognition of the tough side he saw in her.

"I guess I can be. After a year, I caught up to my father in Greece and I've worked for him since then."

"And your mother?"

"Unfortunately, she died giving birth to me," she said with a hint of remorse.

"I'm sorry," Moore sympathized.

"Me, too. I wish I could have known her. Everyone has told me what a proud woman she was."

Moore noticed how the setting sun cast a warm glow on her skin, making it look like caramel. She was a real beauty, he thought to himself.

"How about you? Are you a shipwreck hunter like your friend Willie?"

"Nothing glamorous. I'm a reporter for a daily newspaper. Always looking for stories."

"So, you're going to write about this U-boat?"

"Maybe. I've been keeping notes every night on my laptop. We'll see where this all goes and then I'll decide."

"Married?"

"No." Moore thought he saw a hint of a smile cross her lips

before it disappeared. "My wife and son were killed in a car accident some years back."

"I'm so sorry to hear that. It must have been difficult."

"It was. I think of them often," Moore said.

"I should be going. I know father will want to look at the charts again," Asha said as she turned to leave.

"I enjoyed talking with you," Moore said.

"We should do it again," Asha responded, invitingly.

"I'd like that."

"I would too." She smiled coyly and walked away.

Interesting lady, Moore thought. He watched as the sun sunk over the horizon before heading below deck. He thought he was going to enjoy this trip more than he had planned.

The next morning as the crew finished their light breakfast, Moore excused himself and began heading to the stern when he spotted Asha, who had passed on breakfast. She was in the forward compartment bent over the chart table, studying something. Moore took a detour to stand next to her.

"No breakfast today?" he asked.

"No. I'm too excited about finding the U-boat," she replied. "This is the type that we are looking for," she said as she pointed to a diagram on the chart table.

Moore looked down and allowed his eyes to focus on the diagram.

"It's the *U-235*. It's a type XB. They were mine layers when they were launched. But toward the end of the war, several of them were converted to underwater freighters," she explained.

"How's that?"

Asha pointed to the bow section of the U-boat's hull. "These are the six vertical shafts that held the mines." Moving her finger to point to the side of the U-boat's hull, she added, "There were twelve more shafts set into the saddle tanks on each side. The Germans stored freight containers in the shafts rather than mines."

"That's pretty simple."

"Actually, it was."

Looking at the forward compartment, Moore asked, "What about the torpedoes in the forward compartment? Did they have to reduce the number because of the freight?"

"They didn't have forward torpedo tubes or torpedoes so they could store freight containers on the forward compartment's deck."

"No torpedoes?" Moore asked in surprise. "What if they were attacked?"

Asha moved her finger to point to the stern of the U-boat. "They still had two stern torpedo tubes."

"How many torpedoes could she carry?"

"Fifteen in the stern compartment." She moved her finger to point at the deck armament. "And they had their twin 20mm anti-aircraft guns. But remember, these were long range U-boats and not built as attack vessels. They could stay submerged for most of their voyages to avoid detection."

"What are you two doing?" Karam asked in a belligerent tone as he entered the forward compartment.

The two turned to face Karam and Asha explained, "Oh, Father, I was just showing Emerson the diagram of the U-boat."

"Is that really necessary?"

"Yes," Moore replied. "I have a better sense of how the U-boat is laid out. That's going to help me when we dive on her."

Karam ignored Moore's comment as he glared at Asha. Moore decided it would be a good time for him to leave the two of them. "I guess I'll head on deck," he said as he walked past Karam and left.

Karam walked over to the chart table and looked at the diagram. "He doesn't need to know details about the U-boat."

"He was just curious," she explained as she looked at her father.

"Don't get close to him. We need to focus on our mission, understand?" Karam asked in a tone which meant business.

"I know," she said with exasperation.

Karam looked toward the stern. "It was a mistake allowing a newspaper reporter to join us. A big mistake."

"I didn't have anything to do with that decision," she said defensively.

"I didn't say you did."

"He'll serve his purpose," she added.

"That he will. That he will," Karam repeated as he bent over the charts.

In the stern area, Moore and Wilbanks worked to ready the towfish.

"Shouldn't be long now," Moore said to Wilbanks as he looked toward the bridge where Hopkins and Karam had been conferring after the ship's forward progress had slowed to a halt and it was bobbing in the ocean.

Karam stepped away from the bridge and called to Moore and Wilbanks in the stern. "We're ready to start. Go ahead and release the towfish."

"Right," Wilbanks said as he and Moore started the winch to lower the towfish, which they had unsecured, in the ocean. No more than a minute had passed when Wilbanks asked, "You have this?"

"Piece of cake," Moore said as he monitored the towfish's descent and the cable as they were released.

"I'm going inside and review the data it transmits."

"I'll let you know if there's any problem from my end," Moore said confidently.

Wilbanks disappeared and for the next four hours the ship ran its pattern with the towfish trailing the ship. Moore manned the stern and kept an eye on the cable during the process.

CHAPTER 16

The next day
Straits of Florida

Everyone was up early and had chowed down the light breakfast that Knowles had prepared before starting their search again. The seas were relatively calm and there was a light breeze.

The excitement of the search wore off that afternoon and the monotony of going back and forth in the grid pattern replaced it. The only thing that happened to break the tedium in the late afternoon was Asha appearing on deck in a brief bikini.

"Break time," she announced to the crew on deck as she headed to the bow to catch some rays.

Sloan was standing next to Moore as both watched her disappear. "Whew! Is she built or what?" Sloan observed.

"She definitely keeps herself in shape," Moore said appreciatively.

"If those boulder holders were any smaller, she'd be falling out all over," Sloan cracked.

Moore didn't comment and the men returned to their responsibilities for the balance of the day.

At dinner that evening, Wilbanks questioned Moore, "Boring, huh?"

"In some ways. But it's the anticipation that captures you. Sort of like a jack-in-the-box. You know the jack is in there. You just don't know when he's going to pop up," Moore answered.

Leaning toward Moore, Wilbanks said, "I know what you mean. This stuff never gets boring to me."

"We'll find her. Trust me," Karam said confidently from his seat across the table from Wilbanks.

Behind Moore, Asha, who had changed into a tee shirt and shorts, was standing at the counter offering several beverages. She held a plastic pitcher of ice water and was examining it before pouring a glassful.

"What kind of pitcher is this?" she asked Knowles.

"It's dat ting from my hospital stay. I reused it."

"It's a urinal container," Moore said incredulously after spinning around in his seat and realizing what she was holding.

"Dat's no problem, Missy. I washed it real good," Knowles said in a serious tone while the dining area burst into laughter.

Asha set down the container and poured herself a glass of orange juice from an open carton. "This looks much safer."

"That's nothing, Asha," Hopkins called from his seat at the end of the table. "Until this vessel went dry," he shot Karam a frown before continuing, "Bingo served us shots of whiskey in used urine specimen containers."

Crinkling her face, Asha commented as she took a seat next to her father. "Disgusting!"

"They were clean. He washed them," Hopkins added.

Another roar of laughter filled the room.

"What's so funny?" Sloan asked as he entered the room and plopped into the open seat next to Asha.

Wilbanks caught up Sloan on what had transpired and Sloan chuckled as he cast an admiring glance at Asha.

The clanging of a metal spoon against the top of an aluminum cooking pot announced Knowles' entry from the galley. He was carrying a large pot as he walked.

"What do you have there, Bingo?" Karam asked.

"Chili."

Most of the folks at the table groaned.

"Chili? Bingo, why would you serve us a hot meal like that on a hot day like today?" Sloan asked.

"Then don't eat it," Knowles replied, leaning between Asha and Karam as he set the pot on the table. As he pulled back, he looked at Asha and flirted. "You know dat women tremble when they see me walk into de nightclubs."

Having sensed that Knowles was everyone's favorite target, Moore jumped in with a quick retort. "Bingo, that's because they're afraid that you're going to ask them to dance!"

Everyone except Asha laughed. She was thinking that she needed to put a stop to this teasing.

From the other side of Asha, Sloan decided to jump in. "I just felt something running down my leg."

"What was it?" Wilbanks asked.

"I was hoping it was Asha's fingers," Sloan replied.

"Not my fingers. Maybe my orange juice. When I spilled it, it must have dripped through the table cracks onto your leg," she said.

Not to be rebuffed, Sloan added, "Well, I want you to know that it's okay if you ever get the urge to run those fingers down my legs."

"Not in your lifetime, bud!" Asha replied as her hand closed into a tightly clenched fist.

Seeing that his daughter was beginning to boil over, Karam stepped in. "Stow the chatter, Devlin." Turning to his daughter, he tried to calm her. "Settle down."

"I can take care of myself, Father," Asha countered.

"I know you can, but we don't need a show of your physical prowess here." Karam stood from the table and addressed everyone in a stern tone. "I want this innuendo stuff to end. It's getting out of hand and I don't like it one bit. This is my daughter!"

From the other end of the table, Hopkins spoke. "Devlin, that will be enough."

Sloan nodded his understanding.

"Bingo, did you hear me?" Hopkins called into the galley.

"Every ting be cool, mon," Knowles replied.

With the drama resolved, the rest of the mealtime was relatively quiet. After the meal was concluded, Knowles tidied up while Hopkins and Sloan went to check on the engine. Wilbanks went to the head and Moore found himself on deck. He began to walk toward the bow when his path was suddenly blocked by Asha.

"Where you going?" she asked in a serious tone.

"The bow. Want to come with me?"

"Off limits," she said firmly.

"Off limits? What do you mean?" Moore was surprised by her serious tone.

"My father is busy up there."

Moore looked around her toward the bow. He saw Karam on a satellite phone. "Okay, so he's on the phone," Moore said nonchalantly.

"It's a private call. He doesn't want anyone around."

"No problem," Moore said as he began to retreat.

Realizing that Moore seemed stunned by her tone, Asha added, "We can talk later."

"Sure. No problem," Moore said as he turned and sullenly walked away.

As soon as he could, he walked to the other side of the ship and toward the bow. His curiosity was up. He wanted to know what was so secretive.

He didn't get any closer to Karam on the other side.

"Where do you think you're going?" a gruff voice asked. It was Carpos.

"To the bow to get some fresh air."

"It's just as fresh at the stern," Carpos said with an edge to his voice.

Moore started to push by Carpos who reacted by pushing Moore roughly against the rail. "I told you to go the stern," he growled as his hands closed in a tight grip around Moore's arms.

"Listen …" Moore didn't get to complete his sentence.

"What's going on back there?" Karam asked as he approached and Carpos released his grip on Moore. He was carrying the satellite phone in his hand.

"Your assistant won't let me pass to go to the bow," Moore explained.

Karam placed his right hand on Carpos' shoulder and looked at Moore. "I'm sure that this was just a misunderstanding. Right, John?"

"Right. Just a misunderstanding," he answered although the glare in his eyes spoke otherwise.

"No problem," Moore said. Looking at the satellite phone, Moore commented, "Nice phone."

"Oh, this?" Karam said as he looked at the phone in his left hand. "These things come in handy. You should get one some day," he said as he guided Carpos along the walkway to midship.

"Yeah. That's a good idea," Moore said as he resumed walking toward the bow. He looked down the other side of the ship, but didn't see Asha. No problem, he thought to himself as he took in the evening air, freshened by a slight breeze.

Within minutes, he heard someone approaching. It was Wilbanks.

"You all out here by your lonesome?"

"Story of my life," Moore replied.

"Oh, come on now. A nice-looking guy like you? I'd think you'd have females flocking to you. They flock to me," he grinned. "Must be my Southern charm," he added with a wink.

"Sometimes, I think I'm blind to women coming on to me," Moore said.

"Like that Asha?"

"You noticed?"

"I think everyone on board has noticed, including her father. I see how she looks at you. She's pulling you into her web."

"Great! Like a deadly black widow spider," Moore teased.

"Well, I'll tell you. She could pull me into her web any old time she wanted. Did you see that bikini she had on today?"

"Looked more like some string with three small patches."

"Boy, I'm telling you that I almost had to go get my heart pills," Wilbanks kidded.

"Certainly wasn't much there. Difficult not to notice."

"Yeah, but there was one thing that really weirded me out."

"What's that?"

"Her father."

"How?"

"The way he looked at her after she walked by us below deck."

"He was angry?" Moore asked.

"No. That's what was weird. He stared, too. Like he was enjoying the view. Not what you'd expect from a father."

Moore shuddered with revulsion. "That creeps me out."

"That's a strange thing, for sure."

"Did you know what happened up here tonight?" Moore asked.

"No, what?"

Moore relayed how he was stopped by Asha and Carpos from entering the bow area while Karam was on the satellite phone.

"I don't know if there's anything to that. The guy might just be funny about his phone calls," Wilbanks said.

"Seemed strange to me," Moore added. His gut was signaling that all was not right on board the *Dark Side*.

The two men chit-chatted for another thirty minutes before calling it a night.

The next day, they followed the same routine as the previous day with the same results.

No U-boat.

Leaning against the winch, Moore stared into the night. A nightmare had awakened him at two o'clock and he decided to go topside. He enjoyed the sound of the waves lapping at the side of the ship and the peaceful solitude of the night's sky filled with twinkling stars as a gentle breeze of salt air blew across his face.

"Lonely?"

Recognizing Asha's voice, Moore turned and looked at her. "Not really, but we can talk."

"Your turn on watch?" she asked.

"No, Devlin's up in the bow." Moore noticed that Asha was wearing a skimpy bikini that highlighted her curvy figure. "Going for a swim?"

"Yes. Want to be my lifeguard?" she teased, catching Moore off guard. He was surprised by seeing this side of her.

"I can do that," Moore smiled as he noticed in the moonlight that her ample bosom seemed to overflow her top.

She saw his gaze and smiled to herself. "It's better to take a swim at night after everyone is sleeping. I can only imagine the comments I'd hear from the guys."

"That's for sure," Moore agreed.

Asha stretched. "It feels like my boobs are pushed up to my chin."

"That's better than being at your waist," Moore laughed.

"Turn around."

"Why?

"I'm taking off my top."

"Why should I turn around?" Moore asked good-naturedly.

"I thought you were a gentleman," she responded. "Not like the others."

"Damn. That always works against me," Moore said, feigning disappointment.

"I won't forget," she said, seductively.

Complying, Moore turned around.

"Hold out your hand," she requested.

Filled with curiosity, Moore did as she asked and she placed her top in it.

"Don't lose this. I'll need it."

Feeling the texture of the bikini top in his hand, Moore smiled at the level of trust she had in him.

The next thing he heard was a soft splash as she eased herself off the stern's work platform into the water.

"You can turn around now."

When he turned, he saw her head bobbing out of the water. "Want to join me?" she asked.

"That could be interesting," he replied.

"I'd be glad to," Sloan said. He had walked unheard from the bow to the stern just as Asha slipped into the water. "I would if I wasn't on watch."

"Then I'd be coming out of the water," Asha said firmly.

"And I'd enjoy watching," Sloan smirked.

"Here you go Asha," Moore said as he leaned off the work platform and tossed her top to her.

"Thanks, Emerson. Guess I better put this back on," she said as she glared at Sloan.

"Don't do that on my account. I don't mind," Sloan commented lecherously.

"I didn't think you would, but not today or any day, Devlin," she said coolly.

"Let's go up to the bow," Moore said as he grabbed Sloan's arm and began to ease him forward.

"Ruining the show," Sloan said as he reluctantly allowed Moore to steer him away.

"That was my plan," Moore added.

When the two reached the bow, Sloan asked, "What are you doing on deck? Not your watch yet, Emerson."

"I get these nightmares from time to time. Something to do with a loss of memory I had not so long ago," Moore explained as he unconsciously rubbed his fingers over the scar on the side of his head from the bullet wound that previously caused the memory loss.

"Wish I could forget some things I did in my past," Sloan said.

"Don't we all, Devlin?"

Sloan pointed to a spot west of their ship. "You notice anything out there when you've been on watch?"

Moore looked. "I did a couple of times. I thought I'd see a freighter come into view and then disappear. I could see her silhouette in the moonlight."

"Yeah. I've noticed her, too. She's not running lights. It's almost as if she's shadowing us."

"You say anything to Hopkins or Karam?"

"No."

"We both should in the morning," Moore suggested.

"Okay."

They heard a noise behind them and turned to see Asha reentering the cabin.

"Guess she's done with her swim," Sloan lamented.

Grinning, Moore playfully punched Sloan in the arm. "Sorry you missed the show." Moore turned and headed back to the stern for solitude. Ten minutes later, he headed below deck.

The next morning, Asha was running late. Everyone had risen, eaten breakfast and were at their workstations for the day. Asha hurried into the dining area.

"Do you have anything ready?" she called to Knowles as she poured a cup of coffee.

"I've got some pancakes ready," Knowles answered.

"Perfect," she said as she took a seat at the table.

Knowles appeared and set a plate full of pancakes in front of her, then took a seat across from her.

Asha quickly stabbed two pancakes and placed them on her plate. As she started to cut them, she saw that Knowles' plate was empty. "Bingo, aren't you eating?"

"I tink I lost my appetite," he replied.

"Why? Don't you feel well?"

"Oh no, missy. I feel fine. You're so pretty dat I can't eat a ting," Knowles replied as he ignored the captain's orders.

She shot him a look that could kill.

"Oh good, my appetite, it just come back," he said quickly.

"Good," she said relieved.

"Yep and you look yummy!" he chortled.

Knowles didn't react fast enough as Asha tossed her plate with the uneaten remains of her pancakes at Knowles, catching him squarely in the face.

"Pig!" she yelled as she stood and stormed out of the dining area.

Bingo's face had a large smile as he wiped his face and cleaned up the mess.

The monotony of the search continued throughout the day with the crew taking a quick break for lunch. After dinner that evening, Wilbanks pulled out a deck of cards and several of the crew joined him in a game to pass the time.

When Moore tired of watching the card play, he walked out to the stern deck. A smile crossed his face when he saw that Asha was standing next to the winch. She was staring at the stars.

"Nice evening," Moore started.

She shuddered in surprise and turned to greet him. "I didn't hear you sneak up on me."

"Sorry. I wasn't sneaking."

Looking over his shoulder toward the galley, she asked, "Had your fill of their shenanigans for the day?"

"Something like that," Moore answered. "I just needed a break from that rowdiness and sophomoric behavior."

"Yeah. I know what you mean," she said as she looked at the moon's glow shimmering on the water's surface. "You and Willie don't fit in with this crew," she observed.

"Oh, I don't know about that, at least as far as Willie goes. He's a rascal in his own way."

"Okay. Let me correct myself. You don't fit in with them."

"How's that?"

"You're different."

"In a good way or bad way?"

"Good. You seem more like a gentleman."

"I try, but I have my moments. None of us is perfect."

"Like I've never heard that comment before tonight."

"That's what I believe. I try to accept people for who they are. And I try to do the right thing. I'm not always successful, but I try."

Asha looked closely at the handsome man in front of her. "Pretty honest guy, huh?"

"Try to be."

"I think women sense that in you, Emerson. That's an attractive trait to have." Boy, he was good-looking, she thought. "Did you always want to be a reporter?"

A gentle wave caused Moore to fall against her and their

bodies touched. "Sorry," Moore said as he reluctantly moved his body away from hers.

"Yes. Since I was a kid. I thought it would be fun investigating storylines and interviewing people."

"I guess that would be interesting."

"And there's the travel. You never know where a story is going to take you. I've had a lot of adventures."

"I bet you have," she said suggestively. "Have you ever wanted to do anything else?"

"Yes," he said as he set the bait.

"Oh. Pray tell, what would that be?" she said as her large brown eyes looked deeply into Moore's eyes.

"Be a thief."

"A thief?" she asked in disbelief.

"Sometimes, I think I'd like to be a thief around you."

"Oh?"

Moore looked at her succulent lips before responding. They looked inviting. "Well, you see if I was a thief, I'd steal a kiss from you," Moore said hesitantly.

"Emerson, you are too sweet! You wouldn't have to steal a kiss because I'm giving you one!" Having said that, Asha closed the distance between them and locked her lips on his, stunning Moore.

After they broke apart, a surprised Moore stammered, "Wow, do you know how to kiss!" He liked how aggressive she was.

"Funny man!" Asha said as she ran her finger along Moore's lips. "You have cute lips."

Moore grinned. "And they're ready for another kiss!" He couldn't help himself.

Asha threw her arms around Moore and the two embraced as they kissed a second time.

"Asha?" Karam's voice called as he approached the stern. "Are you out here?"

"Yes, Father," she responded with a slight irritation in her voice at having such a pleasurable moment interrupted. The two quickly separated.

Karam emerged from the shadows and approached the two of them. He had a frown on his face. "Everything okay?" he asked.

"Yep. No problems here," Moore answered hurriedly. He was irritated, too.

Karam eyed Moore suspiciously.

"I was just getting ready to hit my bunk," Asha said as she walked past her father and called back to Moore. "See you in the morning, Emerson."

"Sleep well," Moore responded as he looked at Karam who had a bigger frown on his face. "Guess I'll turn in, too," he said as he left the deck.

Karam was alone at the stern. He didn't like what he sensed was developing between Asha and Moore. He didn't like it at all.

The next day, everyone followed the routine of breakfast and working the grid in search of the lost U-boat. Late in the afternoon, Karam and Wilbanks saw an image appear on the monitor.

"I think that could be our U-boat!" Karam said

enthusiastically, a change from his usually sullen demeanor.

"Maybe," Wilbanks said as Asha leaned over his shoulder to view the image. Wilbanks studied the shadows and the outline that was emerging. After a minute, Wilbanks nodded his head. "That's our U-boat," he said as he noted the GPS coordinates.

A large whoop went up from Carpos, Asha and Sloan, causing Moore and Knowles to join them in the forward compartment.

"What is it? Did you find it?" Moore asked.

"Lock, stock and barrel," Wilbanks grinned.

Knowles grinned. "I tole you all dat every ting is cool."

Karam wrote down the coordinates and went up to the bridge where he relieved Hopkins so he could see the image.

"Job well done, folks," Hopkins grinned as he looked at the pictures on the monitor. "We'll be diving her in the morning."

"Great!" Asha said.

Wilbanks and Moore walked to the stern where they reeled in the towfish and secured it.

For dinner that evening, Knowles celebrated their find by serving fresh chicken. "Celebration," he sang as he placed the serving plates on the table.

"What about our fresh eggs for breakfast?" Sloan asked when he realized that Knowles had killed the remaining chickens.

"I tink we need to party tonight," Knowles said as he twirled in excitement.

Responding to Knowles, Karam commented, "After tonight, you won't need to worry about any eggs for breakfast."

Out of the corner of his eye, Moore thought he noticed an evil glint in Karam's eyes. When he turned to look closer, it had disappeared as Karam allowed a smile to fill his face. Moore suddenly felt uneasy for some reason, but steadfastly shook it off and returned to enjoying the fresh chicken.

Hours later, Moore was tossing and turning in his bunk. He wasn't sure if it was the excitement of finding the U-boat, but Moore couldn't fall asleep. He checked his watch and saw that it was two o'clock. His watch on deck began at four o'clock after Carpos finished his turn. Thinking fresh air and a cool breeze may help clear his mind, he rolled out of his bunk and headed topside.

As he walked quietly past the open door to the pilothouse, he heard a noise. He turned his head to look inside the well-lit pilothouse. He saw a body in a pool of blood on the deck. It was Bingo Knowles. Kneeling over the body and holding a bloodied knife was Asha. Her eyes were wide.

Behind her, Moore could see the ship's radio. It had been destroyed.

Puzzled, Moore asked, "What's going on here?"

"I can explain, Emerson," Asha started as she dropped the knife.

Hopkins' voice boomed over Moore's right shoulder. "You've killed Bingo!" he said angrily as he shoved Moore aside and rushed into the pilothouse. "And my radio, what did you do to it?"

The loud voices caused Sloan to appear in the doorway.

"Secure her, Devlin," Hopkins directed. "And you help him, Moore."

The two men advanced quickly and grabbed her arms, then walked her out to the stern.

Hopkins reached for his cell phone. "I don't know that it will work this far off Key West, but it's worth a try."

"I wouldn't, captain," Karam said quietly, catching Hopkins off guard. He hadn't heard Karam enter the pilothouse.

"You don't tell me what to do," Hopkins said as he spun around to face Karam.

"I might not, but this will," Karam responded sinisterly.

Hopkins looked down and saw that Karam was holding a .45 caliber semi-automatic pistol in his hand. It was pointed at Hopkins.

"That doesn't scare me," he said as he raised his cell phone.

"It should," Karam said as he aimed the weapon at Hopkins' head and pulled the trigger.

Hopkins was killed instantly. His body dropped to the deck as Karam calmly turned and exited the pilothouse.

"Release her," Carpos commanded Sloan and Moore as he walked into the stern area. He was carrying a deadly Uzi 9mm submachine gun.

Carefully, Moore released his grip on Asha as he calculated his next move. There was no way he could close the distance between himself and Carpos without taking a bullet. Sloan didn't think first, he just reacted—and the wrong way. He rushed Carpos and received a burst of bullets from the weapon into his torso.

He dropped to the deck and died.

Stepping across the body to stand next to Carpos, Asha spoke, "Stupid pig." The stern and rugged Asha was back in her true form.

"Need help?" a voice trumpeted through a loudspeaker and everyone on deck turned to look past the stern where a freighter was looming over the research vessel. During the melee on deck, no one had noticed its approach. The name on the bow read *Mongo*.

Karam appeared in the stern, pushing Wilbanks in front of him. "We're in control," he shouted. "Two to go," he said as he pushed Wilbanks to the stern to stand next to Moore.

Eyeing their captors, Moore spoke quietly to Wilbanks. "Interesting twist."

"Understatement, friend," Wilbanks replied in a hushed tone.

"Quiet!" Karam barked. "Sit down and no talking."

Carpos secured the two men's hands and feet with rope.

Over the next hour, the two captives watched silently as the freighter lowered a boat with two armed men. Karam and Asha had disappeared below deck. Carpos held his weapon on Wilbanks and Moore until the freighter's boat tied up and one of the men replaced Carpos in guarding them.

Karam, Carpos and Asha were bringing gear, charts and equipment on deck and loading them into the boat. As they finished, the man at the boat's helm handed Carpos a package and Carpos carried it below deck.

Asha and the guard boarded the boat while Karam pointed his weapon at Moore and Wilbanks.

"What's this all about?" Moore asked.

"It doesn't matter for you. In a few minutes, you'll be blown to pieces with this ship," Karam said.

"Come on. You owe us some sort of explanation," Wilbanks said.

"I don't," Karam said firmly. "What I'm going to do has no impact on you two. You are dead anyhow."

Moore pushed for an answer. "What's on board that U-boat that's worth our lives? The treasure?"

Karam's mind was made up. He wasn't going to give the two captives the pleasure of a response before they died. He had a mortal grin on his face as he remained silent.

"All set," Carpos said as he returned topside.

"Good. We go then."

The two men boarded the boat and it moved back toward the freighter.

Aboard the research vessel, Moore tugged at his restraints. "What is this about? Got any ideas?"

"No," Wilbanks replied as he strained at his bindings. "Other than there's something on that U-boat that is so important that they don't want to risk the chance of us seeing it and revealing it. We did our job; now we're expendable."

"Must be mighty important," Moore commented as he eased his back up against Wilbanks and began to untie the rope around Wilbanks' wrists.

"But not as important as us staying alive right now. I don't know how much time we have before that explosive goes off," Wilbanks said as his hands became free and he turned to untie Moore's hands.

Moore raised his head over the stern and looked toward the freighter. "I'd think they would have given themselves enough time to get far enough away and to the freighter."

"Where are they now?" Wilbanks asked as the two untied their feet.

"At the freighter."

"Think we have time to disarm it?"

"No!"

"Time's up!" Wilbanks exclaimed

"Exactly."

"Abandon ship!" Wilbanks said as he moved to a crouching position.

"My exact thoughts," Moore said as he joined him.

The two men rolled over the side of the ship and into the warm Gulf water. Their escape didn't go unnoticed on the nearby freighter as shouts filled the air. A large searchlight switched on and swept the water, catching the two escaped men as their heads broke the surface for air.

"Not good," Moore said as he bobbed in the water.

"Kill them," Karam shouted from the deck of the freighter.

Before Wilbanks could comment, a hail of bullets from the freighter's crew struck the water near them. The two men ducked underwater and swam toward the bow of the research vessel to put it between them and the freighter. As they surfaced for another breath, the research vessel exploded, sending debris through the air and showering the two swimmers who submerged again.

When they resurfaced, they saw the remains of the vessel's hull burning and heard the approaching sounds of the freighter's boat.

"It's Carpos," Moore said to Wilbanks. The small craft made its way through the floating debris as Carpos fired rounds from his Uzi into anything that floated.

For the next five minutes, the boat searched for Moore and Wilbanks, who repeatedly dived below the surface and carefully resurfaced below debris that had been riddled with bullets.

Satisfied that the two men couldn't have remained alive, Carpos directed the man at the tiller to return to the freighter where Karam was waiting.

"Did you kill them?"

"Yeah. A couple of rounds in both of them," Carpos lied as the small craft was lifted onto the freighter and the searchlight doused.

Meanwhile, Moore heard a hurtful moan. He looked and saw Wilbanks trying to stay afloat. "You okay?" he asked quietly.

"Took one in the shoulder, Emerson."

"Is it bleeding?"

Wilbanks wiped his right hand on left shoulder. When he brought it back to his face to look at it, he replied, "Yeah."

Moore looked around the surface and sighed with relief. "No sharks yet. But that blood soon will attract them."

"You can count on that," Wilbanks agreed.

Moore pulled off his tee shirt. "Let's see what we can do to stop the bleeding."

"You're still going to have a bloody tee shirt in the water," Wilbanks countered as he winced when Moore tried to tie it.

"I need something to hold it in place," Moore said. Then, he took off his belt and used it to tie the tee shirt against the wound. It was while he was tying the belt on Wilbanks' shoulder that he felt something bump into the back of his head. It hadn't taken the sharks long, he thought.

When he turned around to face the threat, he was relieved by what he saw. He even chuckled. Floating in front of him was Bingo's chicken coop. Moore climbed on top of it.

"Give me your arm," he said as he reached out to Wilbanks.

Wilbanks extended his arm and between the two of them, they were able to pull Wilbanks on top of the crate. In the process, Moore ended up back in the water. There just wasn't room for both of them on top of the floating chicken coop. It was only two feet wide and four feet long. As it was, Wilbanks' legs dangled in the water.

"Emerson, you should just let me go. Save yourself," Wilbanks said as he winced in pain.

"Can't do that, Willie. We're in this together."

"I got you into this mess. Let me get you out," Wilbanks said as he tried to flip himself off the coop.

"We'll make it. Don't worry. This could be one of the best stories I'll ever write," Moore said as he tried to remain optimistic about their fate. "We'll take stock of our situation in the morning," he added as he, too, clung to the coop.

As they drifted, Wilbanks asked, "Do you know what started that mess back there?"

"All I know is that I saw a light in the pilothouse and stuck my head in. That's when I saw Bingo on the deck. There was a pool of blood around him and Asha was kneeling over him. She had a bloody knife in her hand."

"Bingo sure taunted her. He had it coming, but not that," Wilbanks mused. "Did you see her kill Bingo?"

"No. I think I arrived right after she did it," Moore said.

Wilbanks winced as he shifted his weight. "That Knowles would wake up at the crack of stupid. What a character!"

"They all were. Like you said—a ship of misfits! But none of them deserved to die."

"That's for sure." Wilbanks groaned as he shifted his body. "There's more to this than what we've seen," he surmised.

"Shooting everyone and blowing up that leased ship with all the equipment on board just doesn't make sense."

"They're hiding something and they don't want any survivors around to tell tales," Wilbanks said. "Hopkins, Sloan and Knowles dead. We're lucky to be alive."

"I'd guess now that they had this planned for some time."

"Ya think?" Wilbanks asked sarcastically.

Moore put off the critical tone as a reaction to the pain that Wilbanks was experiencing. "For whatever reason, Karam didn't want us diving on that U-boat. I wonder what was so special on board that they didn't want us to see it."

"Yeah. Makes you wonder," Wilbanks said.

"What makes me wonder is how I misread that Asha. I thought I had got by her rough façade and was connecting with a nice person. Boy, was I ever wrong. I'll never forget that image of her kneeling over Knowles with that bloody knife in her hand," said Moore.

"I feel sorry for Bingo, but he sure did push himself on her," admitted Wilbanks.

"The guy didn't understand that he needed to back off."

"She got her payback," Wilbanks retorted. "And I didn't see Asha running to your rescue when they left us tied up and waiting for the bomb to blow us up with the ship!"

"Yes. I know," then Moore added, "disappointing."

They passed the night with Wilbanks occasionally moaning and drifting in and out of sleep as they floated with the current.

When the morning dawned, Moore took stock of their situation. "Good news."

"We're rescued?" Wilbanks moaned.

"No, we're floating in a debris field."

"See the freighter anywhere?" Wilbanks asked with mild concern.

Moore raised his head as far above the water as he could and looked around. "No, my guess is that they're on station at the U-boat site. Probably diving on it."

"Probably," Wilbanks agreed. "We're drifting with the current. If they're on station, we should have drifted several miles away from them."

"Where do you think we'll end up? Cuba, maybe?"

"Dead if we're not careful," Wilbanks said pragmatically. "We could drift right out into the Gulf Stream and up the coast. We'd be out too far to try to swim in. Our only hope is to get picked up by fishermen or a passing ship."

After a brief pause, Wilbanks continued, "If I ever see that Karam again, I swear I'll dip his privates in acid."

"I hope you have the opportunity. I'll even help you," Moore offered.

Hearing a moan from Wilbanks, Moore turned and noticed a deep laceration on Wilbanks' back. "Looks like something cut your back. Falling debris, maybe," Moore guessed.

"It hurts like hell," Wilbanks said.

"Let's see what I can salvage," Moore said as he pushed the chicken coop through the floating debris. He found some line and several larger pieces of wood, which he lashed together with the coop. He found a life ring and a cooler.

"We can use the cooler to catch rain water," he said.

"We'll need that. You can only go three days without water," Wilbanks warned.

"I know. Hope we get some rain, Willie," Moore said as he looked hopefully to the sky.

"Well don't hope for a deluge. We don't need no tropical storm to break apart what you've cobbled together," Wilbanks said as his feet rested on part of the makeshift raft.

"I'm not done," Moore said as he swam away from his jury-rigged creation to see what else he could find. About ten feet away, he reached below the water's surface and pulled up the netting that had supported one of the bunk bed mattresses. "Here's a net for fishing," he called to Wilbanks before swimming back with it in tow.

"That will come in handy," Wilbanks said as Moore climbed back on the raft.

"Sure will," Moore said as he pulled the net aboard. "Bonus find!" He then pulled a plastic item from the net.

"What do you have there?"

"Looks like we've got Bingo's urinal container," Moore remarked as he held it up to show Wilbanks.

"I hope it's clean," Wilbanks said.

Moore chuckled as he set it down and turned his attention to another item caught in the net. "And a blanket. I can rig up some shade for you."

"Good. I'll be as red as a lobster in the sun," Wilbanks said. "So will you."

Moore had his eyes focused on a ten-by-six-foot section of the research vessel, floating about thirty feet away. "That piece would be a great addition to our raft," Moore suggested. "I'm going after it."

"I'd wait a bit before you go back in," Wilbanks warned.

"Why?"

"Unless you think you can swim faster than that one."

Moore looked in the direction that Wilbanks was pointing and saw a shark fin breaking the water. "Maybe I'll wait."

"Good idea."

"At least I'm glad that he didn't show up last night when we were still in the water." As the shark passed next to their raft, Moore asked, "What kind is he, Willie?"

"That would be a tiger shark. He's about ten feet long and about a thousand pounder, I'd guess," Wilbanks answered. "You go ahead and swim with him if you want. I wouldn't mess with him. Very aggressive, too."

"I'll just wait," Moore said as he shuddered and watched the shark pass by again.

The shark circled the raft and immediate area for the next hour, then disappeared.

"I think I'll give it a go," Moore said as he clumsily splashed into the water.

"I wouldn't have done that, Emerson. You should have eased yourself into the water. That splashing attracts them."

"Now you tell me," Moore said as he quickly looked around for any sign of a dorsal fin. "I think I'm good."

"The operative word was think," Wilbanks responded. "Be sure it's clear."

"Looks good," Moore called as he swam quickly to the section of debris and climbed aboard. "Uh-oh," he said as he turned and saw an approaching fin. "Maybe this wasn't one of my better moves," he said as he watched the tiger shark circle his precarious float.

After twenty minutes, the shark widened its circle and showed no intention of abandoning its potential meal.

Moore looked overhead and noticed the darkening clouds. "Looks like we're in for a storm," he called to Wilbanks. The waves were beginning to get rougher.

"Hope it's not a bad one. It could separate us. I might lose you," Wilbanks replied. He was weakening from the loss of blood.

"You're not going to lose me that easy," Moore said as he unwrapped the line that he had tied around his waist. He held it up and gauged the distance between himself and Wilbanks. "Too short," he announced.

Lying prone, Moore cautiously began paddling with his hands in the water to close the gap. He made some progress before withdrawing his hands as the shark swam directly toward him.

For the next half hour, Moore played a game of cat and mouse with the shark as he intermittently paddled and withdrew his hands when the predator advanced. Sitting up, Moore gauged the distance to Wilbanks.

"I think I'm close enough now." Moore threw one end of the line towards Wilbanks and it landed in the water next to Wilbanks, but out of his reach. Moore tried several more times before landing the rope end on the raft where Wilbanks was able to grasp it.

"Hold tight," Moore said as he pulled himself to Wilbanks and quickly used the line to secure the new section to their raft, enlarging their rickety float to eight feet by ten feet. "That should give us a little more elbow room."

"What do you have there?" Wilbanks asked as he saw some long pieces of plastic pipe near Moore's feet.

"Found these floating in the flotsam and grabbed it. I can rig a frame to put that blanket on. That'll protect you from the sun." Moore began working on rigging the sunshade. He was able to bend two pieces of the flexible pipe into a u-shape. He tucked the ends between the open slats of the chicken coop and draped the blanket over it.

"This should work nicely," he said as he admired his makeshift shelter as the raft began to ride up and down in the choppy seas and the wind freshened.

Moore held up a three-foot square piece of torn aluminum. "I found this in the debris field. I think I can use it to catch rainwater and funnel it into the piss pot," Moore suggested hopefully. "It'll supplement what we catch in Bingo's cooler."

Within minutes, the sky darkened overhead and a torrential downpour pummeled the men and raft. Moore took the aluminum and creased the edge and gave it to Wilbanks to hold so that the fresh water drained into Bingo's urinal.

"Need to borrow your sunshade," Moore said as he reached

for the soaking wet blanket and started to wring it out.

"You can't drink that water," Wilbanks said. "That blanket was soaked through with salt water."

"But I can try to use the rainwater to rinse it out. Then when it gets soaked again from this rain, we can wring the cleaner water into the urinal."

"Good thinking," Wilbanks said as he opened his mouth to capture as much rainwater as possible.

Moore busied himself alternating between wringing out the blanket and retying lines that threatened to separate and break up their fragile raft. The rain shower was brief, lasting perhaps twenty minutes. As the clouds passed, the sun reappeared and bathed the two survivors with its hot rays. Moore worked quickly to return the blanket to his makeshift shade for Wilbanks.

Holding up the full urinal, Wilbanks took a swallow and handed it to Moore. "I'd suggest that we each limit ourselves to one swallow," Wilbanks said as he lay back on the chicken coop to seek its inviting but limited shade.

"Sounds like a plan," Moore said before taking a swallow and wedging the urinal container between the slats of the coop. Scanning the quieting seas, he happily announced, "No sharks."

"Good."

Moore then grabbed the bed netting and two broken pieces of the plastic pipe. He weaved the pipe through the netting so that he could hold one end of each pipe in his hand and scoop the net into the water.

"Going fishing?" Wilbanks asked wearily.

"Yeah. I think this could work," Moore said confidently as he began to lean over the edge of the raft and dip the net in the water.

Suddenly, the net was torn from his hands as Moore jumped back from the edge and the tiger shark's vicious teeth narrowly missed taking a tasty bite of a *Washington Post* reporter. The shark swam away with the netting caught over its snout.

"That was close," Wilbanks observed.

"Closer than I ever would want to be. Guess that ends my fishing attempt," Moore said as he looked at Wilbanks and noticed how drained Wilbanks appeared. "You okay, Willie?"

"Fine. Just fine, Emerson," Wilbanks responded weakly.

Moore saw through the response. He figured that Wilbanks' blood loss from the bullet wound and the laceration on his back were contributing to his advanced decline. Moore was concerned that Wilbanks would suffer blood poisoning from the laceration, which had been open to the back muscle.

Moore scanned the horizon for any sign of a ship, but saw nothing other than blue water and sky. When he looked back at Wilbanks, he saw that he had fallen into a fitful sleep.

CHAPTER 17

Three days later
Strait of Florida

"Manny, you've got to hide," Fat Freddy screamed at Moore. "Jimmy's on the rampage."

"Who does he want me to knock off now?" Moore asked.

Moore watched as Fat Freddy waddled across the room. He turned and his cherubic face was pointed at Moore. He held Moore's .22 caliber handgun in his hand.

"He wants you to take me out. You wouldn't do that, would you?" Fat Freddy asked.

"No, Freddy. We're buds," Moore said.

"Yeah. That's what I was thinking."

Moore followed Fat Freddy out the front door and onto the farmhouse's porch. That's when he felt something cold against the back of his neck.

"That was a test, Manny. I know you're not Manny Elias. You're Emerson Moore. And now I'm going to kill you," Jimmy Diamonds said as an evil look crossed his face.

When the hammer clicked on an empty chamber, Moore awoke from his nightmare and sat up to check his surroundings. Over the last seventy-two hours, Moore had been sleeping on and off. His sleep was interrupted with nightmares about his recent involvement with Mafioso Jimmy Diamonds. He wished that his bout with memory loss had eradicated that not-so-long-ago chapter in his life.

He saw that he and Wilbanks were still adrift in the water. Wilbanks was in worse shape than Moore. He had been phasing in and out of consciousness, becoming increasingly incoherent and delusional. The limited supply of fresh water in the urinal container and cooler were almost depleted. Moore had reduced his consumption to half a swallow a day while increasing Wilbanks to two swallows a day.

Moore wondered if they would be rescued or if they would die at sea. He was thirsty, suffering from nausea and having nightmares. He experienced a loss of appetite and felt severely fatigued—all symptoms of dehydration.

Looking overhead, he saw a seagull drifting over them. There had been several that had swooped low, but not close enough for him to try to grab one although he thought it would be a fruitless attempt. None of the savvy seagulls would land on their floating home.

A moan from Wilbanks again signaled that he was awakening.

"I'm going shopping, Emerson," Wilbanks said deliriously as he tried to sit up.

"Where?" Moore asked.

"On that island over there." Wilbanks pointed to a spot on the horizon.

Moore looked and saw nothing.

"I can swim there. It's not far. I'll bring you some food and water," Wilbanks said through defeated eyes before collapsing back on the chicken coop.

"You just rest, now," Moore said as his eyes strayed from Wilbanks to the coop. Nails! The coop had nails in it, Moore thought. He decided to pry a nail lose and make it into the shape of a hook for fishing. He could use a piece of line and tie it to the hook.

Moore grabbed one of the pieces of plastic pipe which had a sharp edge and began prying at one of the nails to the coop. Over the next fifteen minutes, his patience paid off, as he was able to work the head of the nail out to the point where he could start to work it in his fingers. Finally, he was holding the nail in his hand.

He carefully bent the nail into a hook. He tore a small strip of the bloodstained tee shirt and wrapped it above the bent nail. Then he optimistically dropped it into the water. In about ten minutes, Moore saw a fish approaching the hook and became excited that he might actually catch it.

When the fish struck at the cloth and hidden nail, Moore jerked on the line, only to see the fish swim away. Hurriedly, he pulled in the line and saw that his hook had disappeared. He cast the line down, frustrated with his lack of success.

An hour went by and Moore spotted a jellyfish floating on the surface. Within minutes, it was floating near enough that Moore was able to scoop it out of the water by using the jagged piece of aluminum. Carefully watching the tentacles and fearing being stung by them, Moore set the jellyfish on the farthest point of the raft.

He poked at the top of the prized quarry and watched as it wiggled. It was food although he was squeamish about eating it. He bent down and bit into the gelatinous top, the bell part of the jellyfish. He sat back up and savored the first food that he had had in several days. His semi-adventurous taste buds discovered a bland taste and a rubbery texture. He swallowed, gagging as he did. Well, he thought to himself, it was protein and watery. He took another bite.

He then used the sharp edge of the pipe to cut a piece for Wilbanks and scooted over to him.

"Here, Willie. Eat this," he said as he raised Wilbanks' head and held the piece of jellyfish to Wilbanks' lips.

"What is it?" Wilbanks groaned with animal-like misery.

"Tofu. Tofu of the sea," Moore grinned as Wilbanks chewed on his portion. "Eat it slowly," Moore cautioned as he stared at Wilbanks' dull and hopeless eyes.

Over the next fifteen minutes, the two men devoured the fresh delicacy, keeping some to use as bait. Then Moore shoved the tentacles overboard.

"That was good. Go to the store tomorrow and buy more of that. Buy some rum, too," Wilbanks said before he slipped back into unconsciousness.

Moore kept his eyes alert for more jellyfish. He was hoping that they would drift into a large group of them so he could harvest them.

Later that evening, Moore woke up with intense stomach pain. He rolled on the raft in agony and began to vomit. When he finished throwing up the contents of his stomach, he continued to have dry heaves. He wasn't sure if he was allergic to the jellyfish or if it was too much for his empty stomach. In any event, the incident advanced his state of dehydration.

Moore collapsed on the raft as a flood of despair overwhelmed him. He was engulfed by the fear of his mortality. He felt like something really bad was going to come from the other side of hell—their death.

When Moore awoke, night had fallen again. He was desperate and in no condition to enjoy the starlit sky. He thought about his deceased parents and how they had raised him. He rekindled fond memories of their love and the solid upbringing they had given him.

He could hear them as if they were seated next to him. They were telling him to pray as they did throughout his youth. He bowed his head and prayed although he felt like God had abandoned him. He thought of Aunt Anne, his shining light and spirit. He thought of his boss and editor John Sedler as well as his trusted confidantes, Sam Duncan and Mike Adams. He believed he soon would rejoin his wife and son, in Heaven this time. His faith in the Lord gave him assurance. The end was near, Moore and Wilbanks were nearly out of time.

Five minutes later, Moore lifted his head and saw dark ominous clouds moving quickly to cover the stars. The wind had freshened. Another storm would be passing through as the waves began to rock their fragile craft.

Within twenty minutes, the craft was bobbing as waves crashed over it, threatening to rip it apart. Moore looked at

Wilbanks. He was unconscious and oblivious to the danger they faced. On his hands and knees, Moore crawled over to Wilbanks. That was when the large wave broke, knocking Moore overboard.

Moore sank. He felt like his lungs were going to burst as he swam toward the turmoiled surface. Breaking through, he gasped for air, but instead ingested gulps of saltwater.

Choking, he tried to spit it out and replace it with air. Waves broke over his head as he fought to breathe. Finally regaining his breath, Moore looked around for the raft. It was drifting away.

Screaming for help was useless. No one would have heard his screams.

As the stormy seas battered him, Moore began swimming after the raft. He knew in his weakened state that he wouldn't last long. He pulled whatever inner strength he had and swam as hard as he could.

He caught up to the bobbing raft, which through some miracle was still in one piece, if one could call it that. He tried to pull himself aboard, but was too weak. He rested for a few minutes as waves continued to break over the raft and his head.

He had a death grip on the raft. Again, Moore tried to pull himself aboard and made it halfway. Exhausted, he passed out.

Two hours later, something brushed against Moore's legs, which were still in the water and attached to his body. Moore's eyes rolled open slowly. He was greeted by the early dawn and calm seas. Feeling relieved that the night's terror had passed, Moore relaxed, but not for long. He felt something again brush against his legs.

When he turned to look, he saw a dorsal fin disappear under the water's surface. Panicking, Moore pulled his lower torso out of the water and rolled onto the raft. Within minutes, he was chuckling as the dolphin jumped out of the water. Relaxing, Moore was relieved to know that it wasn't a shark. He had no intention of becoming shark bait.

Moore cast an eye toward Wilbanks and saw that he was still unconscious and probably now dead. Weakened further by the entire ordeal, Moore fell back to the raft deck and passed out. He had nothing left to give.

CHAPTER 18

Two days later
Lower Keys Medical Center

"You were lucky. Especially your friend," the doctor said as he reviewed the two men's medical charts.

"Is he okay?" Moore asked as he turned to look at his roommate.

"Barely. He wouldn't have lasted another day. We got IV's into both of you. Lucky that a fishing boat spotted you both. They pulled you aboard and radioed the Coast Guard. They sent a helicopter out to bring you here yesterday."

"Where's here?" Moore asked, glad that their tormenting journey was in the past.

"Key West."

Moore's lips were still dry and cracked. He slowly reached for a glass of water on his tray. Holding the glass close to his chest, he sipped through a straw. This was the first time that he felt that he could talk coherently since vomiting the jellyfish. "How long were we at sea?"

"If you tell me when you went into the water, I can answer that," the doctor said.

Moore looked over at Wilbanks. "It was a Thursday."

"This is Friday. Judging from your condition that would put you at eight days. You both suffered from severe exposure, shock, advanced dehydration and extreme sunburns. Your buddy was in worse shape, at death's door. He lost a lot of blood from that bullet wound and laceration in his back. We had to give him a blood transfusion. Still, it was touch and go with him. He must have an iron constitution to pull through the way he did. He should be fine."

"That's good news," Moore said as he breathed a deep sigh of relief.

"You get some rest now. I'll be back later," the doctor said as he started to walk out of the room. He paused in the doorway. "By the way, you've created a clamor in the media. Your rescue and pictures of your raft have been in the newspapers and TV. We had to post a security guard in the hallway to keep the reporters from sneaking up here for an interview."

"That's great," Moore mumbled as the doctor closed the door behind him. We're the story and Karam knows we're alive, he thought as he relaxed under the clean, white sheets in the room's air-conditioned comfort. He was still very thankful for their rescue and briefly counted his blessings before falling into a deep sleep.

Moore's sleep was interrupted twice as he was awakened

to eat a light lunch and dinner. He had no problems falling back to sleep even though Wilbanks was snoring.

Around 3:00 A.M., the elevator doors opened, then shut. They repeated this sequence several times. Must be stuck, the security guard thought as he stood from his chair and walked the short distance to the elevator. As he walked by the nurse's station, he noticed that it was empty. Then he saw a nurse down at the other end of the hall as she walked out of one room into another.

The guard began to enter the elevator when a hand stealthily reached out and pulled him inside.

"What's …?"

He didn't get to finish his question as the butt end of a pistol connected with his head, instantly knocking him unconscious. He dropped to the floor as the dark-complected assailant set the emergency stop button on the elevator's control panel.

The assailant stuck his head out in the hallway and saw no one. Stepping out of the elevator, he walked to the closed door next to the chair formerly occupied by the guard. This was going to be easier than expected, he thought as he opened the door.

He stepped inside the room and with a look of consternation saw that only one bed was occupied. It contained Wilbanks, who appeared to be in a deep sleep. Hearing the toilet flush behind the closed bathroom door, the assailant stepped over to the door and waited for it to open.

Just as an unsuspecting Moore opened the bathroom door, the room door opened and the nurse walked in.

"What are you doing in here?" she asked, startled at seeing

the visitor who was holding a .22-caliber handgun fitted with a silencer.

The man raised his arm and took quick aim at the nurse who screamed. Before he could pull the trigger, Moore rapidly moved into action as he grabbed the assailant's arm with both hands and thrust it downward. He then slammed the arm against the wall as he tried to break the man's grip on the weapon. At the same time, the man's left arm went around Moore's neck in a tight choke-hold.

Moore was in no condition for a fight. He felt like he was going to black out. Suddenly, the man dropped the weapon as he grunted in pain when Moore was able to connect the man's wrist with the corner of a counter.

The nurse reacted without thinking by kicking the weapon under Wilbanks' bed as she continued to wildly scream for help.

The assailant retaliated by placing both hands around Moore's neck and squeezed even more tightly this time. Moore blacked out and fell to the floor.

When he regained consciousness, he felt exhausted. He looked around and saw there were several members of the medical staff and a police officer standing over him as he rested in his bed.

Moore recognized the nurse and asked, "What happened?" Then Moore saw the assailant on the floor in a pool of blood. He was dead. "Did I do that? I don't remember."

"No, I did," the nurse said proudly. "Took my scissors and stabbed him in the carotid artery. I was a Marine. No one tries to kill me and gets away with it."

"Thank you," Moore mumbled appreciatively. "Thank you so very much."

"I know you probably could have handled him by yourself if you had been at 100 percent," she said to comfort Moore's male ego. It was no big deal to her.

"Yep. No problem there," he grinned.

"You know this guy?" the police officer asked.

"Never saw him before," Moore said as he looked at the man's face.

"I thought we had a guard outside the door," Moore said, confused.

"You did. He's recovering from a nasty bump on his noggin. He'll be fine. We've got another guard out there now."

"Good," Moore said as the police forensic team entered, took pictures and processed the crime scene before assisting with the body removal.

"You better get some rest," the nurse said. Turning to the officer, she asked, "Are you done here for now?"

"Guess we are," the officer said as he walked out of the hospital room with the others. The nurse was the last to exit, turning off the light as she did.

Lying in the darkness, Moore felt severely exhausted from the fight and the activities that followed. He was sore. He replayed the tussle and thought about Karam coming after the two of them. What was so important, he asked himself before falling asleep.

CHAPTER 19

Morning
Lower Keys Medical Center

Awaking from the bright sunlight streaming into the room, Moore looked toward Wilbanks' bed. Wilbanks' head was facing him and his eyes were closed. Slowly he opened them and stared blearily at Moore. When he recognized Moore, his lips formed a small smile. They moved soundlessly for a few seconds as he struggled to speak.

"We made it," he said in a half-whisper.

"Yes, we did. How you feeling?" Moore asked.

"Okay. Because my name wasn't in today's obituaries. How about you?" he asked with a faint rasping sound deep in his throat.

"Better than you look."

Raising his eyebrows, Wilbanks muttered, "I look that bad?"

"Actually you do look better than the last time I remember seeing you on the raft. You really looked like you had one foot halfway through death's door. I was worried that you were going to check out on me."

"They got any rum around here?"

"You're on meds. I don't think you'll be drinking rum for awhile."

"I will when I get home," Wilbanks said as he widened his eyes and looked at his IV. Changing topics, Wilbanks struggled to speak, "Glad that we had that chicken coop!"

The two started to chuckle, but were interrupted by a voice.

"No life vests on or any type of approved floatation devices, but you had a chicken coop. I'd like to know how you two came across a chicken coop in the middle of the ocean."

Moore and Wilbanks looked toward the doorway and saw two uniformed Coast Guard officers walk into the room.

"It was Bingo's," Moore explained.

"You're going to have to do much better than that. Tell us who Bingo is," the first officer said as he introduced himself as Dave Brenneis and his fellow officer as Bert Fall.

"In fact, tell us the whole story about what happened to you two."

With Moore doing most of the talking, he explained over the next thirty minutes about his initial meeting with Karam through the research vessel explosion and gunfire. Wilbanks filled in some of the gaps as Fall took notes.

When they wrapped up the session, Moore asked, "Are you going to search the area that we were in?"

"Yes, although I'm not sure that we'll find much. It's been over a week and who knows where that freighter went," Brenneis answered.

"Sure would like you to find them," Moore commented with a disappointed, but imploring tone.

"We'll see what we can run down on this Karam, Carpos and the woman," Fall said as he looked at his notes. "The doctor said you're being released tomorrow and your buddy here the next day if he is fit. You both staying in Key West?"

"No reason. I'm heading back to Ohio to recover for a few days, then I'll see what I'll do," Moore answered.

"How about you, Wilbanks?" Brenneis asked.

"I'm going home to Charleston," Wilbanks murmured. "Time to fly the coop," he joked weakly.

"We're going to need phone numbers for both of you so that we can follow up. I'm sure that we will have additional questions," Fall said.

After the two Coasties left, Moore turned to Wilbanks. "We had a little excitement here last night, sleeping beauty."

"What do you mean?"

"Since we made the news, I'm sure that Karam heard we were alive and wanted to shut us up. Looks like he sent a hit man to silence us."

"What do you mean?"

Moore explained what had transpired.

"You're kidding me!" Wilbanks exclaimed quietly. "I didn't hear a thing."

"You slept right through it. You owe me for saving your life again!" Moore teased.

"Oh no! He owes me," the nurse said as she entered the room.

"Thank you, dear," Wilbanks said. "I'd rather owe you, sweetie!"

The nurse smiled even though she didn't like being called "dear" or "sweetie."

"You're still here?" Moore asked in disbelief as he looked at the nurse. "I'd have thought they would have sent you home."

"Got my duty to perform. Remember, I'm a former Marine," she said proudly as she went about her business.

Moore reached for the phone so he could call John Sedler and update his editor on his most recent brush with death.

CHAPTER 20

Two days later
Put-in-Bay, Ohio

Moore sought an escape by sitting on his aunt's porch where he had retreated from her incessant "mothering." She had gone overboard in babying him since his return. He knew that she meant well, but he didn't need or want that close attention from anyone. Moore was enjoying his solace and the view of Put-in-Bay's harbor as he wrapped up a phone conversation with John Sedler at *The Post*.

"Lucky again," Sedler said after discussing Moore's ordeal and the search for the U-boat. "I'm glad you called me earlier from the hospital to update me."

"When we wrap this all up, I'm going to have quite a story to submit."

"I bet!" Sedler agreed. "Have you heard anything more from the Coast Guard or that Wilbanks fellow?"

"Nothing, although I did get a text from Wilbanks that he's feeling stronger and will be released tomorrow. He'll head back to Charleston."

"What about those folks who chartered the research vessel?"

"Nothing. It's as if they disappeared into thin air."

"Strange."

"There's more to this and I'm going to figure it out," Moore said.

"And what have I told you in the past?"

"You and everyone else who thinks they're my mother. 'Be careful, Emerson,'" Moore mocked.

"Yeah. Yeah. You better. You rest up and make sure you're fully recovered before you start following up on this. Understand?" Sedler asked, knowing that Moore would do as he wished.

"Sure."

"And you keep me in the loop. None of this Lone Ranger stuff. Got it?"

"Got it," Moore grinned as the two ended their call and looked at his watch. Realizing that he had lunch plans with Mad Dog Adams, he went to the garage and hopped in the Ford Model A truck. Starting it, he drove over to Mr. Ed's Bar on Delaware Avenue, but couldn't find a parking spot. He drove around the corner and behind the building to park in the rear. He walked past the Subway restaurant and turned right into Mist, the tropical pool and bar which was a part of the Mr. Ed's complex.

Mist was hopping as usual. Loud music filled the patio and

pool area as scantily clad females gyrated to the music in front of a bevy of admiring male onlookers either relaxing in one of the lounge chairs or standing at the blue and white umbrella-covered tables. The sunken bar in the pool was crowded two-deep as patrons vied for the bartender's attention.

"Over here," Adams called when he spotted Moore.

Seeing Adams comfortably seated at the u-shaped bar under the giant tiki hut, Moore walked over to join him.

"I picked a good spot," Adams said as a couple of bikinied girls near them jumped into the pool.

"You always do," Moore teased as he sat down.

"What happened to you?" Adams asked as he looked at the recovering Moore who then proceeded to catch up Adams on his misadventure, pausing to order one of Mr. Ed's famous hamburgers.

"Nice to hear that you didn't lose your memory again," Adams teased as he sipped his drink.

"I didn't, but I continue to have the nightmares about Jimmy Diamonds and Fat Freddy. Now they've been expanded to include dreams about me being missing, like I'm lost at sea and sharks are attacking me."

"I swear that you have more lives than a cat. That was a close call."

"I have Sam Duncan to thank for more lives than a cat. Yeah, it was a close call all right, too close. Nothing like being lost at sea to make you feel hopeless. One of the worst experiences of my life."

"You could have died."

Moore nodded his head in silent agreement.

"I'm glad you made it back in one piece, my friend," Adams said genuinely as the server appeared with their food.

"Me, too. Sometimes I think I should try a new career," Moore said as he watched two attractive women sit at the table next to him.

"You wouldn't be satisfied," Adams spoke all-knowingly.

"You're probably right." Then Moore sat straight up in his chair. "Maybe I could be an entertainer like you."

Adams looked at Moore over the rim of his trademark sunglasses. "Honestly? You can't sing, Emerson. You don't play an instrument."

"I can be a jokester."

Moaning at the thought, Adams said in a serious tone, "I'd rethink that. Your jokes are anemic. They don't have the punch or the timing."

Knowing that Adams was right, Moore countered as he waved his fingers in an effeminate manner, "I was just being rather whimsical."

"See. That's just what I mean. You need to stick with your shtick!" Adams chuckled and changed the subject. "And nothing more about the freighter?"

"Not a thing." Moore was going to continue, but he was interrupted by his buzzing cell phone. "Key West area code," he said as he looked at the phone's display. "Might be the Coast Guard now."

Answering his phone, Moore nodded to Adams that it was the Coast Guard calling. They conversed for a few minutes and Moore ended the call.

"The Coast Guard searched the coordinates that we gave

them, but couldn't find anything. No freighter. No nothing. The debris field had drifted away. Most likely with Willie and me."

"And nothing about the vessel's crew?"

"Nothing. Not a sign of Hopkins, Sloan or Knowles. You would have liked Bingo. He was such a crack-up."

Adams nodded his head. "The Bahamian guy you told me about?"

"Yeah. And Willie Wilbanks is just as ornery as you. Now, you two could be a great comedy team."

"I'd like to meet him one day. Sounds like he and I would hit it off." Then Adams asked, "What's the Coast Guard doing now?"

"Running down Karam, Carpos and Asha to see what they can learn about them," Moore responded.

"You think they already dived on the U-boat and stole whatever treasure was onboard?"

"That would be my guess. I don't understand why they wouldn't have had us dive and bring up the treasure to help them do the work. Then kill us off. Why kill us off first? Why get a freighter involved? Why get more people involved?"

"Yeah, why?"

"Too many whys. It doesn't fit. Something's amiss here and I can't figure it out."

"It smells." Adams looked at his watch. "It's almost show time," Adams said as he stood and left money on their table to pay the bill. "I need to get over to the Round House. You coming over to see the show?"

"I'd like to, but I'm going to spend the afternoon researching this entire mishap."

"You're missing a good show."

Moore smiled at his friend. "All of your shows are good!"

Adams grinned at his friend. "You should head up my fan club," he joked.

"Is that the one with the fan dancers? That's what I'd expect from you," Moore kidded back.

"I like that. See if you can arrange that!" Adams said as he left.

Moore finished his drink and stood to leave. When he turned around, he almost knocked over an attractive woman with black hair who was wearing a barely-there bikini.

"Sorry," Moore started before recognizing Cheryl Rubel, one of the island residents and local partiers. "Hi Cheryl," he greeted her as he helped her regain her balance.

"Emerson! I've missed seeing you!" Cheryl exclaimed as she planted a kiss on Moore's cheek.

Moore was all smiles. "I've been out on assignment," he responded as he elected not to go into detail. "Where's Jeff?"

Cheryl's husband responded, "Right here."

Moore turned and saw her muscular husband behind him. He was wearing one of his sleeveless Harley-Davidson muscle shirts. Moore was fond of the biker couple as were many of the islanders. The two epitomized coolness.

"Turn around and show Emerson your new tat," Jeff encouraged his wife.

Without hesitation, Cheryl spun around so that Moore could see her new tattoo, which made its way down the side of her back to her hip and under her bikini bottom. "You like?"

"Nice," Moore said appreciatively.

"You should get one, Emerson," she urged as she turned to face him.

"Me and a tattoo?"

"Go for it," Jeff urged.

"Maybe one of those henna temporary tats," Moore grinned.

"No. Do the real deal," she urged.

"Yeah. We know some great tat artists," Jeff added.

"Baby steps first," Moore teased.

"I promised Cheryl I'd get her a huge diamond. Turn around, honey, and show him."

Cheryl turned slightly so that Moore could see her back. Across her lower back was a large tattoo. A large diamond was etched into the bottom of the tat.

"Not quite the type of diamond that I had in mind," she laughed.

Moore smiled at the comment. "Guess you don't have to worry about misplacing that diamond," he chuckled.

"You've heard about the Hope Diamond?" Jeff asked.

"Yes."

"Well, this is the Cheryl Diamond. Can't quite put a value on its worth, even though it's in the rough!" Jeff joked.

"I'm in the rough, too," Cheryl purred as she planted a kiss on her husband's cheek and wrapped her arms around him. "Aren't I, sweetie?"

Jeff answered with a large smile.

"Listen, it was great seeing you both, but I've got some

stuff I need to get done and better run," Moore said.

Cheryl gave Moore another quick peck on the cheek. "Get a tat, Emerson. Do it."

As Moore shook his head and walked toward the exit, Jeff called after him. "Go for it, Emerson."

When he took one last look at the couple, he saw that Cheryl was giving Ed Fitzgerald, Mist's owner, a big hug and a kiss on the cheek. Moore smiled. They were such a nice couple.

Moore retrieved his truck and returned to his aunt's home where he did additional online research on Karam, Carpos and Asha. He found several websites which mentioned their backgrounds and research, but nothing noteworthy. Moore was frustrated. Very frustrated.

He reached for the phone and called Sam Duncan. Moore was anxious to talk to Duncan about the mess into which he had gotten Moore involved. Moore left Duncan several messages, but there were no return calls. He guessed Duncan was out of the country on one of his covert assignments.

Moore next decided to call Wilbanks and check in with him.

"Hello?" a groggy voice answered.

"I wake you from your beauty nap?" Moore asked with a smile in his voice.

"I'm glad that you asked," Wilbanks said as he quickly became alert. "You all are the one who needs beauty sleep. How you doing, boy?"

"I'm fine. I'm more concerned about you."

"Well, you know how it is, Emerson. You just can't keep

a good ol' Southern boy down. I feel younger than a spring chicken."

"Glad to hear that."

"Have you talked to Sam?" Wilbanks asked.

"No. But when I do, I've got a lot of questions to ask him. I've called him a couple of times. No answer. He must be out of the country," Moore guessed.

"Yeah. I'd like to talk to that little cotton picker, too. I got a bone to pick with him about getting you and me into that mess. And we didn't get paid on top of everything!" Wilbanks grumbled. "You ever hear anything about our friends who tried to kill us?"

"Nothing. I've talked to the Coast Guard and they're trying to find the *Mongo*. They've alerted law enforcement throughout Florida's coastal regions to be watching for it."

"Could have headed down to Central America. Could have headed anywhere," Wilbanks mused.

Moore had an idea. "Willie, do you know Steve Nicholas in Washington?"

"No. Never met him."

Moore gave Wilbanks a quick rundown of Nicholas, who had been in a top level position at the National Intelligence Agency and also had worked at the NSA as well as Moore's past encounters with him.

"Sounds like an interesting guy."

"He is, and he has a wealth of contacts. I'm going to give him a call. If I can set up a meeting with him, would you like to fly up to D.C. and join us?"

"Delighted. Those spy spooks always intrigue me," Wilbanks answered.

The two chatted for another ten minutes before ending the call. Moore then called Nicholas and caught him up on his recent misadventures and set a meeting with the three of them in D.C. Next, he emailed Wilbanks so that he could make his travel plans for the meeting.

CHAPTER 21

Three days later
Nicholas' Office, Washington, D.C.

After parking his rental car in front of Nicholas' townhouse on East Capitol Street NE, Moore walked up to the front door and rang the doorbell as he looked up at the camera next to the entranceway. He had taken an early flight from Ohio to D.C. and first dropped his bag at his houseboat in nearby Alexandria before making the drive to Nicholas' place behind the nation's Capitol.

Hearing the door unlock, Moore entered and walked down the hall to Nicholas' study, where he found Wilbanks and Nicholas already chatting. Nicholas was seated behind a large desk, which was a precise replica of the famous 19th century Resolute desk first given in 1880 to President Rutherford B. Hayes and used by many successive U.S. presidents. Nicholas loved the desk, so he acquired an exact replica for his home.

He was splitting his attention between Wilbanks and the two 22-inch monitors in front of him as his fingers flew across the keyboard.

"Good afternoon, Emerson," the 68-year-old greeted the intrepid and oft-battered *Post* investigative reporter.

Nicholas looked as if he was in his early fifties. His full head of hair and bearded face, which was just starting to show a hint of wrinkles, complimented his muscular, trim physique.

"Hello Steve," Moore returned the greeting.

"Willie was answering a few of my questions. Things that I forgot to ask you about," Nichols remarked.

"You're looking much better," Moore said as he gazed at Wilbanks.

"I feel more like myself now," Wilbanks commented. "My wife tells me that I'm back to being ornery. That's a good sign."

"You two had quite the exciting experience," Nicholas said as Moore plopped into one of the deep cushioned armchairs next to Wilbanks and in front of Nicholas' prized desk.

"We survived," Moore said nonchalantly with a sense of bravado.

"Yes, we did," Wilbanks agreed.

Nicholas was not one to waste time on idle chit-chat and got right to the point. "Any news on your missing freighter or the three who hired you?"

"Not one peep. They're making glacial progress on this," Moore answered. "I also checked out Karam, Carpos and Asha. They seem legit as far as I can tell."

"And I checked them through my channels and nothing surfaced that was of any concern, although Karam seemed like a real piece of work."

"That he was," Wilbanks concurred. "And that cotton picker could talk up a storm, too. He had more wind than a sack full of farts!"

They all chuckled.

"We did learn that Karam was born in Turkey and we are running that down for more info," Nicholas added.

Moore nodded as he wished he had access to the closed intelligence channels that Nicholas did.

"How about that guy who was killed in your hospital room? They identify him yet?" Nicholas asked.

"I talked with the Key West police and they are running into a blank wall on him."

"Yeah, that's got me stumped, too," Wilbanks added.

"I wonder if he might have been from that freighter," Moore offered.

"That could make him difficult to identify," Nicholas added. "I'll get in touch with the Key West police and see if I can get some photos of him. Then I can run it through my channels."

Moore nodded.

"I thought about our earlier phone conversation, Emerson. I made a couple of calls and I have several individuals interested in funding your return to the U-boat site and dive even though the treasure may already have been recovered," Nicholas stated.

"That's great," Moore responded.

"Emerson, did you get a chance to talk with Kim Fisher?" Nicholas asked.

"Yes, and he's willing to take us out in one of his boats and dive with us on the U-boat."

"Good," Nicholas said as he looked at Wilbanks. "And you're going?"

"Hell, yes. I wouldn't miss this for anything," Wilbanks replied. "Besides, someone needs to go along and keep an eye on Emerson."

"What do you mean by that?" Moore asked his friend.

"Boy, sometimes I think that brain of yours rattles around like a BB in a boxcar. You do things a man with a brain would think twice about doing."

Moore laughed. "You've got to take chances in life."

"But not some of the stupid ones you take!" Wilbanks growled good-naturedly.

"I agree, Willie," Nicholas added. "I'm very interested, as are my friends, to see what you discover on board. We'll want a video of the interior."

"Shucks, that's no problem at all. I can shoot it," Wilbanks offered.

"When do you head out?"

Moore responded, "Fisher said we should be in Key West tomorrow."

"Good. You two flying out this evening?"

"No, I'm taking Willie over to my houseboat. He'll spend the night there and we'll fly out tomorrow morning. You want to join us for dinner at Indigo Landing?"

"No, you two go ahead and enjoy dinner. I've got dinner with a couple of senators on the Foreign Relations Committee tonight," Nicholas said blankly.

"Imagine that. Stood up because of some hoity-toity senators!" Wilbanks kidded.

The men talked for another ten minutes and then broke up the meeting.

Wilbanks and Moore left Nicholas' home and drove Moore's rental car to his houseboat on the Potomac River. As they turned off of the George Washington Parkway and headed down the peninsula's tree-lined Marina Drive, Wilbanks looked at the large boats riding gently at their dockage and commented, "I think I'm in the wrong business. This has got to cost you an arm and a leg."

"Don't let the surrounding scenery fool you. I actually live in a doublewide here," Moore teased.

"Doublewide, my ass," Wilbanks shot back. "So, which one of these yachts belongs to my rich reporter friend?" he asked as Moore pulled into a parking space near "A" dock.

"The *Serenity*," Moore answered as he pointed to his houseboat.

"Bless your pea-pickin' little heart! That thing has got to be at least 60 feet long," Wilbanks said as he stepped from the parked car with his duffel bag.

"You nailed it," Moore smiled as the two men walked down the dock and boarded the houseboat.

"Boy, I bet you could have some parties here," he said after following Moore through the entryway and inside. "Redskins fan?"

Smiling, Moore replied, "Cleveland Browns fan. Hey, no wonder you and Sam are such good friends. You both like to party like it's nearly your last day on earth."

"You better believe it!" Wilbanks said. "Tell me. Have you had some big parties here?"

"Not really," Moore replied. "I'm not a party animal. Although the previous owner told me he could get 50 people up on the flying bridge," Moore said as he walked up the steps to the bridge with Wilbanks on his heels.

"I believe it," Wilbanks said as they stepped onto the upper level and Wilbanks surveyed the deck. "You let Sam and I organize a party here some time. It would be a lot of fun."

"You two together are dangerous," Moore surmised.

"You have no idea!" Wilbanks said with a mischievous look on his face.

Smiling, Moore said, "Follow me and I'll give you a tour." They returned to the main level and Moore showed him the staterooms.

They filled the rest of the day with securing their plane tickets for the next day to Key West and enjoying the view from the bridge before walking to Indigo Landing on the riverbank for drinks and dinner.

CHAPTER 22

Next day
Historic Seaport, Key West

After landing at the Key West airport, Moore and Wilbanks caught a taxi, which took them across the island to the Historic Seaport where they would meet up with Kim Fisher and his son, Sean. They paid their taxi fare and walked out to the dock where they heard Kim yell, "Emerson, we're over here."

Moore waved and the two men walked over to meet the blond, lanky Fisher and Sean, his son with a chiseled chest and shaved head.

"Been awhile," Kim said as he eagerly greeted Moore.

"It has," Moore responded.

"Not too particular who you hang around with, are you, Emerson?" Kim asked as he shook hands with Wilbanks.

"I know what you mean. I just felt sorry for him and told

him he could tag along."

"Now you wait just one cotton-pickin' minute ..." Wilbanks started.

Kim interrupted. "No explanation needed," he said as he shook Wilbanks' hand. "Willie and I go way back, don't we old-timer?"

"Centuries! We're the ones who found Moses drifting in the bulrushes," Wilbanks grinned.

The men chuckled as they boarded the 90-foot salvage ship, appropriately named *Dare*, and prepared to get underway.

Several hours later, Sean was positioning the ship near the dive site. "You sure about those coordinates, Willie?" he asked.

"Oh yeah. Those coordinates are locked into my pea-brain mind," he laughed as he walked out of the pilothouse to join Moore at the stern.

"Ready to go for a dive?" Wilbanks asked as he approached Moore.

Moore was anxious to go below and search for the U-boat. He began donning his scuba gear as did Wilbanks.

"We've got the perfect day for diving," Moore observed as he assessed the calm sea and cloudless sky overhead.

"Any day is a perfect day for diving in my book," Wilbanks added. Looking at the two large mailboxes hanging above the stern, Wilbanks remarked, "We won't be using those babies today."

Moore turned his head to look at them and nodded, knowing that they wouldn't be dropping them overboard to wash away sand. "But I hope we may have to use that crane and winch."

"I doubt it. If there was anything valuable, it's already gone," Wilbanks guessed.

"Willie."

Wilbanks looked up and saw Kim approaching.

"You probably want this," Kim said as he handed Wilbanks a medium-sized box.

Wilbanks bent over and opened the box, then pulled out a bright yellow handheld object.

"Christmas come early this year?" Moore asked.

"Oh baby, you know it," Wilbanks said as he admired the device in his hand.

"What do you have there?" Moore asked.

"Oh, just a little something I had express shipped to Kim."

"What is it?" Moore asked again as he curiously watched Wilbanks attach it to his dive belt.

"It's an IdentiFinder U SeaSpec," Wilbanks grinned, looking at Moore.

"And what are you going to use it for? Identifying the U-boat?" Moore asked.

"No, I'm probably going to use it to make sure you don't end up frying your ass," Wilbanks poked at Moore.

"Seriously, what is it?"

"It's a digital gamma spectroscopy and dose rate system. It integrates a multi-channel analyzer, an amplifier, a high voltage power supply and memory together with an integral scintillation detector."

"That was quite a technical response for a cracker to give!" Moore grinned.

"Surprised you, didn't I? You didn't have a clue that I could talk that technical jargon crap, did you?"

"No, I didn't." Moore had a puzzled look on his face. "What's it really do?"

Wilbanks replied, "It's going to tell you whether you're going to live or not. It's a radiation detector, Emerson."

"Oh, come on. There's no need for that. The Germans didn't have nuclear-powered U-boats."

"You just listen to Uncle Willie now. I just have a hunch. That's why I had this shipped down."

"Okay, knock yourself out," Moore said in an exasperated tone.

Wilbanks handed Moore an underwater video camera. "You know how to work one of these?"

Examining the camera in his hands, Moore answered, "I've used this brand before."

"Good. I want you to film what we find below."

Within minutes, Wilbanks and Moore were underwater and making their way toward the U-boat's location.

As they approached the sunken craft, they swam past the stern. Wilbanks pointed toward the stern and Moore looked to see the damage caused by the explosion from the Avenger's torpedo. Moore filmed the stern and they moved toward the conning tower where they saw the Nazi swastika and U-boat number. It read *U-235*.

Moore gave Wilbanks the "okay" signal when he saw that the number confirmed that this was their target. He also saw that the forward deck had been cut open halfway between the bow and the conning tower. There was a gaping hole about eight feet in circumference.

The two men swam to the opening and switched on their flashlights, then dropped through the hole. As they did, they used their flashlights to examine the U-boat's interior.

Suddenly, Wilbanks focused on a metal rack bolted to the deck. He motioned for Moore, who continued to video the dive, to join him as he bent to pick up a piece of broken wood. There was an inscription in Japanese.

He handed the wood piece to Moore and reached for the meter affixed to his dive gear. Turning the meter on, he scanned the metal rack as he watched the readings. After returning the meter to his dive gear, he looked at Moore and motioned to him that it was time to ascend.

After taking their safety stops during their ascent, their heads broke the ocean's surface.

Both men dropped their masks below their heads. Moore was the first to speak.

"What was that all about?"

"My suspicions are confirmed."

"What do you mean?"

"I'll tell you when we get aboard. Do you still have that wood fragment?" Wilbanks asked as he turned and swam towards the nearby ship.

"Right here," Moore replied as he followed him.

After they boarded the stern and removed their gear with the assistance of Kim and Sean, Wilbanks munched on an orange slice from the plate of oranges that Sean had prepared.

"You're killing me," Moore began, anxious to hear what Wilbanks had learned from their inspection of the U-boat.

Wilbanks stalled, allowing the moment to dramatically build as he finished a second slice before beginning his explanation.

"Somebody was down there before and used a cutting torch to cut open that bow deck. From the looks of things, it wasn't too long ago."

"Must have been that ghost ship *Mongo* that we saw appear on our last night aboard the *Dark Side*," Moore suggested.

"Probably."

"So what was the deal with the metal rack and the radiation detector? Did you find any radiation?"

"Absolutely."

"That's interesting," Kim said with raised eyebrows.

"What was it from?" Moore asked.

"I can give you an educated guess," Wilbanks said as he picked up the wood fragment and examined the Japanese characters. "We'll need to get this translated."

"I've got a couple of friends in Key West who should be able to help," Sean offered.

"Good. You boys better make yourselves comfortable because I'm going to tell you a little-known fact about the German war effort."

"Go ahead," Moore urged, still anxious.

"It really came to light after the war when *U-234* surrendered in Portsmouth, New Hampshire."

"Why did it surrender?" Moore asked.

"The *U-234* was informed of Hitler's suicide on May 1, 1945. On May 4th the German Naval High Command ordered all U-boats to observe a ceasefire. That was followed a few days later with the order from the Third Reich to surrender. The *U-234*'s captain contacted U.S. naval authorities in Halifax, Nova Scotia, that they wanted to surrender and the *USS Sumter* was sent to escort them in to Portsmouth. But the U-boat captain had a problem."

"How's that?" Moore asked.

"He had two Japanese senior officers on board and they didn't have orders to surrender. Remember, Japan did not surrender until several months later, in August. When they learned that the German U-boat captain was surrendering his ship and crew, the two Japanese officers committed suicide and the captain buried their bodies at sea."

"Why were the Japanese on board?" Moore asked, perplexed.

"To keep an eye on a very special cargo," Wilbanks continued. "The *U-234* was built to be an underwater mine-laying U-boat just like the *U-235* below us was. Later she was made into an underwater freighter to carry much larger cargo than a regular U-boat. That's why this class of U-boat was selected for this project. Besides carrying air defense radar and jet engine equipment to Japan, the *U-234* had a special cargo."

"Okay, break the suspense. What was the special cargo?" Moore urged.

"The Golden Torpedo. She carried eighty gold-lined cylinders marked in Japanese lettering For the Japanese Army. The cylinders were filled with enriched uranium oxide for the Japanese nuclear development program. The U.S. government didn't know during World War II how advanced the Japanese were in developing a nuclear weapon. However, the discovery of this radioactive uranium oxide sped up our development of the atomic bomb and our decision to drop it on Japan."

"I didn't know that," Sean offered as he listened intently.

Wilbanks continued. "There was a rumor going around that the uranium oxide from the *U-234* was used on our atomic bombs. So, the uranium oxide actually made it to its destination, just not in the manner which the Japanese expected."

"Interesting twist," Kim observed.

"And how does this tie into the *U-235*, which I now realize is the designation for uranium-235?" Moore asked.

"Funny how coincidental that is," Wilbanks said. "I did get a radioactive reading down below. The racks we saw were the same style as the *U-234* had. So, I'm guessing that the *U-235* had a cargo of golden torpedoes that she was secretly transporting to Japan. I really didn't want to spend any time examining the remains of the crew, but I'd venture there were remains of a couple of Japanese officers on board."

"Why did they line the containers with gold instead of lead?" Moore asked.

"Uranium is a highly corrosive metal and can be easily contaminated if it comes into contact with other unstable elements. So, you need a stable element like gold. You see, gold has radioactive shielding properties like lead, but unlike lead, is a highly pure and stable metal. That's why they used the golden torpedoes and shipped them in large wooden crates with Japanese lettering and characters," Wilbanks said as he looked down at the wood fragment in his hand.

"And the *U-235*'s golden torpedoes are missing," Moore stated.

"Yep. I'd venture that our buddy Karam and his lot dived to the U-boat, cut her open, winched up the crates and took off with the golden torpedoes," Wilbanks suggested.

"To sell the uranium oxide?" Moore asked.

"Maybe. Depending on how much they had on board, they could make several dirty bombs."

"Isn't that complicated?" Sean asked.

"Not really, Sean. If you can build a conventional bomb, you could build a dirty bomb with relative ease. You just combine dynamite or TNT with the enriched uranium."

"Do they need a plane to deliver it?" Kim asked.

"Nope. Not these dirty bombs. You could use a van or a backpack depending on what you want to accomplish."

Moore shook his head. "Karam could be building a weapon of mass destruction," he suggested.

"More like a weapon of mass disruption," Wilbanks responded. "You're not going to kill a lot of people, but you can expose them to contamination from the radioactive dust from which they can die over time.

"The explosion would contaminate the buildings and land surrounding the blast area. The land could be unusable for long periods of time. It'll put people out of work and cause businesses to shut down. It could have a huge economic impact on the area as well as psychological impact on people—filling them with fear."

"Not a good thing," Moore offered.

"Not at all. We've got to find that freighter." Turning to Kim, Wilbanks spoke. "Take us in, Kim."

Hearing the request, Sean moved quickly to hoist the anchors as his father prepared to pilot the vessel home to Key West.

CHAPTER 23

A waterfront warehouse
Tampa Bay

Karam smiled. After years of planning, he was on the verge of completing his mission. Two weeks had passed since he and the crew from the *Mongo* cut open the *U-235* and winched the golden torpedoes aboard. They had then sailed to rendezvous with a large fishing trawler named *Floating Funds* in the Gulf of Mexico near Tampa Bay. There, they secretly transferred the golden torpedoes to the new vessel that Karam had recently purchased and was being crewed by Karam's men.

After paying the *Mongo*'s captain, she sailed south toward Brazil while Karam, Asha and Carpos headed to a waterfront warehouse on Tampa Bay. When they reached the warehouse, it was after midnight as Karam had planned. He didn't want anyone seeing them arrive or transferring the golden torpedoes inside.

The crew secured the trawler to the dock and prepared for the next step as Karam, Asha and Carpos stepped ashore to oversee the work. Using the trawler's winch, they quickly transferred the golden torpedoes to the dock where a forklift transported them inside the cavernous warehouse and near a room that was going to be their lab.

Two of the crew armed themselves with Kalashnikov AK-47 assault rifles and took up positions to guard the building while the remaining members went to the makeshift living quarters. Karam, Asha and Carpos walked into another room that would serve as their office. It opened to yet another room set up with cots.

The office was spartanly furnished, except for the surveillance equipment. It was state-of-the-art. Karam eyed the monitors that were linked to covert cameras attached to the outside of the building. There was no way that anyone could approach the building without being seen.

Karam nodded his head with satisfaction as he repositioned one of the cameras. He was pleased.

"Looks good," Carpos said as his dark eyes peered through their partially closed slits.

"I think this will work just fine," Karam agreed. "Asha, you need to get some sleep," he said.

"I will. I'm going to get some food," she said as she opened the office door and started to head to the makeshift kitchen area.

"Send one of the men down here. I want someone watching these monitors all the time," Karam instructed her.

"Will do."

Carpos headed to the back room with the cots. "Big day tomorrow."

"Yes, it is," Karam said. "I'll be in once we get someone on the monitors." When one of the men appeared, Karam gave him strict instructions about watching the monitors, then headed to grab a cot. The next week would be busy.

CHAPTER 24

Coast Guard Station
Key West

After returning the *Dare* to her berth in Key West the next morning, the four men drove to the U.S. Coast Guard station on Trumbo Road where they reported their findings and suspicions. The station commander immediately contacted the FBI and Homeland Security as the four men gave details to one of the officers.

During a break and before agents from the FBI and Homeland Security arrived for a meeting, Moore called his boss, John Sedler, and Steve Nicholas to update them. He tried to get in touch with Sam Duncan, but ended up leaving a voicemail.

The men spent most of the day in meetings with authorities as they explained what had transpired, and answered questions. Several conference calls were conducted with senior agents in

Washington. Finally, the men were excused for the day.

The Fishers dropped Moore and Wilbanks at the Crowne Plaza hotel on Duval Street at the intersection with Fleming. They dropped their bags in their room and met up in the lobby.

"Jack Flats?" Wilbanks asked.

"That's where all of this started," Moore smiled. "Sure. I love their grouper sandwiches."

"I could eat two of them," Wilbanks grinned. "Maybe we'll see my beautiful server again!"

The two walked across the street and a half block to the sports bar across from Jimmy Buffet's Margaritaville where they grabbed seats in the front, overlooking Duval Street. They placed their orders with another server much to Wilbanks' chagrin, and were enjoying their grouper sandwiches and drinks when Moore's phone rang.

"Hello," he answered.

"This is Ensign Kissel at the Coast Guard station."

"Yes?"

"We wanted to let you know that the *Mongo* has been located in the western Gulf of Mexico and has been boarded. We're currently conducting interviews of the crew."

"Do you need us to come over to the station?" Moore asked.

"Nothing you can do here. If we have anything to pass along, we'll get back to you."

"Thank you. We appreciate it," Moore said as the call ended.

"Found the *Mongo*, huh?" Wilbanks asked after he swallowed his beer.

"In the west end of the Gulf," Moore replied.

"I bet she's empty," Wilbanks guessed.

"Why?"

"Freighter like that moves too slow. They wouldn't take a chance in having the enriched uranium on board."

"You think she went into a port and unloaded?"

"Nah. Too risky. I'd guess she unloaded at sea and a smaller craft took the uranium into port."

"When we were aboard the *Dare*, you mentioned it was simple to build a dirty bomb and it could be easily delivered."

"I did," Wilbanks confirmed.

"And you said you don't necessarily need a plane, right?"

"Right. You don't need a dirty bomb to create disaster. You could just fly a plane into the side of a nuclear reactor and cause a massive release of radioactivity." Wilbanks took a sip from his beer before continuing. "As far as a nuclear bomb, you could deliver one in a suitcase."

"A suitcase!" Moore was stunned.

"Yep. A nice portable and unsuspecting way to cause destruction. You could take uranium and manufacture enough critical mass that would cause an explosion ranging from ten to twenty tons. If you used one in Washington, D.C., it would destroy everything within a half-mile radius of the explosion. The winds would carry the radiation to an even greater area, contaminating the whole region."

"That's different from the dirty bomb we were just talking about."

"Yes, and the nuclear bomb takes a whole lot more expertise to build," Wilbanks answered.

"I have to admit that I'm completely blown away by your knowledge."

"I get that pun. So, you just thought I was a Southern cracker, didn't you?" Wilbanks grinned. "It's worked for me so far. Keeps me under people's radar."

Reluctantly, Moore nodded his head. "How come you know so much about this stuff? I thought you were an underwater archaeologist," Moore probed.

"I am, but I dabble in other areas, too."

"Is that how you know Sam Duncan?"

Wilbanks carefully eyed Moore over the rim of his beer glass. "What are you getting at, boy?"

Moore smiled. "I was just trying to determine whether you and Sam worked together on some of those clandestine operations he works."

It was Wilbanks' turn to knowingly smile as he stood up from the table. "I guess it's time to get back to the room before I get your feathers ruffled."

"I'm not upset, Willie. It just dawned on me that you and Sam have worked together before on that covert stuff he's involved in."

"Ain't that the berries?" Wilbanks asked in a firm tone.

"I guess you're not going to answer my question," Moore pushed.

"Like I just said, I'm beat and looking forward to hitting my mattress."

Moore knew that Wilbanks wasn't going to give him an answer. The two men paid their bill and walked the short distance to the Crowne Plaza.

The next morning the two men met in the hotel lobby and checked out of the hotel.

"Had an interesting call from that Ensign Kissel this morning," Moore said as he spoke with Wilbanks while departing the hotel lobby.

"How's that, Emerson?"

"The boarding crew didn't find the missing golden torpedoes, but they did find traces of radiation on board the *Mongo*. Primarily in one of the cargo holds."

Wilbanks grinned. "That doesn't surprise me one iota!"

"No one on the ship's crew is talking."

"That doesn't surprise me either."

"They're bringing the ship into Station Sand Key in Clearwater. And, he said that they have contacted NSA to view satellite imagery to retrace the path of the *Mongo* to see which port she may have entered to unload her cargo."

"Good. We should catch a flight to Tampa and we can grab a rental to Station Sand Key."

"My exact thoughts," Moore said as he sat in a nearby chair and took out his iPad to find flights. In a matter of minutes, he looked up and spoke, "Got us booked on a flight to Tampa in two hours."

"Perfect." Looking at his watch, Wilbanks said, "We better head to the airport."

Moore grabbed his duffel bag and followed Wilbanks out to the curb in front of the hotel where they caught a cab.

CHAPTER 25

Coast Guard Sector
St. Petersburg, Florida

Six hours later, the two men were seated in a conference room with three Coast Guard officers, two members of Homeland Security and three members of the Tampa Police Department's anti-terrorism team. Over the next thirty minutes, Moore and Wilbanks briefed everyone on what had transpired.

"You two have been through a lot," the senior Homeland Security team leader said. His name was John Wisse. The medium-build, sandy-haired and bearded Wisse had significant experience in anti-terrorism; much of his training came from overseas assignments with a number of other government agencies.

"That is an understatement, sir," Wilbanks cracked.

"I'm sure it is." Wisse turned to one of his men who was

viewing information on a laptop. "We've got to find that missing uranium. Anything from NSA, Stan?"

"It's just coming in," Stan promptly answered as Wisse leaned forward to look at the screen.

"Track it backwards to trace its route," Moomaw suggested. Randy Moomaw, who had a medium build with close-cropped dark hair and a large confident smile, was the leader of the Tampa Police Department's anti-terrorism unit.

Stan's fingers flew across the keyboard as he typed in a number of commands. Within minutes, he sat back. "Looks like we have something."

"That's for sure," Wisse said as he studied the image. "Looks like a fishing trawler met up with them and they transferred cargo to it."

"The golden torpedoes," Moore suggested as Wilbanks nodded in agreement.

"Can you track the trawler and see where she heads?" Moomaw asked.

"Yes," he responded as he bent to the task.

"How long ago did that transfer take place?" Moore asked.

"The date on that image was a few days ago," Wisse replied before turning to Stan. "How's it going?"

"I'm losing her. It looks like there was thick cloud cover that day. Can't see through it."

"How far could you track her?"

"She was entering Tampa Bay when I lost her."

"Great!" Wisse said in disgust. "She could be anywhere."

"How about the guys at NSA? Can they pierce the clouds

with their technology?" Moore asked.

"I hope so. We sure will give them a shot at it. Not sure that there's much more for you two to do," Wisse answered.

"Can you keep us in the loop?" Moore asked as he and Wilbanks stood.

"Sure. Give me your phone numbers and I'll give you a call."

The men exchanged numbers and the two left the meeting. When they exited the building, Moore let out a deep sigh. "What a mess!"

"Sure is, boy. And that ain't the half of it."

"What do you mean, Willie?"

"If they're making a dirty bomb, they've got ample targets here. Tampa is the home of the Tampa Bay Rays, Buccaneers and Lightning. You could expose a lot of people easily."

"Yep."

"Let's get a hotel close by," Wilbanks suggested as the two approached the car.

An hour later, they had checked into adjoining rooms. Wilbanks was in the shower when the phone rang. It was Wisse.

"Did you break through the cloud cover?" Moore asked eagerly as he answered his cell phone.

"No, but we may have another type of break."

"How's that?"

"A Tampa police car pulled over a white commercial van on a routine traffic stop. It looked like it was running stolen plates. The four occupants didn't take kindly to the stop and opened fire. As they raced to a nearby office building, the van's driver was killed and he dropped a large backpack. We've got the bomb squad there now and we have a hostage situation in the building. Moomaw is on site."

"Can you give me the address?" Moore asked and hurriedly wrote it down. "Thanks, John."

"I told you I'd keep you updated. Not sure if this is related, but thought I could let you know."

"Thank you," Moore said as he ended the call. "Willie, we've got to go," Moore said as Wilbanks entered the room with a towel wrapped around his waist.

"Go where?"

Moore quickly explained. "Now get dressed."

"I'm moving. I'm moving," Wilbanks repeated as he walked briskly from the room and dressed. Within five minutes the two were in their rental car and driving to the office building on the north side of Tampa.

Packed into a sweltering back room barricaded with chairs and wooden tables, the three terrorists had taken refuge with five extremely scared female hostages.

The three wide-eyed terrorists were jumpy as they toted their Kalashnikovs in one hand. Nothing had gone to plan. Not only did they not make it to their targeted destination because of being pulled over by the police, but they had also lost the backpack. And on top of that, Omar, their leader, had been killed.

Shaheen was now in charge. He looked around the room. He had made a mistake in leading his remaining team members here. He thought it was an exit to the back of the one-story building, but it was a dead end. Shaheen was thankful that he had snatched the hostages as his team first entered the building.

Outside the building, SWAT team members positioned themselves strategically. A mobile command post had been set up with Moomaw in charge. A police negotiator was preparing to contact the hostage takers.

Moore and Wilbanks arrived on the scene and, after identifying themselves, were directed to the command post. When they entered, Moomaw greeted them.

"Didn't take you two long to get here."

"We flew," Moore said.

"You each can take a seat there while we work through this."

Moore and Wilbanks plopped into two seats where they could observe the negotiator who was reaching for the phone.

Inside the building, the phone rang unexpectedly, startling Shaheen. When one of the other terrorists began to walk over to answer it, Shaheen directed him. "Ignore it. Don't answer."

One of the older hostages boldly spoke. "I'd be happy to answer it," she said in as firm of a voice as she could muster.

Shaheen glared at her, thinking as he did. "What is your name?" he asked.

"Sandy Hammer. I'm the office manager."

"Go ahead Sandy Hammer the office manager. But be careful what you say," he said as he joined her at the desk. "I'm listening very closely," he said as he stuck the barrel end of the Kalashnikov firmly under her chin.

"Hello," Hammer answered, stammering slightly as her bravado quickly evaporated.

"This is Kent Weimer with the police department. I'd like to talk to whoever is in charge of the hostage holders."

Hammer turned to Shaheen. "He wants to talk to you."

With a look of hostility, Shaheen grabbed the phone from her. "Yes?"

"Hello. This is Kent Weimer with the police department," he started. "We wanted to see if …"

Shaheen cut him off. He didn't have time for this hostage negotiator's methodology. "Stop. You listen to me. I want all of your police to leave. I want my backpack and I want my van back. I plan to leave here in five minutes with my hostages." Shaheen wanted to see if he could get his mission back on track and fulfill it.

"But these things take …" Weimer started before he was abruptly cut off.

"Do it now. You have five minutes or I will kill the woman who answered the phone, Sandy Hammer the office manager," Shaheen barked before slamming down the phone. Shaheen's face had an evil grin when he looked at the panic-stricken Hammer at hearing the death threat. Shaheen motioned her to return to the other hostages.

Inside the mobile command post, Moomaw and Weimer huddled. They agreed that they were not going to submit to the kidnapper's demands as they were certain that the hostage takers intended to complete their deadly mission if they could get away. They also knew the mission was deadly since a preliminary analysis of the backpack had revealed that it contained a dirty bomb.

As the five minute deadline approached, Weimer called again.

When the phone rang, Shaheen stepped back from where he stood near a window. He had been watching the lack of activity by the police. Not answering the phone, he motioned for Hammer to join him.

With tears in her eyes, she stood motionless and defiant with the other hostages. She shook her head from side to side, showing her noncompliance.

"Okay Sandy Hammer the office manager, I will pick someone else," he said as he pointed to a visibly pregnant woman standing next to Hammer. That action provoked Hammer to act. She stepped forward and walked to him as the other hostages cried for her.

"Watch them," Shaheen said to his two companions as he pushed Hammer through the open door and into the front room. They walked to the front door of the building and Shaheen instructed Hammer. "You may leave. You are free."

Hammer's head turned quickly to look at Shaheen with disbelief.

"You go now before I change my mind, Sandy Hammer the office manager," he said with a crooked smile.

Hammer turned and opened the door. Casting one last look over her shoulder, she bolted through the doorway with fear. She had seen Shaheen leveling his weapon at her. Three shots rang out and she fell to the ground. Within seconds, she died.

"This is what happens when you don't listen to me," Shaheen yelled, before returning to the back room.

It was difficult for the snipers to hold back, but the on-scene commander wouldn't allow them to take a shot in fear of the other hostages being immediately killed.

When Shaheen entered the rear room, the phone was ringing. He grabbed it and without waiting to hear the negotiator speak, Shaheen snapped, "This is what happens when you don't do what I say. You have five minutes. Otherwise, I have a pregnant hostage who I will set free in the same manner." He slammed down the phone.

In the command post, SWAT commander Moomaw issued orders for immediate action. Several SWAT team members crawled to take position below the windows of the back room. Others squatted behind adjacent cover near the office entrance as one officer carefully made his way to the front door and worked to unlock it.

Shaheen moved close to a window in the back room, but not close enough to make himself a target for any sniper. His darting eyes keenly searched for movement or a target. Seeing none, he stepped away.

Suddenly, a number of SWAT team members dashed through the unlocked front door and through the front office to the entrance to the barricaded back room. They lined themselves against the wall with their gun barrels pointed forward as they poised to end the siege.

A moment later there were several flashes and small explosions in the back room as the SWAT team broke the windows to the back room and tossed in flash and smoke grenades. The hostage takers and hostages started screaming as a cloud of pale smoke filled the room and began to dissipate.

Seconds later there was another loud boom, this time from the direction of the door to the room leading to the barricaded hostage takers. Panic erupted inside the back room.

As the hostage takers swiveled and pointed their weapons at the debris-filled entrance, the SWAT team members below the broken windows stood and poked their weapons into the room. They quickly identified targets as the smoke cleared and fired several rounds into the three hostage takers. One round caught Shaheen in the eye socket before he could finish turning to shoot the pregnant hostage.

As the noise and smoke settled, one of the SWAT team members shouted after inspecting the hostage takers' bodies to confirm they were dead. "All clear." Four officers helped the remaining hostages to their feet and comforted them as they walked them into the front office for questioning.

Following at a short distance, Moore and Wilbanks trailed Moomaw into the building where he spoke briefly to each of the rescued hostages and then entered the rear room to survey the damages and the three dead terrorists.

"Did you find anything?" he asked one of his men.

"Nothing significant. We're still going through everything," the officer explained.

"Let me know."

"I will," the officer replied.

Moomaw, Moore and Wilbanks walked out of the entrance door and stood as medics and law enforcement officers scurried in and out of the building.

Moore asked Moomaw. "What did the bomb squad find?"

"Backpack bomb," Moomaw answered.

"Like a suitcase bomb?" Moore queried.

"Yes. This one has three 'coffee can-sized' aluminum canisters. Looks like they were on their way to set it off."

"Do you know where?"

"The van is being processed. Maybe we'll find some maps or a GPS with the directions set."

An approaching policeman called out to Moomaw. "The plates were reported stolen this morning."

"Have you run the VIN?" Moomaw asked.

"Yes. It's registered to EK Enterprise."

"Sounds like Eli Karam," Moore suggested. "Not too smart of him."

"Have an address?" Moomaw asked the officer.

"I wrote it down," the officer said as he handed the paper to Moomaw. Moore edged closer to peer at the address. "You might be interested to know that there are four more commercial vans with sequential VIN numbers registered to that address."

"Thanks. That's good to know," Moomaw said as he reached for his cell phone and called John Wisse. "John, I'm going to give you an address. It might be where the missing golden torpedoes are. I'd like you to use one of your radiation sniffing drones and fly it over this address to see what you can pick up."

Wisse took the address and hurried to have the drone launched.

"What's next?" Moore asked.

"We'll wrap this up and meet with Wisse's team. In all likelihood, we will be paying a visit to that warehouse within twenty-four hours."

"Mind if we tag along?" Wilbanks asked, beating Moore to the question.

"That's fine, provided you stay in the background."

"We can do that just fine. Right, Emerson?" Wilbanks asked.

"Sure."

Wilbanks stared at Moore. Something troubled him about Moore's staid response. It was the way Moore answered. Something about the solemn tone.

"I'll let you know when we plan to move on that address." Moomaw then leaned his head to his left. "It looks like I have a bevy of reporters lined up to get a story. I better head over there."

"Good luck," Moore grinned.

"And Emerson, I trust that you're not writing anything on this," Moomaw said as he stopped and looked directly at Moore.

"Nothing until we have this all wrapped up," he assured Moomaw, who smiled assuredly and walked over to the waiting reporters.

Moore and Wilbanks headed for their rental car.

"What are you up to?" Wilbanks probed.

"What do you mean?"

"Don't go and get coy on me, boy. I know you better. I don't know if you ever can stay in the background."

"But I just did. I sat with you in the command post while the hostage situation was underway."

"Like you had a choice! Did you get the address for that company that owns the vans? I saw you peeking over his shoulder."

Moore grinned.

"You answer me now. No Cheshire cat grinning at me!"

"I didn't see the address." Moore wasn't being truthful to his friend.

"And the sun isn't coming up in the morning. What do you think? You think I just fell off the turnip truck?"

"You saw right through me," Moore chuckled as they reached their rental car and entered it.

"Darn straight I did! Promise me that we're going straight back to the hotel."

"I promise," Moore said as he drove the car.

Within fifteen minutes, they parked at the hotel and grabbed lunch. For the rest of the day, they talked, spent time on their laptops and made several phone calls. After a late dinner and several rounds of drinks, they walked to their rooms where Wilbanks offered Moore a warning.

"Don't get any ideas about sneaking out tonight and checking out that building. I'm a light sleeper and I swear I will jump out of bed and run into the hall and strangle you."

"You have nothing to worry about," Moore responded to the threat.

"And just to underscore to you why you don't want that to happen, I want you to know that I sleep as naked as a jaybird. So, if you don't want my old naked body out here in the hall late at night and strangling you, you better not try anything," Wilbanks warned.

"Not only don't I want that, but I'm sure the other hotel guests wouldn't want that either," a smiling Moore replied.

Wilbanks walked into his room and shut the door. Two

seconds later, he opened the door and peered into the hallway to see Moore inserting his keycard into his room door. "I'm warning you. I'm watching you."

"I get it," Moore said as he entered his room, closing the door behind. He heard Wilbanks' door close and was surprised how well he could hear it close. He planned to rest and leave his room in the middle of the night to check out the building by himself despite the warning. Moore was like a kid being told not to touch the hot stove, then going ahead and touching it. Some things one has to learn the hard way.

Moore stretched out on the queen size bed to relax for a few hours. He awoke suddenly as if his internal clock signaled him. His mind felt jostled, almost alarmed. Moore glanced at his watch and saw that it was after midnight. Jumping from his bed, he took a quick shower and changed into a black tee shirt, black jeans and a black pair of Converse All-Star high-top sneakers.

Feeling refreshed and perhaps a bit nostalgic, Moore walked to the door of his room and carefully opened it. He felt like the secret agent man in the Johnny Rivers song of the same name. Thinking that, according to the song lyrics, "with every move he makes, and every chance he takes; odds are he won't live to see tomorrow," Moore realized he had no idea what danger may await him in his pursuit of the golden torpedoes.

He cautiously stuck his head into the hallway and carefully listened. He chuckled softly as he heard the sound of Wilbanks snoring. He closed the door and walked quietly to his car where he entered the warehouse address in the car's GPS. He was pleased that it was only twenty minutes away from his hotel.

Starting the car, he drove along the route to his destination. When he saw that he was within two blocks of the warehouse, he found a spot to park. The time was 1:15 a.m. and it was beginning to rain. Not hard. Just a passing shower.

CHAPTER 26

A waterfront warehouse
Tampa Bay, Florida

Leaving his car, Moore walked through the light rain, trying to stay in the shadows as best he could as he deftly made his way toward the warehouse. Nearing the rather nondescript building, he scanned it for any signs of surveillance cameras. He didn't see any, and breathed a quick sigh of relief. It would be short-lived, as the surveillance cameras were hidden.

He made his way to the waterfront side of the building and spotted the trawler, *Floating Funds*, at its dockage. He looked it over quickly, but turned to focus on finding an entrance to the warehouse.

He elected to bypass trying a door and walked over to one large window. When he tried to raise it, he found it was locked. Looking around, he pulled a small knife out of his pocket and opened it. He then began to jimmy the window and was able to pop it open. After returning the knife to his pocket, he slowly raised the window and slipped inside the open warehouse. He paused and listened intently for any sound within.

Hearing nothing to cause him alarm, Moore slowly eased the window shut behind him and wandered over to a number of boxes. He reached into his pocket and grabbed his cell phone. Using its light, he illuminated the writing on the side of the box. It read Freefly Systems Alta 8 Commercial Drone. He counted several more empty boxes, guessing that they each contained the same type of drone.

In the shadowy light and the noise from the rain on the roof, he spotted several other containers and wondered if they might be the golden torpedoes. He crouched as he padded across the warehouse floor to check them. Halfway across the open space, the overhead lights suddenly came on. Moore stopped dead in his tracks.

"I am very amazed to see you, Mr. Moore," Karam's voice boomed in the massive warehouse. It did not sound very happy. "Especially alive, I should add," Karam continued as he glared briefly at Carpos, who had told Karam that he had killed Moore after the *Dark Side* exploded.

Squinting his eyes in the bright light, Moore's head turned. He saw Karam, Asha and Carpos standing in front of him. Carpos had a Kalashnikov assault rifle pointed at Moore. Karam's fists were angrily clenched, his complexion had darkened with rage, his eyes were glaring and his lips were clamped in a thin line.

"I have an odd habit of popping up when people don't expect to see me again," Moore grinned in a show of bravado.

He thought that Karam looked like he was a top candidate for an instant coronary. Moore's gaze shifted briefly to Asha and he thought that she gave him a slight smile, but it quickly disappeared.

"Is that so? I can help with that. I specialize in helping people break habits. There's nothing that I'm going to enjoy more than breaking your habit—or should I say, you!" Karam emphasized *you*. "I'm stunned that you survived your adventure at sea."

Moore smiled at Karam's discontent. "My friend Willie Wilbanks survived, too."

"I'm sorry to hear that, but I'm sure that you won't survive tonight." Karam had a sinister look on his face. "As a matter of fact, I am confident you won't survive the night," Karam said sternly.

"We'll see," Moore popped off.

Karam ignored Moore's comment. "My, my. But you are out late tonight and you've interrupted my sleep. You interrupted the sleep of all of us, especially when we have a very big day planned," Karam said.

Moore looked around the warehouse and saw the open gold-lined containers. "Did you get your uranium?"

"You knew about that? You surprise me, Moore." Karam said, genuinely startled.

"I know more than you think and so does law enforcement." Seeing the four white vans parked inside the warehouse and a white Jeep Laredo, Moore commented, "Looks like you're ready to attempt some more deliveries. My guess is that you won't get far. They'll end up just like your attempted delivery today."

"I saw that on the TV news," Karam responded. "Were you involved with that little misadventure?"

"No, but I was there when they took out your guys. The same will happen here. We can make this easy for you and you could just surrender to me."

Karam laughed loudly. "I should surrender to you? You're unarmed, right?"

Before Moore could answer Karam, Asha and Carpos moved closer to Moore and Carpos frisked him, then signaled to Karam that Moore was unarmed.

"Looks like you're not armed. You're becoming a nuisance, Moore," Karam sneered as he nodded at Carpos.

Before Moore could comment, Carpos swung his weapon down and sharply against Moore's skull, knocking him unconscious. Moore instantly dropped to the ground.

"Asha, you and John take him to my lab and secure him."

"As you wish, Eli," she said before bending to help Carpos. The two dragged the unconscious Moore down the hall and lifted him onto a lab table. Then they bound him to the table.

Carpos left the room as Asha busied herself.

Hearing a groan from the table, she turned to face Moore. "Are you okay?"

Moore painfully turned his head to the right so he could see her. "I don't like that Carpos."

"None of us do," Asha softly said.

Her comment bewildered Moore. He wasn't sure which side she was on. "So, what's your part in all of this? You seem like a round peg in a square hole. You don't fit." Moore was perplexed by the woman to whom he had been deeply attracted.

"Thank you for the observation."

"But then again, I saw that you knifed Bingo," Moore added in a cautious tone. "I think."

"No. What you saw was me kneeling over Bingo and holding the knife I found in him. I didn't kill him. Carpos did. He's like Karam."

Moore was surprised to hear her refer to her father by his last name.

Asha continued. "They both kill accurately and without hesitation. You're the exception. You're still alive after they tried to kill you twice. You are very lucky."

"I guess so. But—that's quite an observation to make about your father," Moore said incredulously.

"He's not."

"What?"

"He's not my father. It's been our cover for years. It allows me to go with him a lot easier."

"I don't get it. What do you mean cover?"

"Come on, Emerson. You're a smart man," her brown eyes flashed as she spoke.

"So all of this background stuff was manufactured as a cover so you could get the golden torpedoes?"

"Well, it looks like you do have a brain!" she teased.

"That would be a very elaborate cover. I mean with all of the backgrounds you had to manufacture and substantiate."

"Not that hard when you have money," she said. "And an

important mission that certain parties want to see completed."

"Who are those parties?"

"You guess. You know where we are from."

"The Mideast."

"Bingo. Oops, maybe I shouldn't have used his name."

Moore probed further. "So who are you, Asha? Is Asha even your real name?"

"That's not important now. I'm on a mission."

"A mission?" Moore probed. He wanted to hear more.

Asha stared at Moore. It was as if she wanted to tell him more, then she shook her head. "Nice try. I'm not that easy," she said as she shook off a fleeting thought. She really did like Moore and wished their circumstances were different.

Moore thought back to the time together they spent at sea. "What about us? I thought we had something going?"

"What did you expect? Pretty girl. Handsome man. Sparks can fly," she said as she tried to put an emotional wall between them.

Moore was disappointed. "So you really are part of this dirty bomb terrorism?"

"I told you I was on a mission."

"And your mission was so important that you were willing to let Willie and me be blown to pieces on the *Dark Side*. You didn't lift one finger to help us!" Moore stormed quietly.

"I wanted to help, but I couldn't. The mission was too important," she responded firmly.

"Boy, did I misjudge you," Moore said, disgusted with his senses that were clearly very off this time.

Asha turned her back to him. She didn't want him to see the hurt look in her eyes. Allowing a few seconds to compose herself, she faced Moore. "Life can be like that at times, Emerson," she said as she patted the side of his face.

Now Moore was really confused by the intimacy of the face pat. He wanted to ask her more, but the sound of someone entering the room interrupted him.

"Is he firmly secured, Asha?" Karam asked as he walked to the table and inspected the bindings.

"Yes," she replied.

"Not quite," Karam said as he saw that Moore's head had not been secured. "I'll hold his head while you bind it to the table."

Asha reached for two straps on a shelf beneath the table and began to secure Moore's head while Moore fought against Karam's tight grip on it.

Within two minutes, Moore's head was secured tightly against the table. Try as he might, he couldn't move his head as the straps cut red marks into his face.

"What's this all about, Karam?" Moore demanded as his captor walked away.

"Tsk. Tsk. I don't like that demanding tone of yours. You are in no position to be demanding," Karam observed with a sly smile as he stood next to a lab workbench. "Tell me, Mr. Emerson Moore. Have you ever heard of *Naegleria fowleri?*"

"Some kind of chicken dinner?" Moore asked sarcastically.

"You would only wish that it was. No. Not quite. You see, *Naegleria fowleri* is an amoeba."

"Nope. Can't say that I have," Moore responded as he

wondered where the conversation was headed.

"Maybe this will help. It's a brain-eating amoeba."

Moore cringed. He had read about the dangerous amoeba. "What about it?"

Karam held up a vial. "The amoeba goes through three stages. This vial contains amoeba in the second stage, the tropozoite stage. It's the feeding and dividing stage. And the most dangerous stage for humans."

"Okay, I believe you," Moore said as he tried to move his head to look toward Karam, but couldn't.

"Normally, the amoeba enters a human through the nasal passage when a human is swimming underwater in an infected pond, lake or river. It travels through the nerve to the brain, its new food source. Over two weeks, the infected human begins to have symptoms like a headache, fever, vomiting, confusion and hallucinations. Then death."

"And why are you telling me this?" Moore asked with growing concern.

Picking up a syringe, Karam stuck the needle into the vial and filled it. He set the vial in a holder and turned to face Moore as he held the syringe in his hand. "Because I have found a way to shorten the two-week period to a matter of hours by injecting the amoeba directly into the brain."

"Good for you," Moore said unabashedly as fear began gripping him.

"I'd like to show you. It would please me much more than shooting you."

"No, that's okay. I believe you," Moore said as he struggled against his bindings to no avail.

"You're going to do more than believe me, Moore. You're going to see firsthand how it works," Karam said as he approached Moore with the syringe.

Karam talked as he walked, "There are a number of ways I can get this amoeba quickly into your brain. I could drill into the bone of your skull and inject it through the opening. I could inject it into your cerebrospinal fluid through one of your intervertebral spaces like a spinal tap. Or I could inject it into your blood stream, but I'm not sure that it would pass through the blood brain barrier."

Karam seemed exhilarated as he mentioned each method and saw the horrifying look in Moore's eyes.

"But I have an alternative method. I'll inject the amoeba directly into your brain by going through your eye socket."

Moore panicked and tried again to escape, but his bindings were tight and held him securely as Karam reached the table. A bit of vomit filled his throat, out of intense and uncontrollable fear, but Moore seemingly controlled the urge and was left with an incredible acid reflux burning sensation that nearly ceased his ability to breathe.

"Stop," Asha said firmly from where she was standing.

"What? What do you mean?" Karam asked, angered at being interrupted.

"Let me do it," she responded.

"Why?" Karam asked, astonished by her request.

Asha looked from Karam to Moore. She smiled. It wasn't a normal smile. It was deadly. "I want to be the one responsible for his death. I want to see him suffer. He said nothing when the ship's crew harassed me, and has been nothing but trouble for us."

Moore was shocked by her unexpected comment. In his years of working with people and assessing their character, he'd missed this one by miles. "Why?" he asked as he helplessly looked up at her.

"You're a journalistic pig. Nothing more than a parasite feeding off the lives of others. Now, I want to give you a parasite to feed off of you!"

"But, but," Moore stammered. "I don't understand. I've never done anything to you to deserve this type of reaction."

Karam was enjoying the exchange between the two.

"Had me figured wrong, didn't you?" Asha asked with a flippant attitude. She looked at Karam and held out her hand for the syringe. "May I?"

"Yes. Only inject half of it through the eye socket," Karam said as he handed the syringe to Asha.

"No!" Moore shrieked as he struggled again to free himself from his bindings, but without any success.

"Should be no problem," she said as she positioned the syringe above Moore's eye as directed.

Suddenly the door burst open and Carpos entered the room. "Eli, come quick."

"What is it?" Karam asked, agitated at being interrupted.

"The surveillance cameras. We've got company."

A blood-curdling scream from Moore caused Karam to turn around and glance at Asha who was staring down at Moore. She had an evil smile and was holding the syringe. It now was half-full.

"Did you inject him?" Karam asked, frustrated at not witnessing the event.

"Yes. I didn't want to waste any time."

"Eli. Come with me," Carpos insisted.

Karam looked at Moore who was still struggling at his bindings. "I'll be back to watch you suffer and die," he said with deadly glee. Looking at Asha, he said, "I'll be back shortly. This won't take long."

Asha nodded as Karam rushed out of the room to follow Carpos.

After Karam left, Moore stopped struggling and looked up at Asha. "I don't understand. Why did you fake it?"

"You will see," she said as she quickly released him from his restraints and helped him to his feet. "Careful and don't step in that amoeba I squirted on the floor beneath the table."

"You don't have to warn me twice about that. Thanks for whispering that I should scream bloody hell! How did I do?"

"Very believable," She said as she started for the door. "Follow me."

"Wait." Moore grabbed her by the arm. "I want to know what's going on. Who are you?"

"I shouldn't say anything, but I'll give you a name."

"A name?"

"Sam Duncan."

"You know Sam?" Moore was flabbergasted at the revelation.

"We've worked together, but I've been deep cover on this assignment with Karam for a number of years."

"Karam works with Sam?"

"No. Karam is the real deal in bad guys, especially after he was radicalized." Asha looked around. "We've got to get out of here."

"You're not going anywhere," a familiar voice boomed from the doorway.

When they looked at the doorway, they saw Carpos. He was holding a pistol and it was pointed at Moore. "What's going on here?"

"That seems to be a popular question," Moore quipped as he tried to distract Carpos.

Asha had slowly edged to the corner of the room. When Carpos turned to face her, Moore suddenly rushed him, knocking his pistol to the floor. The two men followed the gun to the floor as they wrestled. Charging toward them, Asha grabbed the weapon and lifted it over her head before bringing it down hard on Carpos' head, knocking him unconscious.

"Help me," she directed Moore as she dragged Carpos to the table. "We need to put him on the table and restrain him."

Moore looked worriedly toward the door. "Do we have time?"

"We'll make time. This one is a killer. You have no idea what I've witnessed him do to people. The man is evil personified," she said as Moore helped her lift Carpos on the table and restrain him. "Get his pistol," she said.

Moore picked up the handgun and turned back to Asha. What he saw shocked him. Asha had plunged the syringe's needle into Carpos' eye socket. Leaving the syringe embedded in his head, she turned to see Moore staring in bewilderment.

"He deserves a horrific death." Looking at the gun, she reached for it.

"I know how to use this," Moore said, reluctant to let go of the weapon.

She eyed Moore cautiously, then shrugged her shoulders. "Okay, Mr. Hero. Let's go." She led the way to the door and opened it. Seeing no one in the hall, she led Moore down the hall.

They didn't get very far before they heard the sound of approaching voices. Karam's voice was barking orders. Before they rounded the corner, Asha opened the door to a room and shoved Moore into it.

"Hey! What are you doing?" Moore asked startled by her action.

"Saving your butt again! Just wait," she ordered.

Reluctantly Moore did as instructed and stood next to the door with his weapon ready while she closed the door. And just in time as Karam and two armed men rounded the corner.

"Where are you going?" Karam demanded.

"I was coming to help. What's happening?"

"The police are breaking in. Looks like a tactical unit."

"And there's a police boat at the dock," one of the armed men added.

Before they could continue, they were distracted by a large door being breached at the end of the hallway. Police began pouring into the building.

One of the armed men let loose a burst from his Kalashnikov as the others ran around the corner. The police returned fire, killing the man.

Seeing the man drop to the floor, Karam shouted at the remaining gunman, "Hold them off as long as you can!"

The man nodded and eased up to the corner where he began firing upon the oncoming police officers.

"Where's Moore?"

"Still on the table. He's dying," Asha lied.

"I will miss watching his agony, but we have to go. Follow me."

As gunshots filled the air, Karam led Asha through the large warehouse where the remaining golden torpedoes were stored and into an adjoining building that was connected to the warehouse.

"Did you see Carpos?" Karam asked as they hurried.

"No," Asha lied again. "Maybe he ran to the dock."

"That idiot!" Karam said.

Once they cleared the second building, they entered another adjoining building and Karam smiled. He saw four white vans parked there. Each contained a dirty bomb mounted on a drone. His four drivers were waiting for his instructions.

"We are moving up our plans. Today is the day." Karam looked at Asha and instructed her. "Open the garage doors, then join me in my vehicle." Looking at the drivers, he said, "We will commence our operation in one hour. Drive to your assigned positions."

The drivers raced to their vans and drove through the open garage door into the early morning rain. Karam jumped into a Jeep Laredo and drove it to the garage door where Asha entered it. He then quickly drove away from the police-filled warehouse two buildings behind him.

Inside the warehouse, the police advanced down the hallway using suppressing fire on the gunman who unwisely poked his head around the corner at the wrong time and caught a bullet in the head. He dropped to the floor. As the police advanced down the hall, they cleared each room.

When they entered one of the larger rooms, they found Carpos on the table. He had regained consciousness and was twisting, trying to break his bindings. He could feel the needle embedded in his eye socket and screamed in agony. He was frantic about his upcoming painful death.

"Got one in here, Randy," an officer called to Moomaw, who stepped into the room.

Moomaw eyed Carpos with a look of skepticism. Was he a good guy or bad, he wondered.

"This one surrendered to us. Found him in a room down the hall. Says he's working with us. You know him, Randy?"

Moomaw swung around and saw Moore standing in front of him. He smiled. "What are you doing here?"

"That's what I want to know, too," a voice bellowed from the doorway. "For crying out loud Emerson, you just get yourself in a bunch of crap any time I turn my back."

"Hello Willie," Moore greeted Wilbanks.

"You disappeared on me last night and I didn't know where in tarnation you were going although I kind of wondered if you might be headed here."

"I couldn't wait. I thought it would be too dangerous to allow any more time to expire."

"Dumb ass!"

Moore grinned, then looked at Carpos on the table. "I don't think there's much you can do for him, Randy. Asha injected him with a brain-eating amoeba meant for me."

"Lucky you," Moomaw quipped.

"Yeah and unlucky him. Might have an hour or so to live," Moore suggested.

Moomaw turned to one of his men. "Call in the medics and have them take him to the hospital and see if they can do anything for him."

"I think it's too late," Moore commented.

"Who is he?"

"Karam's top henchman, John Carpos. Nasty guy."

Moomaw pointed to one of the officers. "Stay with him." He then led everyone out into the hall. As they walked, another officer called, "Building secured."

"Do you have Karam or the woman?" Moomaw asked as they rounded the corner and entered the cavernous warehouse.

"No. They've disappeared, but we are still looking for them."

"There's your source of radiation," Moore said as he pointed to the golden torpedoes where two law enforcement technicians in radiation suits were already at work scanning the golden torpedoes to confirm the radiation source.

The group walked over to them and saw that only one remained unopened. The others were empty.

"Karam must have taken the U-235 from the open ones." Moore pointed to the empty boxes. "The drones were in those boxes. They're gone, too."

Moomaw walked over to the boxes and examined them. "I'm familiar with this type of drone. It's the Freefly Systems Alta 8. It's a high-end market drone, which allows you to fold the arms and propellers and carry it in a backpack. It can carry up to forty pounds."

"So something like that backpack dirty bomb wouldn't be any problem for it to carry, right?" Moore asked.

"Piece of cake. A dirty bomb payload wouldn't weigh forty pounds," Moomaw replied.

Moore looked at the markings on the box. "This came from Amazon?"

"Yes. Surprising that you can order heavy lift commercial drones that easily," Moomaw said.

"One more thing, Randy."

"What's that, Emerson?"

"The four white vans that were parked here last night are gone."

"Vans like the one we stopped the other day?"

"Exactly the same. Plain, white commercial vans. No markings. Can blend in anywhere."

Moomaw turned to the police officer next to him. "Call that in, would you? I want everyone looking for those vans. They could have left here early this morning before we got here."

"Got it." The officer stepped aside to call it in to the mobile command post which was now parked outside of the building.

"One other thing, Randy," Moore started.

"What?"

"That woman."

"Asha?"

"Yes. She saved my life. Karam was going to inject that brain-eating amoeba into me and she butted in, saying that she wanted to do it. Scared me to death. But when Karam was distracted, she squirted half the syringe's contents on the floor and then told Karam that she had injected me. After Karam left the room, she freed me and helped save me when Carpos came in. She's the one who injected the syringe into Carpos."

"She's on our side?"

"Looks that way to me. She shocked me when she mentioned my friend, Sam Duncan. He does a lot of black ops work. And he's the one responsible for getting me involved in this mess."

"That makes two of us," Wilbanks chimed in as he recalled Duncan's invitation to join Karam's crew to look for the lost U-boat.

"Come with me to the command center," Moomaw said as he began walking out of the building, noticing that the rain had stopped and the sun was shining. "Let's see what we have here."

When they entered the mobile command center, an officer approached Moomaw. "We've got choppers looking for the white vans. Sure are a lot of them on the road."

"Have them look for any that might be driving together like a mini-convoy, although I'm sure that they would be smart enough to separate."

"On it already," the officer said. Then, he added, "We've got radiation sensing drones up, too."

"Good." Moomaw walked to a table where a large map of Tampa had been spread. Several men were studying it.

"Have you identified any potential targets?"

"Not yet. I mean that we've got the usual soft targets like

schools and hospitals," one of the officers answered.

"Are the Rays playing today?" Moore asked.

"Nope," the officer replied.

"How about any special events? Concerts? Festivals?" Moomaw asked.

"Nothing but some small street fairs in the suburbs," the man answered.

An officer who had been speaking on his headphones turned in his chair. "We've located an eyewitness about a block from here. He saw four vans leave a building half a block from here about an hour ago while the firefight was taking place."

"Good. They don't have a big start on us," Moomaw said.

"We've got our guys going over to check out the building."

"Good," Moomaw responded.

"One more thing, Randy. The guy said he also saw a white Jeep leave that same building and follow them. The Jeep had a man and a woman with dark hair in it."

"I bet that's Karam and Asha," Moore interjected.

"Probably," he said. "Put out an alert for the white Jeep with a male and dark-haired female passenger."

"Got it," The officer said as he turned back to the console to do as he was instructed.

Moomaw scratched his head as he thought. "We've got to determine where they could do the maximum damage. What would be a target of preference?"

Moore reached over one of the seated officers. "Is this Tampa's airport?"

"No, but you might have just picked the juiciest target for them," Moomaw said.

"What do you mean?" Moore asked confused.

"That's MacDill Air Force Base. It's the home of CENTCOM."

"CENTCOM?" Moore asked.

"U.S. Central Command. It's the combatant command for the Middle East, North Africa and Central Asia. They've deployed troops and directed military operations like Desert Storm in the Persian Gulf War and are involved in operations in Afghanistan and Iraq now."

"They'd be a perfect target," Moore said.

Moomaw barked orders to his team. "Alert CENTCOM to lock down and watch for the four vans. Tell them to keep their eyes open for any drones approaching the base. They could have dirty bombs aboard. And get me a chopper. Be quick about it! We may not have much time. It's only four miles southwest of downtown Tampa."

"Got a chopper here by the dock, Randy."

"Tell the pilot we're on our way and we're going to MacDill. Let's go."

As Moomaw rushed out of the mobile command center with Moore and Wilbanks, he explained, "Exploding four dirty bombs over MacDill would cost lives and contaminate the grounds and equipment for years."

The three men walked briskly to the waiting chopper and boarded it. As soon as they strapped into their seats and put their headphones on, the chopper took off for MacDill, located on a peninsula jutting into Tampa Bay.

In less than a minute, a voice filled their headphones, telling them that one of the white vans had been pulled over off of

South Dale Mabry Highway near MacDill. Gunfire had been exchanged and the van's occupant had been killed. Officers on the scene found a drone in the van and were waiting for the radiation inspection team to arrive.

"One down. Three to go," Moomaw spoke seriously.

"Why do you think they were using four vans? Backup?" Moore tried to answer his own question.

Wilbanks took a shot at answering. "I'd guess they were going to ring around the base as best as they could so they could saturate it."

"I think you're right, Willie," Moomaw commented.

Before Moomaw could continue, another message filled their headphones. A second van had been pulled over and followed with a gunfight. One officer had been wounded, but the occupant had been slain. The van contained another drone.

"That's two," Moomaw acknowledged.

"And we still have Karam and Asha," Moore reminded him.

"Right," Moomaw agreed as the chopper circled the air base.

"There. On the right!" Wilbanks spoke into his mouthpiece.

The men saw a white van pulled behind a building about a block from MacDill. A man had unloaded a drone and was unfolding the wings.

"Circle them," Moomaw instructed the pilot as he barked orders to the mobile command post to send officers to the site. In a matter of moments, two patrol cars arrived and the men in the chopper watched the exchange of gunfire below. One officer was struck and fell. A hail of bullets struck the terrorist, killing him. Several of the officers rushed to secure the drone.

"One to go," Wilbanks said as the chopper continued to make its way around the air base's perimeter.

"Too late," Moore called as he pointed to a low-flying drone approaching MacDill.

"I wouldn't be too sure," Moomaw said with a tone of hope.

Suddenly a bright beam of light shot up from the ground at the air base, destroying the drone in a ball of fire.

"What was that?" Moore said, stunned by what he had witnessed.

"Not sure that you have the clearance for me to tell you," Moomaw responded. "We'll see if they want to tell you." Turning to the pilot, he asked, "Can you see if they'll clear us to land?"

"Will do." The pilot then radioed MacDill and identified themselves, then received clearance. Once they landed, the three men exited the chopper and were greeted by the base commander. He and Moomaw had been friends for years.

Moomaw introduced a trim and fit General Nick Cleveland to Moore and Wilbanks, then gave Cleveland a brief background on the two men and what had transpired.

"Randy, we appreciate what you and your team have accomplished for us in keeping the base secure and safe," Gen. Cleveland said appreciatively.

"It's a partnership," Moomaw smiled.

"Were you anxious?" Moore asked.

Gen. Cleveland chuckled. "I'm never anxious. We have the systems and processes in place to protect the base."

"I'll say. What was that explosion? How did you shoot down that drone?" Moore asked.

Cleveland looked at Moomaw who nodded his head that it would be okay to explain if he wanted. "This is not for publication or to be repeated. Understand?" he asked as he looked from Moore to Wilbanks.

The two men affirmed their understanding.

"There are a couple of things that I'll share with you. We actually have the technology to jam or take control of drones that enter our airspace. What you witnessed is something more lethal. Based on the possibility of a dirty bomb aboard the drones, it was more expedient for us to ensure that we protected the base as effectively as possible. We used a particle beam weapon."

"A what?" Wilbanks asked.

"It's a high energy beam of atomic particles that disrupt and destroy the molecular structure of the target. It vaporizes the target. So there's no radioactive residue left to contaminate the area."

"I didn't know such a weapon existed," Moore said with a stunned look.

"It's been rumored to exist for years. Some of it has leaked out, but no one has been able to confirm its existence. I expect you both will maintain the confidential nature of this information. National security."

Again, Moore and Wilbanks agreed.

"We still have one more to find," Moore suggested.

Cleveland's eyes widened. "I thought we had dealt with the four drones."

"We have. Emerson is referring to the leader, Karam. He's still on the loose. He's got a woman with him and then we still have to find the man and the van from which that last drone was launched," Moomaw explained.

"I see," Cleveland said. "It does sound like the base is out of the woods for now."

"It does and we should be heading out," Moomaw said.

The men bid Gen. Cleveland farewell and reboarded the chopper that returned them to the mobile command post. On the way, they learned that the fourth van had been found abandoned.

Meanwhile, a white Jeep Laredo was racing north. It contained Karam, Asha and Zaman, the driver from the fourth van. He had launched the drone that was vaporized over MacDill before it could detonate. Karam was livid. Everything that he had planned and worked so hard to accomplish over the last several years had been ruined. His anger boiled over as he took it out on his two passengers.

Asha interrupted his rage as they neared the ramp leading to I-275. "You're not taking 275 are you? They'll be watching all of the major highways."

"No, we'll take a roundabout way to Pensacola," he said as he headed for FL-589 which he'd follow to Route 19N. He had one more backpack dirty bomb. It was in the rear of the Jeep.

"The naval base in Pensacola?" Asha asked in a low voice.

"Maybe. I'm not sure. It could be protected like MacDill was and we're not going to waste the only one we have left."

The three occupants rode in silence as Karam thought about potential soft targets. A couple of times, he had Asha

Google cities along I-10. He had several ideas, thought about them and discarded them.

But one potential target seemed to be sticking with him. He looked at his watch. He had plenty of time to drive and think.

Karam looked in the rearview mirror and asked Zaman, "Is my satellite phone back there?"

The passenger looked down and replied, "Yes. Do you want me to hand it to you?"

"Not yet. I may want to make a call in the next hour. I'll let you know."

CHAPTER 27

SWAT Headquarters
Tampa, Florida

Sitting up on the cot that had been provided for him in the ready room, Moore looked at his watch. It was almost 2:00 P.M. He'd been asleep for five hours and was restless. Stretching, he stood and walked into the adjacent kitchen where he found a pot of brewed coffee and poured a cup. He savored the taste and saw a package of Ritz crackers, which he quickly opened and wolfed down. Having satisfied his hunger pain, he walked into the operations center.

"Good afternoon, Sleeping Beauty," Wilbanks said when he saw Moore enter.

"I was bushed."

"You had reason to be," Wilbanks said. "Every time I turn around, you seem to be causing some sort of ruckus."

"Great material for my reporting," Moore tried to stifle a yawn, but couldn't help himself. "Anything new on Karam or Asha?"

"Not a doggone thing," Wilbanks answered. "They put up a checkpoint on I-75. Caused a massive traffic backup, but no Karam. They also have a number of drones up over highways to see if they can pick up any radiation from any vehicles in case that Jeep has uranium in it. Nothing yet."

"The problem is that no one knows where they're headed. They could go anywhere or go to ground and hide out for a few days."

"And if they have another terrorist cell around, they could link up with them—and who knows what kind of horrors they could dream up," Wilbanks pondered as Moomaw walked over to greet Moore. "If Asha is on our side, I wish she would let us know—or stop it herself."

"Yeah. We can't count on that though. Feeling rested?" Moomaw asked.

"Somewhat."

"You looked beat," Moomaw added.

"No news on Karam or the Jeep?"

"Not a thing, although we've alerted every law enforcement agency in Florida and surrounding states and it's being pushed out through the news media. We've got choppers up, too."

"And no luck?"

"You'd be surprised how many white Jeep Laredos are being pulled over today."

"That's kind of funny in a way," Wilbanks interjected.

"The public is getting involved. Calling in tips and we're

wading through them," Moomaw added. "Homeland Security and the FBI are coordinating everything. Chances are Karam is moving out of our jurisdiction."

"I hope your guys can find them," Moore commented.

"NSA is involved. Using satellite imagery to try to track them from MacDill. On a time-elapsed basis they might be able to help." Moomaw looked around the operations center, then spoke again. "You two are welcome to stay here and observe."

"How about some chow, Emerson?" Wilbanks asked. "I haven't eaten since dinner last night. I'm so hungry I could eat the north end of a south-bound polecat."

"Yeah. I am, too."

"Guys, there's a little place about a half a block from here. A little café," Moomaw suggested. "Be sure to keep those visitor badges so you can get back in here."

"Will do," Moore said as he and Wilbanks walked out of the SWAT operations center and headed to the café.

Two hours later, they returned to the operations center and tracked down Moomaw.

"Any developments?" Moore asked.

"One of particular interest," Moomaw answered. "There was a call from the Clearwater Mall. They found a white Jeep Laredo parked inside one of the covered parking decks. A patrol unit was dispatched and they checked the vehicle. Their portable detection device showed traces of radiation."

"You think the mall is a target?" Moore asked.

"It could be. We're evacuating the mall as a precaution. Homeland Security and the FBI are on site and manning every door with local police and state police so they can eyeball everyone leaving. Then, they'll go through the entire mall to look for anything suspicious. They also have a team going over the Jeep and a team checking the surveillance camera videos."

"I already know what you're going to say, Emerson," Wilbanks spoke.

"What?" Moore asked his friend.

"We're heading over there," Wilbanks grinned.

"You've been hanging with me so much you know my thoughts."

"Sort of like a long-time married couple," Wilbanks chortled.

"Perish the thought!" Moore countered. "Ready to go?"

"Yep."

"Thanks, Randy."

"Stay out of trouble," Moomaw cautioned.

"Impossible." Moore smiled as the two men left the room to go to Clearwater Mall.

CHAPTER 28

A Rampart Street warehouse
New Orleans, Louisiana

The long brick building used to be a cotton warehouse. It offered 14,000 square feet of storage with a fenced parking lot. Karam was relaxing in one of the offices and thinking how well his escape plan had worked. He was watching the TV news reports and the fear and misdirection he had caused at the Clearwater Mall. He had a large smile on his face as he sat with Saab, the leader of the New Orleans terrorist cell he had contacted.

After abandoning the Jeep at the Clearwater Mall, the three had entered the mall, with Karam carrying the backpack bomb. They walked into a store specializing in hats where they bought caps for Karam and Zaman and a floppy hat for Asha. They wore the hats out of the store and into the mall.

Karam produced a set of keys for a blue Chevy commercial van and handed them to Zaman while telling him where the van was parked. When Zaman went to retrieve it, Karam and Asha walked through one of the mall's anchor stores to a street level exit door. They waited there until Zaman drove up in the van and then entered it. In a matter of minutes, they were on the road for the 10-hour drive to New Orleans. Along the way, Karam used the SAT phone to call his contact in New Orleans. They spoke briefly and cryptically, but his contact knew to expect them.

Karam's reflection was disrupted when Asha entered the room. "Everything okay?" he asked.

"Yes. I just walked around the warehouse to make sure the guards were alert."

"You don't need to worry about my men," Saab said with an irritated tone. He was miffed that a woman would be so bold as to check his four men.

Asha ignored his comment. "Where's Zaman?"

"He's catching up on his sleep," Karam answered with a nod to the room next door. "You should do the same."

"I think I will," she said as she walked into the next room and closed the door behind her. Rather than taking one of the cots, she stood next to the door and listened. She hoped to hear what Karam had planned for the remaining dirty bomb. She didn't have to wait long.

"Do you want to tell me what your target is?" Saab asked.

"Not so much what, as who," Karam responded. He leaned in. "I was thinking about exploding it on Bourbon Street to destroy the hedonistic partying there."

"That would be good," Saab nodded his head.

"That was what I planned until I saw the local news."

"Oh?"

"I see there's an international trade conference here."

"That's true. It's attracting leaders from all over the world," Saab commented with growing interest.

"And the President of the United States will be attending in two days."

"Yes, that is correct."

"He will be speaking at a luncheon on the *Natchez* sternwheeler."

"That's what I heard."

A thin smile appeared on Karam's face. "Exploding a dirty bomb above the *Natchez* as she is traveling down the Mississippi River would shower the boat and its occupants with radioactivity."

"It would," Saab agreed.

"We would cause the death of many of the world's leaders in one deadly attack," Karam stated proudly.

"We would."

"There's just one problem."

"What's that?"

"I don't have a drone."

"I can get you one."

"Are you sure? I would need it by the end of the day tomorrow at the latest."

"I'm positive," Saab assured Karam.

"It must have the cargo-carrying capacity of my dirty bomb's weight."

Saab looked to the table where three small canisters had been placed. "I will make sure of it."

"Good." Karam and Saab stood and walked over to the table where they huddled, discussing the details of the plan.

On the other side of the door, Asha stepped back. She needed to find a phone. She scurried from office to office in the back of the warehouse as she searched for a phone to use.

When she couldn't find one, she decided to take a big chance. She walked to one of the rear doors of the warehouse and started to open it.

"Where do you think you're going?" a voice asked from the shadows. Out stepped one of the terrorists who had been keeping watch on the rear approach to the warehouse through one of the large windows.

Startled, Asha turned to face the man who stepped forward. "I was just going to run to that corner market. I was hungry and thought I'd pick up some food for us all."

"Okay. Be careful," he said before he melted back into the shadows.

Relieved, Asha unlocked the door and exited the building. She walked the block to the market and was pleased that a telephone booth was around the corner and next to the market. She looked back to make sure that she hadn't been followed, then ducked around the corner to enter the telephone booth. Calling the operator, she placed a request to reverse the long distance charges to the number she wanted to call.

The operator made the connection and left the call.

"Sam?"

"Yes?"

"It's Asha."

"Asha, are you okay?" Duncan asked.

"Yes, but I only have a few seconds. I don't want to be gone too long or I'll arouse suspicions."

"Do they suspect you at all?"

"No."

"Good. Where are you? Still in Florida?"

"No, New Orleans."

"You guys have covered some ground. What do you have for me?" Duncan asked.

"Karam is planning to explode a dirty bomb over the *Natchez* when the president is on board two days from now. They'll be using a drone."

"Like at MacDill?"

"Yes. There's some sort of conference going on and the *Natchez* will have a number of world leaders on board."

"Where's Karam and the dirty bomb?"

She gave him the address. "And there's six of them, plus Karam. All are armed."

"Okay. We'll move quickly. We'll target tomorrow night after midnight."

"Good. I'll do what I can. I better go."

"Be safe."

"Sam?"

"Yes?"

"Did Emerson make it out of the warehouse?"

Duncan sensed a tone of concern in her voice. "Yes. He's fine."

"Good," she said relieved. "Got to go." She hung up and stepped out of the booth. She had been worried about Moore's well-being. She liked him.

Focusing on the matter at hand, she repressed the urge to look around the corner to see if anyone from the warehouse was walking toward the market. Quickly entering the market, she scooped up various groceries and walked over to the counter to pay the dark-skinned clerk.

"As-salaam'alaykum," a voice spoke suddenly behind Asha, who spun to see Karam standing behind her. She hadn't heard him walk into the market.

"Wa 'alaykum salaam," the clerk returned the greeting of "peace upon you" as he finished bagging Asha's purchase and gave her change.

Nodding toward Asha, Karam asked, "Has my friend been here long?"

Before responding the clerk looked at Asha whose eyes seemed to be pleading. The clerk turned back to Karam and answered, "Yes. You know women. Sometimes it takes them a while to decide what they want to buy," he said as he covered for her. He didn't like Karam. There was something about him that conveyed danger and he knew about danger. His store had been robbed six times.

"Thank you," Karam said as he motioned for Asha to pick up the two grocery bags. "Let's go."

After the two walked out, the clerk took a deep breath and

crossed himself as he thanked God for not getting mixed up with the two of them.

Outside the store, Karam turned to Asha. His face was filled with anger. "Why did you leave without telling me? You know the rules. I'm to be informed whenever anyone wants to leave the warehouse!" he stormed furiously.

"You were busy. You were in a meeting and I was hungry," she started to explain.

"There was food in the lunchroom!"

"Nothing appealed to me," she answered, not cowering in front of him.

Karam's dark eyes seemed to stare through her. He didn't like this traipsing off by herself. They had too much at stake with their plans in two days. They finished their walk in silence.

CHAPTER 29

The next morning
Tampa, Florida

The buzzing from Moore's cell phone woke him. "Hello?"

"E! What in the world have you been up to?" a cheery voice greeted him.

"Sam, I have a bone to pick with you," Moore responded, irritated.

"I'm sure you do," Duncan answered without hesitation. "I can explain."

"You have a lot of explaining to do!" Moore muttered as he contained the anger beginning to well up inside.

"I will, but in time. I called you because of your involvement in this enriched uranium adventure."

"You mean misadventure. Do you know how many people have been killed? You almost got Willie and me killed!" Moore started.

"Whoa! Whoa, my friend. Are you going to listen or just explode like a volcano?"

Moore simmered down. "Go ahead."

"I got a tip from Asha and ..."

Moore couldn't hold back and cut right in. "And that's another thing. What's with this woman and you working together? You didn't tell me anything when you invited me on this U-boat search."

"Hold your horses, E." Duncan was getting exasperated with his friend's pent-up frustration.

"Listen, I thought you and Willie might want to catch a plane and meet me. We're wrapping this whole mission up tonight."

"We would, and then you can explain in person what in the world is going on and why you didn't clue us in!"

"I'd be glad to explain."

"Where am I flying?"

"New Orleans."

"New Orleans?"

"Yep. That's where Karam is."

"Asha, too?"

"Yep.

"Is she okay?"

"Yep, and she wanted to know that you also were okay."

Moore's eyebrows arched when he heard the comment. He was pleased that she was concerned for his ongoing welfare. "I'll get Willie and we'll get a flight right over."

Duncan provided information as to where Moore and

Wilbanks should meet him in New Orleans. A command post was being set up near the warehouse that housed Karam and his men.

"We are moving in tonight. If you want to be part of this, you'll need to be here."

They ended their call and Moore ran over to Wilbanks' room and pounded on the door.

"Just a cotton pickin' minute," Wilbanks called. Within seconds, he was opening the door. "Thank you for interrupting the sweet dream I was having. I had a hard time falling asleep last night. The couple in the room next door sounded like two raccoons breeding in a barn. Kept me up half the night."

Moore stepped into the room. "We need to catch a plane to New Orleans. Now. Sam finally called."

"Wait until I see that egg-sucking dawg. I'm going to give him a piece of my mind, what little I have left of it."

"Me, too. They found Karam."

"They did? That's good news. How did they do that?"

"Asha tipped off Sam," Moore said.

"That's good. I was hoping she was a good one. I knew that pretty lady had more going for her than we realized."

"They're going in tonight and we get to be a part of the team."

"Good. You take care of the plane tickets and I'm going to shower some of this old, dry skin off my body. I'll be ready to leave here in twenty minutes."

"Great. I'll get moving."

Thirty minutes later, they were in their rental car headed for the Tampa airport to catch a flight.

CHAPTER 30

Rampart Street Police Department
New Orleans, Louisiana

After arriving at the New Orleans airport, Moore and Wilbanks rented a car and drove into the French Quarter and to the rendezvous point at the Rampart Street headquarters for New Orleans Police Department's District 1.

As they parked, Moore looked across the street at the Louis Armstrong Park where he saw a number of law enforcement vehicles parked and officers and agents talking.

"Getting ready for a major assault," Moore guessed.

"I'll say," Wilbanks agreed as they exited the car and entered the building.

Checking in at the front desk, the two men were ushered toward a large meeting room. As they followed an officer down a hall, Sam Duncan popped out of a nearby doorway and yelled, "Hey E! How you doing?"

"I feel beaten like a bowl of eggs!" Moore responded sardonically to the powerfully built, blond-haired, 39-year-old man. The confident grin on his face went well with his cocky attitude. Moore was ready to give Duncan a piece of his mind.

"You sound like you've been hanging around Willie too long!" Duncan laughed.

"I don't care if I sound like him. I just don't want to look like him," Moore quipped back. He had planned to be sterner with his friend, but Duncan's mischievous charm worked its magic on Moore, who softened.

"Oh, I don't know if you could be as good looking as me," Wilbanks teased back. "It took years to look like this!"

"And a lot of rum!" Duncan added.

"So why did you get me in this mess?" Moore asked.

"That's what I want to know, too," Wilbanks said in a somber tone.

Duncan could see the good-natured joking was done. "Fellas, please step in this office with me," he directed as he opened the door to a small, unoccupied office.

Moore and Wilbanks walked into the office and Duncan shut the door after he entered.

"We were running an operation—and don't ask who the 'we' was because I can't divulge it."

Moore and Wilbanks were keenly focused on his explanation.

"We had been watching Karam for years, even before Karam began using that name. Carpos used an alias, too. Karam and Carpos had been members of a terrorist sect bent on nuclear terror. It was known as Ansar el-Hezb. We were able to infiltrate it a few years ago with one of our operatives who you know as Asha."

"They accepted women?" Moore asked.

"This group did. We had developed a strong background for Asha and gave her a substantial amount of cash to contribute to the group. A key part of her cover story was that she wanted revenge against the United States for the death of her husband who was a nuclear scientist. They were wary of her, but after a couple of years, they accepted her."

"How did all of this end up focusing on the U-boat?" Moore asked.

"Karam had experience in shipwreck hunting before he became radicalized. He also had nuclear experience. From what we understand, he learned about the U-boat from a friend in Turkey. This fellow Uzun was going to lead an expedition to find it. Karam wanted the glory for himself so he had Carpos kill Uzun in Istanbul."

"Ruthless," Moore interjected. "To kill his own friend."

"Ruthless and cunning," Duncan said before continuing. "Carpos had already stolen the plans from Uzun's apartment, then set a trap for anyone who entered the apartment. We lost two CIA operatives that evening who were killed when they walked into that trap. I understand it was a huge fireball."

"But how does this tie into Willie and me getting pulled in?" Moore asked.

"I had positioned myself and Willie to be invited on the U-boat search."

"But you didn't tell me any of this nonsense about terrorists!" Wilbanks spoke indignantly.

"No, I couldn't Willie. But I knew that I needed your expertise to find the U-boat. I had no idea that it was going to go down the way it did and I apologize," Duncan said. "Really, I do."

"You're not getting off that easy," Wilbanks responded. "This is going to cost you a lot."

"I sensed it would."

"What about pulling me in?" Moore asked again.

"As we got closer to the go date, we had a concern that I may have been compromised. We couldn't take the chance so I thought of you, E. I remembered the training you went through with that Special Forces guy in Cedar Key and knew that you could handle a weapon and step up in a fight, plus you're a diver. We just needed someone along so that Willie wouldn't be playing Lone Ranger."

"Lucky me," Moore retorted.

"If there's anyone who likes to play Lone Ranger, it's Emerson. You should know that, Sam," Wilbanks retorted.

Duncan eyed Moore and grinned. "He does have that habit, doesn't he?"

"More than we can ever imagine. And he'll probably have a story or two out of this when it's over. So you both owe me," Duncan said with a smile.

"I will and what a story it will be. But if there's any owing to be done, I still say it's you who owes me, Sam."

"What's the plan for Karam?" Wilbanks pointedly asked as he focused on the matter at hand.

"We're going in tonight. We have to go tonight. Asha overheard Karam planning to detonate the final dirty bomb tomorrow. It's going to be used when the president is in town to meet with a number of world leaders. They're going to explode it over the riverboat *Natchez* while they're taking a lunch cruise."

"I've been on the *Natchez*," Moore said, thinking back to a prior adventure in New Orleans and a fight he had on board it.

Ignoring Moore's comment, Duncan continued. "You guys can come into the conference room with me and hear the details. We're going in at midnight. We're going to crush some walnuts!"

The men left the small office and walked into the conference room, which was located two doors down the hall. After spending the next two hours going over the plans, the meeting broke up and the attendees split up. Some went to other offices to follow up on details. Some went to Louis Armstrong Park to meet with their respective teams. Moore and Wilbanks walked around the corner to grab dinner.

After dinner, Moore insisted that they walk the few blocks to Royal Street so that he could drop in at James H. Cohen and Sons. Moore had forged a friendship over the years with the family who collected and sold antique weapons and coins.

While Wilbanks was distracted by Cohen's grandson as they looked at a pair of dueling pistols, Moore went with the senior Cohen into the back office to make a request. Cohen smiled as he produced a key to unlock one of his cabinets.

"Will this do?" Cohen asked as he handed Moore a .22 handgun.

Moore examined the loaded weapon, popping the magazine to verify the number of rounds it contained. It was just like the one he had been trained to use in Cedar Key. "Perfect."

"I do expect you to return it tomorrow," Cohen commented.

"I will. If all goes well, I won't need to fire it. It's just that I'm used to a .22 now. I don't know what they'll give me tonight."

"No problem. I'll look forward to seeing you tomorrow," Cohen said as he relocked the cabinet and Moore stuffed the weapon in the rear waistband of his slacks and under his shirttail.

Moore returned to the front of the store without Wilbanks realizing that he had disappeared briefly. After fifteen minutes of chatting and admiring Cohen's weapon collection, Moore and Wilbanks left the store and headed for the rendezvous point in Louis Armstrong Park.

CHAPTER 31

Karam's warehouse
Off Rampart Street, New Orleans

Dark clouds hung over New Orleans, making the night darker as a fine misty rain began to fall. It obscured visibility in the park and throughout the city.

Duncan looked at his watch, which showed five minutes to go.

"It's not fair," Moore stormed quietly.

"Life's not fair, E. Whoever said it would be fair?" Duncan asked.

"I don't like sitting on the sidelines," Moore said, frustrated when he learned he couldn't be in the crush of officers assaulting the warehouse.

"Not me. I'm just fine being safe," Wilbanks said with assurance. He seemed to be relieved that they wouldn't be in the mix.

Duncan tried to soothe Moore's feelings. "Sometimes the best players have to set out when specialists are needed. That's all this is."

"Yeah, yeah," Moore grumbled, frustrated that they wouldn't be gearing up for the assault on the warehouse.

"You'll get your story, don't worry."

"I like to be in the front lines."

"I know you do and that's part of the reason you're not going in with us. Besides, you were upset with me earlier because you said I took advantage of you."

"This is different, Sam."

"You'll be close enough to come right in after we secure the building," Duncan explained.

"Let's go," one of the Homeland Security officers called from the lead vehicle. The vehicles pulled out of the park and followed each other to their prearranged positions. Twenty minutes later, the vehicles parked a block from the former cotton warehouse.

"You two stay here. Got it?" Duncan asked.

"You go ahead and do your business," Wilbanks said. "I'm quite comfortable standing right here."

"E?" Duncan asked.

Moore was chomping at the bit. He eyed Duncan with a pleading look.

"Nice try, E. Those sad puppy dog eyes might work on your lady friends, but they don't work on me. Stay! Got it?"

Moore shook his head. "I guess."

Duncan walked away to join the men assembling for the

raid. He cast one last look at Moore and Wilbanks to make sure they hadn't moved, and then turned to the business at hand.

The lead team approached the brick building from the corner. They crouched as they crept to the front door where one member stood with a battering ram and struck the door lock. He was greeted by an explosion from the booby-trapped door and was blown fifteen feet away. The officer suffered massive injuries and died at the scene.

The explosion launched the attack as team members broke windows and threw in flash grenades as others streamed through the breached doors, their weapons pouring out a withering stream of bullets.

Heavy bursts of gunfire began crackling in return as Saad and Zaman led the terrorists in trying to repel the armed intruders. The outnumbered terrorists squatted and fired from behind the limited safety thick pillars offered as live rounds swooshed around the building. Saad furiously waved his arm and screamed orders at his men as he fired his Kalashnikov.

One by one the terrorists were struck and died. Saad and Zaman were among the first. Three law enforcement officers also were killed.

As a cloud of pale smoke dissipated inside the building, the law enforcement teams examined the bodies and attended to their wounded brethren while others searched and secured the warehouse.

Within five minutes, Duncan was walking out of the building toward Wilbanks. "We got the dirty bomb and we found a commercial drone that they were probably going to use."

"I'm mighty glad that you did," Wilbanks smiled.

"But we didn't get Karam or Asha," Duncan lamented. "They're nowhere to be found. We searched the entire building and we know that they couldn't have escaped." Duncan looked around. "Where's E?"

"He took off running like a screaming banshee." Wilbanks pointed down the misty sidewalk. "He told me to stay here and wait for you."

"You think he spotted Karam and Asha?"

"How would I know? I thought they were inside. Besides, my eyes aren't so good for seeing through this mist. I even hate driving at night."

"I'm going after him," Duncan said as he broke into a sprint down the street.

"I'll stay right here in case he comes back."

Minutes earlier, Karam and Asha were returning from a walk in the cool evening air when they heard the explosions and gunfire at the warehouse. Karam guessed what had happened.

"Asha, turn around. We'll go farther into the Quarter," Karam said as he stopped and half-dragged her around when he turned.

"Think they're onto us?" Asha asked.

"Yes," he growled.

The two scurried down the sidewalk toward the riverbank. They hadn't gone far when a familiar voice shouted at them.

"Karam, stop where you are."

Karam and Asha stopped and turned to face Moore. Karam was stunned to see Moore. His surprise was quickly replaced by raging anger. "You were supposed to be dead. Asha, you told me he was dying!"

As Karam then put two-and-two together, his mind fast-forwarded to Asha lying to him. He felt undeniably betrayed. There was no room in his world for traitors! Without hesitation, he placed the muzzle of his .45 semi-auto pistol against Asha's temple.

"Eli, wait! I can explain," Asha said as she panicked and her mind raced to find some plausible explanation to make up. She ran out of time right there at that precise moment on the dark, rainy street.

"Liar!" he said with no remorse as he pulled the trigger and she fell to the ground.

"No!" Moore yelled as he fired off a round from his borrowed .22.

The bullet whizzed by Karam's ear as he turned and ran into an abandoned storefront.

Moore ran to Asha and knelt next to her as blood drained out of her head and mixed with rainwater in a nearby puddle. "Asha! Asha!" Moore said softly as he stroked her face with his left hand. It was too late. She was gone.

Moore stood and looked toward the storefront that Karam had entered. His feeling of deep loss was replaced with a strong sense of anger and revenge. His jaw was set and he had a determined look on his face. He was going to make Karam pay.

Holding his .22 waist high, Moore carefully advanced on the brick-faced building. There was no way that he would allow Karam to escape. It was not an option.

Inside the three-story building Karam had found the rear door gated and locked with a padlock. There was no obvious escape from the first floor. Making his way through the shadows, Karam ascended a set of stairs to the second floor where the windows were boarded shut, letting in no light from the street lights outside. That's when he heard the door to the first floor slam shut as Moore entered the building.

Seeing no escape route on the second floor, Karam climbed the stairs to the third floor. It had large windows overlooking the street below and received light casting upward from the street lights to partially fill the room with eerie shadows. Several of the windows were missing panes of glass and allowed the mist to seep into the room. Karam heard the stairs to the second floor squeak. He knew Moore was coming up after him.

Looking above him, Karam saw a ladder that went up the wall to a trapdoor which he imagined opened onto the roof. Moving quickly, Karam climbed the ladder and opened the trap door. He crawled up and onto the roof where he sprawled next to the opening. He peered over the edge, thankful for a moonless night so that he wouldn't be silhouetted from where he awaited his approaching prey.

Climbing the stairs to the second floor, Moore was disturbed by the squeaking noise they made. He muttered under his breath as he further ascended. He cautiously peeked over the top at floor level and then ducked down. It was so dark on the second floor, he could barely see anything.

Moore slowed his breathing and listened for any noise that would signal Karam's presence. Waiting two minutes, Moore threw caution to the wind and crouched as he finished walking up the stairs. He took a couple of steps into the room, his senses fully alert as his eyes squinted, trying to pierce the veil of darkness.

Up above, Karam had an evil grin. He knew that he had the advantage like a panther stalking its victim. He sharply tapped the metal ladder once with the side of his .45. The noise reverberated through the building, attracting Moore's attention. Satisfied that Karam was above him, Moore walked to the stairs to the third floor.

Approaching very carefully and walking on the sides of the stairs in an effort to minimize any more squeaks, Moore looked up and pointed his gun. As his head broke above the floor level, he ducked back down. He then carefully raised his head again to look around the partially lit room. The slight breeze coming through the broken panes refreshed him as he methodically surveyed the room.

Seeing no signs of Karam, Moore finished his climb to the third floor and stepped off the top step. Again, he carefully looked around the room, which was empty except for a couple of overturned chairs, which had cobwebs on them.

Moore felt a downdraft and looked at the wall where he saw the metal ladder. He guessed that Karam had escaped up the ladder and the noise he heard was of Karam running away from the ladder and across the roof to escape. Moore turned and started for the ladder when he suddenly stopped as a floorboard squeaked under him. It was a good thing it did as Karam then quickly fired three shots through the opening toward the base of the ladder where Moore would have been standing.

Moore moved to the ladder and fired off two quick shots upward, missing Karam who had retreated. Before Karam could fire again, Moore shot three more times, but through the plaster ceiling as he hoped to hit Karam with a lucky shot. He did. Karam briefly screamed in pain as one bullet shot through a rotting piece of underlayment and pierced his abdomen. As a red rose of blood bloomed on his side, Karam swore viciously and in contempt.

Angered by the painful wound, Karam pulled himself partly over the edge of the trap door so that he could see Moore. He fired twice and Moore jumped toward the center of the room. When he did, he landed on rotting floorboards. The floor quickly gave way, dropping Moore with pieces of wooden floor and plaster to the dark second floor room below.

When he landed hard, a very shaken and beaten Moore felt a stab of pain in his left calf. He quickly switched on his cell phone light and checked. Sticking out of his calf was a six-inch wooden splinter. It was painful and bleeding. Moore shut off his cell phone light and rolled over to see if he could see Karam above him.

When Karam heard the crash, he smiled wickedly. He hoped that Moore was hurt as he imagined Moore helplessly lying on the second floor. Bleeding from his abdomen, Karam pulled himself over the trap door opening and painfully climbed down the ladder to the third floor. He groaned as he stepped off the ladder and with his .45 pointed in front of him, he looked for the area where Moore had broken through the floor. Seeing the hole, Karam turned, wincing as he did, and began walking carefully down the creaking stairs to the second floor.

As he descended, he began to twist to his side to try to hide behind the stair rail as much as possible. He looked into the dark room, trying to see Moore. Suddenly, Karam saw Moore's cell phone light turn on and move across the room.

"Stupid move, Moore," Karam shouted with glee as he stood up and leaned over the railing, emptying his weapon at the light and around it in hopes of hitting Moore. When he finished, Karam intently listened. He didn't hear anything but his own excited breathing. He reached into his pocket and pulled out his cell phone and switched on its flashlight. He then shone it in the direction he had fired, expecting to see Moore's dead body. Instead, he only saw Moore's cell phone.

A single shot rang out from the floor in the middle of the room where Moore was sprawled from his fall. The shot caught a surprised Karam in the shoulder and caused him to lose his balance. He tumbled down the remaining four steps to the landing.

"I'm not that easy to kill, Karam," Moore said as he crawled with biting pain closer to Karam.

"Neither am I, Moore," Karam screamed as he struggled to his knees and swung a nearby two-by-four at Moore, just missing Moore's head.

Moore was acutely focused. He wanted Karam to hear these last words. "This is for Asha, Hopkins, Knowles and Bingo!" Moore said quietly and deliberately as he gave a double tap from his .22 to Karam's heart. Karam fell over, dead.

Moore dropped back to the floor as the surrounding atmosphere became extraordinarily quiet and subdued. He noted the partial illumination from the streetlights outside, the smell of gunpowder inside the building following the gunfight and his own sense of personal satisfaction that his revenge was now settled.

The sound of the door slamming below and footsteps rushing upward toward him caused Moore to turn and aim his .22 at the new intruder.

"E! E! Are you okay?" a voice called before Duncan's head poked over the top of the stairs followed by a beam of light from his cell phone flashlight.

"You took long enough to get here," Moore said, biting back the pain in his calf and his body.

Duncan bent over Karam's body and flashed his light to examine Karam. Confirming he was dead, Duncan flashed his light back to Moore. "He's dead."

"Don't expect to see any tears from me," Moore said, wincing at the pain in his leg.

"I wasn't," Duncan replied stonily. Seeing the debris scattered around Moore, Duncan flashed his light up and saw the gaping hole. "Did Humpty Dumpty have a great fall?" Duncan asked as he walked over and knelt next to Moore.

"Yes, I did," Moore groaned as Duncan helped him to a sitting position. "I feel like I was run over by a truck."

"What do we have here?" Duncan said as he directed his light beam at Moore's calf.

"It could be a lot worse," Moore said. He grunted in pain when Duncan suddenly pulled the wooden splinter out of his calf.

"E, I have never seen anyone as lucky as you," Duncan said as he opened his small medical pack and extracted a wrap. He cut off Moore's pant leg below the knee and applied the wrap to the calf. "That should hold you until you can get checked out."

"Did you see Asha?"

"Yes. I heard the shots and ran over, but didn't know where you went. I guessed Karam was involved. I called for medical attention, but it was too late. She was gone."

"You have no idea how ruthless Karam was! He just turned and shot her point blank. No explanation other than calling her a liar before he pulled the trigger. No remorse. Nothing. She didn't have a chance."

"That was his modus operandi. And that's why he was so dangerous and successful. We explained the risk to Asha when she volunteered for the mission, but she didn't care."

"Did she have any reason motivating her to volunteer for the assignment?" Moore asked.

"She did. Revenge. Her brother worked for us. He was infiltrating Karam's team and they discovered him. His death wasn't pretty."

Moore was silent. His mind took him through a series of flashbacks of the positive encounters he had with Asha while at sea and at the Tampa warehouse.

After a couple of minutes, Duncan spoke. "Let's stand you up and get out of here."

Together the two men rose to their feet.

"She saved my life, Sam. Karam wanted to inject me with that brain-eating amoeba and she took the syringe from him, but didn't inject me." Moore was lamenting her death. He would carry her loss for some time.

"She was a good woman."

"She was," Moore agreed with a deep sense of loss.

The two men descended the stairs to the first floor and exited the building where two police cars had pulled up. "Karam's body is on the second floor," Duncan said as two police officers rushed into the building.

Two more patrol cars arrived as well as an ambulance. When the ambulance's passenger door opened, Wilbanks stepped out and walked over to Moore and Duncan.

"What are you doing here?" Moore asked as a paramedic ran over to him in response to Duncan's hand wave.

"Why should I walk when I can ride?" Wilbanks asked with a mischievous twinkle in his eye. Looking at Moore's calf, Wilbanks continued. "What in tarnation did you do to yourself? Good thing I brought the cavalry."

Moore quickly brought Wilbanks up to speed on what had transpired.

"Sorry to hear about Asha. I liked that girl," Wilbanks said in a more serious tone.

"I did, too, Willie," Moore added as he winced when the paramedic twisted his calf. "More than I imagined."

"I am glad to hear you got that polecat, Karam," Wilbanks said.

"Pretty clever how you used your cell phone, E," Duncan interjected.

"It worked," Moore's mind was focused elsewhere. "Did they get Asha's body?"

"I'm sure they're putting her in the ambulance now," Duncan replied.

"I'd like to take another look at her," Moore requested.

"Sure."

The three men walked to the rear of the ambulance where the medics were securing the gurney.

"Mind if I step in?" Moore asked.

"No. Come on in," one of the medics said.

Moore winced as he stepped in and eased over to the gurney. He pulled back the sheet from her face and gazed for a moment at the woman who had saved his life. "Thank you, Asha," Moore said as he ran his fingers down the side of her bloodied cheek.

Slowly he pulled the sheet back over her head and exited the ambulance.

"You okay?" Wilbanks asked.

"Other than feeling a huge burden of grief, I am," Moore said.

As the medics began removing another gurney, Moore guessed it would be for Karam's body and he stopped the medic. "Could you please do me a huge favor?"

"What's that?" the medic asked.

"Don't transport the guy in that building in the same vehicle as her. She doesn't deserve that," Moore said firmly.

"We can do that," the medic said as he turned to the driver and asked him to call for another ambulance.

Moore, Wilbanks and Duncan walked away into the misty evening toward the warehouse where their vehicle was parked.

CHAPTER 32

East Point
Put-in-Bay, Ohio

Five days had passed since the shootout in New Orleans. Wilbanks had returned to his home in Charleston and Moore was at his aunt's house, writing his story for *The Post*. Up early, Moore had grabbed a quick cup of coffee in the kitchen and retreated to the enclosed front porch to continue working.

After two hours, he decided to take a break and walked out on the long dock extending into the bay. Taking a seat on one of the two white wicker chairs, he relaxed. His respite didn't last very long before his cell phone rang.

Moore looked down and saw that Steve Nicholas was calling.

"Hello, Steve," Moore answered.

"Morning Emerson," Nicholas greeted Moore.

"Hi E!" another voice piped in on the speakerphone in Nicholas' office.

"Sam?" Moore asked hesitantly as he warily identified the source of the second voice.

"You got it, buddy," Duncan responded.

"I can tell this call is going to be dangerous," Moore said, imagining his two friends being in cahoots.

"Now, why would you think that?" Duncan asked sarcastically.

"Mixing you two is a recipe for trouble. And I'm usually getting the brunt of it."

"No. No, Emerson. Not this time," Nicholas said.

"Yeah, E. We owe you and we decided to repay you," Duncan chimed in.

"This is going to be good," Moore said as he wondered what they had up their sleeve.

"Did you ever do anything more on linking those Kreigsmarine daggers to Roosevelt's death?" Nicholas asked.

"Like where would I have had any time to do anything? In case you two didn't notice, I've been busy the last few weeks," Moore said with a tone of sarcasm.

"Well, we felt like we owed you," Nicholas said.

"Big time," Duncan added.

"Understatement," Moore retorted.

"Sam, go ahead and tell Emerson what you did," Nicholas urged.

"E, do you remember Peter Nehrebecky?"

"Yes, the director at Roosevelt's Little White House."

"Right. I paid him a visit and, with a little arm twisting from Steve over the phone, we were able to convince him to loan us the Kreigsmarine dagger from the museum."

"You did?" Moore was stunned.

"Yes. I brought it back to Washington and gave it to Steve."

Moore was listening intently.

"I called a couple of friends of mine who specialize in forensics and they stopped by. I gave them the dagger from Warm Springs and the one you left with me from Put-in-Bay. They ran several analyses on the two daggers, including DNA," Nicholas explained very nonchalantly.

"Anything concrete?" Moore asked as his curiosity grew.

"Yes. The DNA from both daggers matched. So, it looks like your Dieter Gabor had his hands on both of them."

"That would put him in Roosevelt's bedroom," Moore exclaimed.

"Possibly. It shows that a dagger found in the museum under questionable circumstances was in the possession of a man in Put-in-Bay. No one knows or is willing to reveal how the dagger showed up in a safe at the Little White House," Nicholas said.

"I have the letter from Roosevelt's cook and her signature was authenticated," Moore offered.

"Circumstantial, Emerson," Nicholas commented.

"I'm writing the story!" Moore said with determination.

"Go ahead. You've already discovered that there were numerous conspiracy stories surrounding Roosevelt's death. Yours will simply be one more."

"So it may be, but I'm writing it nevertheless."

"If I were in your shoes, I would," Nicholas offered.

"Me, too," Duncan added.

"I should mention that I stumbled across something interesting before I caught the Miller Ferry back to Put-in-Bay," Moore said.

"What's that?" Nicholas asked.

"I stopped by the Liberty Aviation Museum at the Port Clinton airport to see Dick Rathmell. He let me climb up on his Avenger so I could look inside the cockpit."

"What were you looking for?" Duncan asked.

"I wanted to check the coordinates for the U-boat it sunk. It was off Sunset Island on the same date that the *U-235* was sunk. I bet this is the Avenger that sunk the *U-235!*" Moore said proudly of his discovery.

"What a coincidence!" Nicholas said.

"Too cool!" Duncan added.

"I better go. Need to finish my story and submit it."

"E?" Duncan wanted to ask one more question.

"Yes?"

"I feel bad about all of the messes I've gotten you into."

"You should." Moore didn't hold back.

"I'd like to make it up to you. Ever hear of Chincoteague Island?"

"Sure. It's off the eastern shore of Virginia."

"Yeah. About a three-hour drive from your place in Alexandria."

"What about it?" Moore asked.

"How'd you like to join me there soon for a few days of

fishing, crabbing and clamming?"

"What's the catch?" Moore asked suspiciously.

Duncan chuckled. "I guess I deserve that question. Honest. I have no hidden agenda. Just some time relaxing, you know, R and R."

For a few seconds, Moore mulled the offer. Then he replied, "As long as this is on the up and up, Sam."

"It is. It is," Duncan repeated himself.

"Okay. Let me finish my story and I'll call you to go over the details."

The three continued talking for a few more minutes before ending the call. Moore stood from his chair on the dock and took one long look at the bay. Then he turned and walked to the enclosed porch. He had a story to write and was looking forward to a peaceful visit to Chincoteague Island.

Coming Soon:

The Next Emerson Moore Adventure

Chincoteague Calm